About the Author

Diao Dou was born in 1960 in Shenyang, Liaoning Province, China. Since graduating from the Beijing Broadcasting Institute in 1983, he has worked as a journalist and latterly as a literary editor. Although his first book was a collection of poetry, *Aiqing jishi* ('Chronicles of Love', 1992), he is best known as an author of novels and short stories. His five novels are *Siren dang'an* ('Personal File', 1998), *Zhengci* ('Testimony', 1999), *Youxifa* ('Playing the Game', 2002), *Wo ge Diao Bei nianbiao* ('My Brother, Diao Bei: A History', 2008) and *Qinhe* ('Close to You', 2011). He has also published five collections of short stories: *Duzi shangsheng* ('Ascending Alone', 1996), *Shaizi yi zhi* ('A Roll of the Dice', 1996), *Shijishang shi hujiu* ('A Cry for Help', 2006), *Qingshu kao* ('Love Letters: A Study', 2014) and *Chuchu* ('Points of Origin', forthcoming). He has also published one collection of essays, *Yi ge xiaoshuojia de shenghuo yu xiangxiang* ('The Life and Imagination of a Novelist', 2012). In 2003, he was awarded the ninth annual Zhuang Zhongwen Prize for Literature. This is the first appearance of his work in English.

About the Translator

Brendan O'Kane spent a decade in Beijing, working mostly as a freelance translator and the co-host of the Mandarin-learning podcast *Popup Chinese*, reviews of which have described him as 'only slightly annoying.' He is currently a Ph.D. student at the University of Pennsylvania.

First published in Great Britain in 2015 by Comma Press.
www.commapress.co.uk

A CIP catalogue record of this book is available from the British Library.

ISBN 1905583621
ISBN-13   978 1905583621

This book has been selected to receive financial assistance from English PEN's
'PEN Translates' programme, supported by Arts Council England.
English PEN exists to promote literature and our understanding of it, to uphold
writers' freedoms around the world, to campaign against the persecution and
imprisonment of writers for stating their views, and to promote the friendly
co-operation of writers and the free exchange of ideas. www.englishpen.org

The publisher gratefully acknowledges assistance from Arts Council England.

Set in Bembo 11/13 by David Eckersall
Printed and bound in England by CPI Group (UK) Ltd, Croydon, CR0 4YY.

POINTS OF ORIGIN

Diao Dou

Translated from the Chinese by
Brendan O'Kane

Contents

Cockroaches

MY FATHER'S MIND WAS clear the night he died, as my mother remembers it. He had gone right back to normal. He handed her a neat stack of handwritten pages and made her promise that she would take me away from Zhangji by sundown the next day. 'I can smell the cockroaches again,' my father said. Then he closed his eyes.

For as long as I can recall, I knew Zhangji as the place our family was from. My mother told me stories about Zhangji and my father again and again, until I knew them at least as well as she did. Her feelings about the place were a complicated mixture of love and hate. Even if the people of Zhangji drove my father to his death, she said, it was still the place where she and he had grown up, where they had lived. She still held out hope that she would live to see Zhangji saved. 'Go there yourself,' she said, 'And maybe now they'll be ready to listen to what your father tried to tell them.' She didn't have long left. I couldn't say no to an elderly woman at the end of her life, especially my own mother.

But did the people of Zhangji think they were living amid disaster? I asked her before I set out. I already had a sort of premonition. I am my father's son, after all.

My mother looked at me anxiously. 'Don't think the people of Zhangji are bad,' she said. 'They're just fools.'

Before the cockroaches came, Zhangji was just another remote, impoverished little city, not the renowned tourist destination it is today. People lived straightforward, uncomplicated lives, unambitious and perhaps a little indolent

1

in their simplicity. And then one evening, as the bitter winter was preparing to set in, my father said he could smell the cockroaches. He was lying on top of my mother at the time. This put a dampener on the mood, but my mother was understanding enough not to hold it against him. She just told him not to get carried away. My father rolled off her, but instead of falling asleep as usual, he tossed and turned in the dark for a while before finally getting dressed and leaving the house. He returned, exhausted, late the following night. My mother went to heat up some food and some liquor for him, but he stopped her in her tracks, saying he was in no mood to eat.

'I went to City Hall,' my father told her. 'I went to Health and Sanitation, I went to the official news agency – I went looking for anyone in Zhangji who might have a bit of clout or influence. I told them that the cockroaches are coming, that the people of this city need to act now to stop the attack. But none of them listened, not a single one. They completely ignored my warning.' My mother comforted him silently, not knowing what to say. Later she told me that she hadn't paid my father's prediction much attention either, that it had sounded like fairy tales to her. But the next morning, when the sky grew light and my mother got up to prepare breakfast, she saw a film of dead cockroaches in a shallow puddle of water on the floor. The cockroaches had all gone black, and they floated gently atop the water like toy boats. She swept them away, stifling her disgust, and then began searching every nook and cranny of the apartment. She found more cockroaches, and she shuddered even though it wasn't cold, thinking of my father's prediction. She swept the cockroach carcasses into a basin, which she carried out through the yard and through the streets to the Dazhanghei River at the southern edge of the city, where she dumped them in. Something kept her from telling my father when he woke up.

Zhangji was as quiet and untroubled as ever that day.

The days were always quiet and untroubled in Zhangji. I even found them to be graceful and beautiful on my arrival there. For three pleasant seasons out of four the temperature was neither too hot nor too cold, I learned, and even in winter the sky above Zhangji remained a clear, crisp blue. It wasn't until I'd spent some time there myself that I realised why people from Zhangji were so enamoured of that troubled, tormented, impoverished patch of country. Arriving in the tourist season, I spent many nights going from home to home with group after group of sightseers, taking in the majestic, otherworldly sight of the cockroach army. We asked almost everyone we met if it wasn't hard to bear, living alongside the cockroaches year in and year out. They always gave the same apparently spontaneous response: 'The cockroaches took over. Wasn't any fault of ours.' Our tour group didn't have anything to say to that. I'd say that when my father and mother elected to flee Zhangji, they were almost certainly the only ones.

Many other Zhangji residents found an unusual accumulation of cockroach corpses in their homes that day, just as my mother had – but this didn't make much of an impression on them. Zhangji had always been a place where roach and rat roamed free, where mosquito and housefly swarmed. My father sat alone at home, not knowing that his prophecy was being fulfilled but ill at ease all the same. He gazed out the window at the Dazhanghei River, murmuring to himself: 'Where do you come from, river, and where are you going?...' After nightfall, when my mother had locked the door and was getting ready to turn out the lights, my father withdrew his gaze from the dark window and a string of desperate, indistinct moans rose from deep in his breast: '*Now* will they see? Now they *must* see! See...'

They did see that night, everyone in Zhangji: the rank and file of the cockroach army surged in and unfurled like the tide, seizing and occupying every single home. It happened too quickly for anybody to do anything. New homes and old houses, hutches and high-rises, all filled with the constant *sha-*

sha-sha-sha of cockroaches skittering and chewing. The sudden appearance of the cockroaches cast an enormous black shadow that dimmed and blurred the lamplight of Zhangji from that day on. The cockroaches were not actually black, of course; it was the sheer scale of their massed, teeming platoons that made them look so oppressively dark. Their carapaces were actually a deep brown, and if you focused on a single cockroach and watched closely, you could see its scurrying body catch the lamplight and give it back in a rich, multicoloured metallic glimmer. The roaches' bodies were all roughly the same size – about half as big as a grown man's little finger – and gracefully slender, with sharp thin heads and legs, and two delicate translucent, saw-toothed wings on their backs.

My mother, who was completely unprepared, was too shocked to do anything but shriek and leap up onto the bed. She held my father tight, curling as nearly into a ball as her plump figure would allow, and babbled: 'What's happening, what's happening, what's happening…?' My father was unable to manage any greater degree of equanimity, premonition or no. His face burned red with shock, and his gaze went green with revulsion and hatred. He paid no heed to my mother beside him. He lay flat on the bed, face turned toward the floor, holding aloft the single leather shoe that he had been able to reach, and beat madly at the teeming cockroaches that already covered the floor. It was to no avail: the swarming invaders continued to fill the spaces where their comrades had fallen, heedless or fearless of my father's flailing. My father continued his frenzied activity until he had exhausted every ounce of physical strength. When he could no longer raise his arm, when blind action gave way to second thoughts, he saw the mess of dead cockroaches he had left beside the bed. The flattened and broken little creatures lay in a foul, sticky mess all over the floor, cemented together by the pale ichor that had been crushed out of them. My mother, hearing that my father had stopped beating at the cockroaches, opened her eyes to see the wreckage. The instant she laid eyes on the mess, a powerful spasm racked her body, and with an ear-splitting retch she emptied the undigested contents of her stomach onto the deceased cockroaches.

You can imagine how that evening went. Fortunately, the cockroaches' incursion went no further than the floor, and the bed, tables and chairs, walls, and cupboards remained friendly territory. Seeing this, my father was able to compose himself. He slowly coaxed my mother to sleep, then began silently and unhurriedly surveying his surroundings. The cockroaches showed not the slightest awareness of their comrades' deaths, he found; they milled and jostled over their corpses and my mother's vomit as if it were level floor. As far as he could tell, they had no fixed targets or plans beyond nibbling and teeming. They changed direction whenever they encountered walls or other obstacles, for no apparent reason other than that it was easier than climbing. My father's initial observations of cockroach behaviour held true on subsequent occasions, and remain true of the cockroaches in Zhangji today.

It was a sleepless night for my father. When the sky grew light and my mother awoke, she saw him still lying there, staring intently at the floor. Sleep had restored her spirits, and she mustered up the courage to look at the floor herself. In addition to the ruined bodies of the dead cockroaches and my mother's vomit, there was a dense layer of cockroach droppings: a speckled, grainy sheet of black. My mother grabbed my father: 'Gone! They're all gone!'

My father shook his head wearily: 'They'll be back come evening.'

Fear and confusion reigned in Zhangji that day. The cockroach invasion was all anyone could talk about. Health and Sanitation issued emergency chemical kits to every household, and the airwaves were filled with broadcasts telling residents not to be alarmed. My father also received a notice from the city government appointing him a special delegate to the first ever 'Cockroach Conference,' at which Renowned Experts and leading scholars would be in attendance.

I too took part as a special delegate in a Cockroach Conference during my time in Zhangji, but it bore little resemblance to the first Cockroach Conference as described by my mother. With its interminable speeches – about the climate, about soil composition, about asexual reproduction, about dredging plans, about expansions to sightseeing venues, turning trash to cash and making lemonade out of the catastrophic lemons Zhangji had been given – the Cockroach Conference had long since lost all actual meaning – or rather, you might say that it had long since taken on another meaning. A tourist who had visited Zhangji many times told me that these had been the only topics under discussion at any Cockroach Conference for years. At a banquet we were invited to during the Conference I attended, I found myself seated next to one of the city leaders. Trying to make conversation, I said, 'It looks like the cockroaches have a pretty strong foothold here in Zhangji.'

The city leader was teetering between drunkenness and sobriety. He patted me heavily on the shoulder with his soft hand and said – with something of an air of mystery – 'How many years has it been now? The cockroaches act like they own Zhangji too these days…'

I stopped chewing and looked at his fat face, startled. He seemed to remember something then, and asserted in a loud, declamatory tone, 'Our city has no greater enemy than the cockroaches. We will not rest until we have completely and utterly and totally and absolutely exterminated every last one of them.'

I knew those words well. They had been the slogan of the first ever Cockroach Conference. Public opinion in Zhangji had been unusually clear: no efforts would be spared in driving the cockroaches out of Zhangji. Many of the Renowned Experts at the symposium had been on the receiving end of my father's warnings, and when they saw him there they offered their deepest apologies. They said that their failure to heed my father's premonition and take timely action was an abiding source of regret. They secretly hoped my father would give them a good balling-out on behalf of the people of Zhangji. 'I didn't want my prediction to be true either,' my father said. 'But things are what they are and what's done is done. The important thing now is to face the facts and figure out what our next move should be.'

My father didn't see anything wrong with saying this; he really meant it, without the slightest bit of condescension or sarcasm. But for the Renowned Experts it was a blow to their self-esteem. Blame and resentment they could deal with, but not my father's sincere forgiveness. Sneers came to their faces. My father was feverishly earnest, almost reverent, now that he was here among the Renowned Experts. He threw himself into their discussions and debates with utter abandon, offering detailed reports on the findings of his sleepless nights. After he got home, he said happily to my mother that the scientific analyses presented by the Renowned Experts had been most enlightening – and that he had a lot of work to do. But afterwards the Cockroach Conferences became little more than a regular holiday gathering for the great and the good of Zhangji, and they never invited my father again. My father's study of the cockroaches became a solitary, unsupported effort.

How to drive off the cockroach invaders was the primary concern – at first. Every morning, as the sky grew light and the cockroaches withdrew by the billions, the people of Zhangji, men and women, old and young, would gather in the streets and argue about what was to be done. They offered suggestions, hatched plans, talked about their own findings, and floated ideas, most of which sank without a trace. A fondness for idle talk was a feature of the Zhangji character, and the latest shocking turn of events with the cockroaches satisfied some deep-rooted spiritual need on their part. As time wore on, however, the unchecked cockroach incursion wore down their faith. Things weren't nearly as straightforward as they had imagined. The chemical compounds issued by Health and Sanitation, for instance, were completely useless. People would scatter powder over the floor by day, or spray pesticides, or scrape blocks of compressed poison across the floor, but come nightfall the cockroach army would rise again in wave after unimpeded wave and mockingly bury every trace of the chemicals beneath a layer of black droppings. The official news agency's overwrought reports, meanwhile, were becoming increasingly difficult to credit. Their descriptions of all the counter-cockroach measures were strained and unconvincing; the on-air discussion and analysis of the situation had no appreciable connection to reality, and the attempts to rouse people to steely determination were even more clearly a load of rubbish. Bit by bit, the people of Zhangji grew indifferent to the cockroach problem, and accustomed to a daily routine that included living side-by-side with cockroaches. Besides, the throngs of cockroaches on the floor would pose no threat as long as people went to bed and fell asleep before nightfall. And there was more to Zhangji than just the cockroaches, after all. Before long, life in Zhangji resumed its normal pace. The city government was resolved not to allow the cockroaches to affect its meetings, banquets, official visits, or ribbon-cuttings. Health and Sanitation could hardly ignore lung cancer, syphilis, hemorrhoids, athlete's foot, or rabies. The official news agency naturally couldn't go on beating the same old drum, and soon enough they returned with gusto to airing light music on the radio and running human interest pieces and humorous anecdotes in the papers.

The only one who couldn't join in was my father. There were months when my father, engaged day and night in battle with the cockroaches, never left the house. He had my mother get as many different poisons as she could, and he tested them on the cockroaches by night, night after night. The double bed he and my mother slept in was piled so high with bottles and vials that in the evenings my mother had to climb up onto a chest, holding me, in order to sleep. My father had no laboratory equipment; his tools and methods of experimentation could hardly have been more rudimentary. To better understand the cockroaches' startling resistance to poison, he even tried eating them by the bowlful, raw, steamed and stir-fried, boiled and brined. To understand what if anything the cockroaches could do to people, he stripped naked and let the cockroaches nibble and crawl and skitter and suck and swarm all over him. Half a year later, when he handed my mother the handwritten draft of his exhaustive report on cockroach removal, my father was barely recognisable as human. Our household was the first to completely eliminate the cockroach infestation, the only one that the cockroaches no longer invaded at night. Night after long, brightly lit night, my father's form was the only one that could be seen flitting from room to room. By that time, as my mother described it later, my father's long hair stood on end like antennae. His pointy head and sharp lips quivered atop his skinny neck, pointing forward as if he was searching for something. He had developed a preference for crawling on all fours, his quick, complicated motions possessing a strange grace. His limbs were unusually delicate, and when he moved it looked as if he had far more than the usual complement of arms and legs. He had lost so much weight that he was little more than skin and bone, but his skin wasn't at all pale, as one might expect; it was flecked with small, densely clustered brown spots that looked like matte scales. If he stepped outside, it was enough to throw all of Zhangji into an uproar.

I don't imagine he would draw any attention if he were to return to Zhangji today. When I went there, I found that everyone in the city was the same. They were sluggish and dull-witted. Alone, they would appear and disappear without warning; in larger numbers, they would mill around with no apparent purpose. When I accepted the invitation to take part in the lavish gala event that was the Cockroach Conference, when I held up the handwritten draft of the report on cockroach removal that my father had written 30 years before,

I saw that all the specialists and scholars and worthies and political leaders displayed, to a man, the mannerisms of cockroaches, though they did their best to maintain appropriate posture and dignified speech. Their forced laughter and dry, papery voices were of the same timbre as the faint skittering of cockroaches on long nights. They went to great lengths to express their respect and gratitude, but their obvious lack of interest made me feel that I was being left out in the cold. In that instant of recognition, I realised that I had been wrong, and my mother had been even wronger. After that flash of sudden comprehension, I contemplated the destruction and ruination that my father's experimental findings had brought him 30 years before.

Thirty years ago, when my mother submitted my father's report to the relevant organs of government, it rekindled the long-dormant hopes of the people of Zhangji that they might be rid of the cockroaches. The newspapers and the radio blanketed the city with reports of my father's fearless sacrifice and selfless dedication to science; out in the streets, the good simple people of Zhangji spoke in hushed tones of my legendary father. Looking back on it now, I can see that it was the shortfall between the elevated hopes and the subsequent disappointment that outraged the people of Zhangji. When the report was dismissed as a fraud, the people of Zhangji had no target for their anger but my father. My mother told me many times that she had never understood – and that my father had never understood – why after reviewing my father's report, the relevant organs of government had pronounced it to be sheer hocus-pocus, or why they insinuated in the media that if the city were to declare outright war on the cockroaches, as my father's plan recommended, it would only lead to even greater disaster for the city and its residents. That was the authorities' final verdict, and nothing my father and mother could do or say would convince them otherwise.

The good, plain people of Zhangji were utterly despondent after the Renowned Experts' opinion was announced. Other reports that were circulating at the same time reminded them of a number of strange occurrences. They knew that my father had been the first to predict the cockroaches' invasion, and rumour had it that at the first Cockroach Conference he had displayed a measure of satisfaction at his prediction coming true. My father's cockroach-like form pointed to some sort of close connection with the cockroaches, they thought, and they determined that if our home was the only one in Zhangji to have been spared the cockroaches, this could only be a sign that my father was planning to use the cockroaches to take control of the entire city. It was my father, they said, who first brought the cockroaches to Zhangji; it was my father who was the brains behind the cockroach operation. It was my father, the angry people of Zhangji decided, who was their common enemy. Every morning at first light, they descended upon our house in droves. They brought basins full of dead cockroaches and dumped them on our house. They spat curses at my father. A few times, my father went out for a stroll and returned battered and bleeding from rocks and clubs. Physically and mentally exhausted, he sank into a long depression. Again and again, hoping that the authorities might reconsider his findings, he got my mother to go lobbying the relevant organs of government on his behalf. 'Nobody else would ever do experiments like mine,' he told my mother. 'And they'll never find a real solution to the cockroach problem unless they do. You have to convince them.' My loyal mother was forced to gather up countless copies of the report and go, day after day, to government agencies, to Health and Sanitation, to the news agency. Every time she returned, my father's despair deepened, until it seemed that it would kill him.

One day, my mother made contact with an old friend who happened to be a distant relative of one of Zhangji's leaders. My mother's tenacity and determination must have moved the kind-hearted woman, for she leaked a piece of top-secret information. My father had been determined to be an agitator who was sowing discord among the residents of Zhangji. My mother knew there was no truth to the charge, but she could hardly ignore information from such an unimpeachable source. With uncharacteristic firmness, she demanded that my father cease all his efforts to exterminate the cockroaches. My father hadn't much time left at that point; my mother's daily labours on his behalf, however fruitless, had been the only thing keeping him alive. Now that she, too, had turned her back on him, he had no strength left to fight. He smiled at her sadly and turned to gaze out the window at the Dazhanghei River.

I paid a brief visit to the old family home while I was in Zhangji. I crossed the bed of the Dazhanghei River to reach the low house with its spacious yard. The Dazhanghei was no longer as I had imagined it: its waters had long since been replaced by garbage that gave off a ferocious stench at every step. I had intended to walk around the refuse, which mostly consisted of cockroach bodies, but I found that my old family home was now a lonely little island surrounded by garbage. The masters of the island were an unkempt old couple who kept slyly shifting position while I talked to them, as cockroaches do, so that I was never quite able to focus on them. A momentary terror flashed over their faces when I asked if they remembered the old owners of this house. 'No,' they said, making exaggerated waving motions with their hands. 'We don't remember.' They locked eyes, as if seeking confirmation from one another.

I said, 'I heard there was one house that got rid of the cockroaches once – do you know which one it was?'

'No,' they said. 'The cockroaches never really went away in Zhangji, not a single house has been freed of them.'

I said, 'Do you still remember the first Cockroach Conference?'

'Sure,' they said in unison. 'Of course we remember. Our city has no greater enemy than the cockroaches.

We will not rest until we have completely and utterly and totally and absolutely exterminated every last one of them.'

I couldn't help smiling coldly at this, which seemed to make them uneasy. We were standing next to the rubbish-heap in the yard, and the deep brown scales on their bodies glinted dizzyingly in the sunlight. There was no point in continuing the conversation, and after a long look at the house that had been my father's tomb, I turned and walked out of the yard.

On that other night, in that very house, my mother was afraid my father would be hurt by her insistence – but she was careful not to let slip what her friend had told her. Still in great distress, she fell asleep. In the middle of the night, when my father roused her from her nightmares, she was startled to find him suddenly cured, the marks the cockroaches had left on his body almost completely vanished. My father was still as gaunt as ever, and the scales had flaked off to reveal distressingly pale skin. He sat ramrod-straight on the bed, his limbs stiff and sluggish where before they had been lithe and nimble. He was smiling at her, and her spirits rose so suddenly that she dived into his arms.

'You're better? You're better! You're really better!' My mother pounded on my father's fragile chest, sobbing and laughing.

My father kissed her deeply, and for the longest time he said nothing at all. Later, after my mother had stopped sobbing and laughing and had settled down to stroking his arm, he said: 'Listen to me. I don't want you to be sad. I won't be getting better; I'll be dying very soon. Right now, this is the last glint of light before the sun goes down.'

It was the last time my mother and father ever talked. As the still, quiet night drew to a close, my father forlornly told her, 'I can smell the cockroaches again.' He was dead before sunrise; at dawn, my mother packed up everything we owned and left Zhangji with my father's body and little me.

On my way out of Zhangji, I took what must have been the same road that my mother took. It was the off-season, and all the tourists and sightseers had left the city, which stretched out cheerless and desolate behind me. The cockroaches would continue to come out in the evenings, but the locals had long since seen more than their fill, and the outsiders would have to wait for the next tourist season. I turned my head to look back at Zhangji, but it had vanished into the mist. I had entered the world beyond, where I could no longer smell the cockroaches; nor could my dead father or my living mother. At the side of the road, I took out the stack of papers that my mother had given me – my father's manuscript – and ripped the sheets to pieces, one by one, holding them up to scatter wherever they might go in this world beyond. I felt better after that, much better. If my mother asks about Zhangji when I get home, I thought, I will tell her, poker-faced and leaving as much room for misinterpretation as I can, that Zhangji doesn't need my father's plan, not anymore.

Vivisection

Neck

'I'LL TWIST YOUR NECK!'

This was, for a time, as commonly heard around Unit 362 as the catchiest lines in the *Quotations from Chairman Mao*. It sprang to the lips whenever two men, or two groups of men – or in a minority of cases, women – faced off, no matter whether they were grey-haired and grizzled or still wet behind the ears, no matter whether they were planning to exchange words or blows. For added effect, speakers could preface the phrase with set gestures: a cocked head; narrowed eyes; a haughty air; a contemptuous glare; a cold sneer.

The line came from a Soviet film that had recently been screened internally as part of the campaign against Khrushchev's revisionist line. The film was about a group of munitions plant workers who were fighting back against German Fascism. Unit 362 was a munitions production base too – though we were easily a thousand times bigger than the one in the film – and we adopted the catchphrase out of a sense of professional solidarity. It seemed a natural fit, even though we were red warriors protecting Chairman Mao's revolutionary line, and the line in question was the catchphrase of the film's villain, a blustery *Standartenführer* who went around threatening to twist people's necks. He never made good on the threat, though, and at the end of the film it was his own long, thin neck that proved fallible when a munitions worker twisted it until it went ka-*cha*. Also, the line had originally been 'I'll *wring* your neck,' but our reprisals – though perfect in every other aspect – invariably substituted 'twist'. This was intentional: we were simply correcting a mistake the voice actor had made when dubbing the film. We understood the two words differently at Unit 362: 'wringing' was soft, something you did to laundry. 'Twisting' was something you did to rebar.

'I'll twist your neck' first gained currency in the speech of plant workers in their 20s and 30s, particularly in situations where two groups were facing off, when tension hung in the air and all nerves were wired to hair-triggers. At first it was only the leaders of the groups who would say it. But everyone wants to be a leader, and everyone needs to vent, and soon it could be heard coming from the mouths of teens and middle-aged workers too, and from then on it became a common saying. Those of us who were too young to take part in revolutionary activities could only use it when horsing around, or fighting over girls, or trying to act tough, or when we wanted to express our anger or gather up our courage. We threw it out as viciously as we could. Sometimes a clearly weaker party would make so bold as to challenge an obviously stronger party with a cry of 'I'll twist your neck!' If the stronger party was magnanimous enough to laugh this off, the weaker party would walk away with a smug sense of having gotten away with something; otherwise, when the stronger party responded with the usual posturing and sneering, the weaker party would have to swallow their pride and back down, giggling nervously – 'Kidding! Kidding! I mean, it's you who'd be doing the twisting…' – before the stronger party could even say 'I'll twist *your* neck.' To hear us speak, you'd think there was an epidemic of neck-twisting, but not one of us ever did any actual twisting. In any real fight, the phrase was nothing more than a rhetorical flourish. I should clarify: none of us had actually seen the scene of the *Standartenführer* getting his own neck twisted; we had only heard about it. Only a select few people in all of 362 (and their friends and relatives) were privileged enough to see movies for the purpose of fighting revisionist thought. In time, the phrase lost most of its menace, and although we continued to use it – the grown-ups still did, and we were the children of grown-ups after all – it quickly became nothing more than bluster, an empty slogan, just as it had been in the mouth of the *Standartenführer*.

We gained a new measure of respect for the phrase after hearing one of the grown-ups say that the Tao girl's father, Big Tao, really had twisted a man's neck, and that the other man died right then and there.

The Tao girl was a boy too, but he was so fair-skinned and fine-featured, with long eyelashes and big round eyes prettier than any girl's, that we had bestowed upon him the nickname 'girl.' He did not take after his father, Big Tao, who was broad-shouldered and burly, with a permanent five o'clock shadow and a penchant for exaggeration that got him the nickname Big Talk. As the story went, when the ideological conflict between the 'East Is Red' faction from Plant 9 (our plant) and the 'Sun Rises' faction from Plant 7 turned physical, Big Talk got a man in a headlock with one arm and twisted until the man's neck went ka-*cha*. The person who told us this described it in such detail that it was as if we had front-row seats at the clubhouse cinema, and when he got to the end, his 'ka-*cha*' rang out as loud and sharp as a test detonation at one of the plants.

It was all anyone could talk about at first, 'ka-*cha*'s ringing out left and right, but soon doubts began to set in. In the heat of the moment, amidst the fog of war, with people either smashing the enemy or slinking away with their tails between their legs, who'd have time to notice other people and their 'ka-*cha*'s? In the end the verdict was that it was just Big Talk talking big again. The grown-ups made fun of Big Talk, and we made fun of the Tao girl, who really did look like a delicate little girl. But of course he was no such thing, and he didn't take well to being laughed at. He insisted that he'd asked his dad when he got home, and that his dad really had broken the man's neck, and that he really had heard the 'ka-*cha*.' 'Maybe your father *did* snap the man's neck,' we said, 'but there's no way it went "ka-*cha*."' We had asked around and been informed that the 'ka-*cha*' in the movie was what was known as a sound effect.

We argued back and forth with the Tao girl until someone suggested that we could try twisting a neck ourselves to settle the question. From our own considerable fighting experience we knew perfectly well that none of us had any chance of snapping anyone else's neck, let alone producing a 'ka-*cha*.' 'But we're just kids,' someone said. 'Of course we're not strong enough to snap another person's neck, but we could try it with a baby or a small animal.' This was an idea, we all agreed. But babies were hard to come by, and no one had the stomach to steal a baby and kill it, so we decided to try an animal instead. The Tao girl suggested a chicken. 'Why bother?' we said. 'A neck that thin, you might as well be strangling a grasshopper.' In the end we settled on a cat.

Mrs Qiu had a mid-sized grey cat who knew us and wouldn't be too hard to catch. That afternoon, we got some fish heads and lured it into an abandoned old swimming pool to make sure it wouldn't escape. The Tao girl wore gloves to protect against scratches and bites. He tried to conceal his nervousness by stroking the back of the cat's neck, then raised his hand to wipe his brow, leaving a few cat hairs plastered to his forehead. It wasn't a hot day: an autumn breeze cooled the air. 'Get on with it,' we told him. 'I will, I will,' he said, but his face was as grey as the cat's fur and he kept not doing anything. The cat snuggled into his arms, peeking up at him drowsily and purring. 'Now!' we yelled. And the Tao girl, seeing his chance, leaned over, pinned the cat's body between his knees, grasped the cat's head in his hands, took a deep breath, and wrenched it sharply clockwise. But he must have been focusing so intently on his hands that he forgot to squeeze his knees together, or perhaps he did squeeze but the cat struggled more forcefully than he had expected. Either way, the drowsy grey cat instantly transformed into a cannonball and shot out of the Tao girl's arms with an almost audible blast. The Tao girl's hands continued wrenching the cat's head, but its body dangled free and spun along with the head, making neck-twisting impossible. The Tao girl froze, panicking, and the grey cat used the force of the Tao girl's wrenching to curl its back upwards like a gymnast on the parallel bars and whirl its tail aside to clear the way for its rear paws, which it lashed – sharply, precisely, powerfully – at the Tao girl's sweaty face. He had gloves to protect his hands, but his face was unguarded. If he had been leaning backwards he might have avoided the attack, but he had leaned forward in his effort to twist the cat's neck. Things went much as you would expect, and by the time he let go in defeat, the Tao girl's pale, fine-featured face was running red with blood.

We were glad the Tao girl's experiment had ended in failure, but angry about what the cat had done to his face – he was one of us, after all. The cat yowled and ran for all it was worth, but it was trapped in the swimming pool. We had chosen the venue for our experiment carefully: people are smarter than cats. We caught the grey cat, and with shouts of 'We'll twist your neck' we avenged the Tao girl with sticks and knives and spades and bicycle chains. After beating it to death, we were going to try snapping its neck to see once and for all whether it would go 'ka-*cha*,' but by then it was a disgusting mass of blood, just like the Tao girl's face, and nobody wanted to touch it.

After the Tao girl's face healed we stopped calling him 'girl' and started calling him 'Dazhai', after the production brigade in the northwest where the workers had brought forth arable fields from barren wasteland. It wasn't the most obvious nickname, but if you remembered the slogan 'In Agriculture, Follow Dazhai!' and thought of the workers standing on rugged mountainsides, braving the elements and taming the wilds, then you'd get the idea.

Heart

Only one person in every 100,000 is born with their heart on the right, and Sha Guangming was one of the lucky few. Sha Guangming was Sha Sha's father.

One time, when I was trying to get in Sha Sha's good books, she asked me quietly if I harboured feelings for her and whether I intended to pursue her. Sha Sha was the only one of the 50 children in our year who could or would or dared use grown-up language like 'harbour feelings' and 'pursue' when talking to a student of the opposite sex, which was the main reason that I wanted to make her like me. The other reason was that she was pretty. Other boys tried to flatter her, but the only thing they had on their minds was that she was pretty. I ranked slightly higher in her estimation, since my flattery had altogether different motivations behind it.

I looked around to make sure we were alone, and then I blurted: 'Yes.'

Not that I was that mature beyond my years, or that I was capable of asking myself the same question. I was trying to get her to like me because it felt like the thing to do, like trying to win when you get on the football pitch. I said 'yes' partly because I couldn't think of anything else to say, and partly because I was sure that any of the other boys would have been so flustered by words like 'feelings' and 'pursue' that even if they wanted to say 'yes,' their lips would have been sealed or rather spot-welded shut. I didn't want to be like the other boys.

'So... is your heart on the right too?'

'Wh–what? I'm not a Rightist or a reactionary or a–'

'I mean is your heart on the right side of your chest – most people have their heart on the left and their liver on the right, but some people have their heart on the right and their liver on the left.'

'I – I don't know. My mom says the heart is *here*.' I patted the left side of my chest.

'Then you can keep your feelings to yourself and forget about pursuing me. My mom says that when my little sister and me are big we have to find a man with his heart on the right. When we grow up, I mean, not now.'

'Why? I mean, I know why not now, but why does the man's heart have to be on the right?'

'Because that's how my daddy is.'

Everybody in 362 knew how good Sha Guangming was to his wife, Wen Ju. In some households not an argument could go by without the woman saying, 'Why can't you be more like Sha Guangming? Look how he treats Wen Ju – and she's certainly no prize.' This was true: Wen Ju was skinny, sickly, no good around the house, and nothing much to look at, while Sha Guangming, in addition to being strikingly handsome, worked as a technician at the plant and made small-bore pistols that were masterpieces of craftsmanship.

I didn't learn about the medical condition of *situs inversus* – having one's organs reversed – until years later, but I confirmed with my mother that afternoon that Sha Guangming's heart really was on the wrong side. As soon as she said so, I began pestering her to take me to get my organs checked. 'They're all where they should be,' she said, cutting me off. 'No need to check.'

Years before, when Sha Guangming had first 'harboured feelings' for Wen Ju and 'pursued' her, he'd got into a fight over her with a bully from 362 who had been pushing her around. The two men fought right there in the workshop, in the middle of all the tools, and when Sha Guangming rushed at his opponent, the other man stuck a screwdriver into the left side of his chest. Everyone there thought that would be the end of Sha Guangming: the screwdriver went in so deep that they could only see the red handle sticking out of the left side of his chest where his heart was. Even Sha Guangming thought it looked pretty bad, and before he lost consciousness

21

he told the people around him to take a message to Wen Ju: 'I regret nothing – and if I don't die, I'll protect you as long as I live.' He didn't die; he made it through with nothing worse than a collapsed lung, and his heart, safe on the other side of his chest, came through unscathed. The two of them were married, and Sha Guangming, as good as his word, quickly gained a reputation as a model husband. Nobody could ever figure out what he saw in Wen Ju, though there was plenty of speculation. The predominant opinion was that people who got their insides backwards must get everything backwards, including ugliness and beauty.

The sickly Wen Ju had been a technician too, but her class background kept her from having any direct contact with military materiel, and she was soon reassigned to work as a ticket-taker at the base clubhouse, a job that offered none of the perks or prestige of being a technician. She never complained. Someone with her class background was in no position to pick and choose. Later, when the movies stopped and the clubhouse was used only for meetings, she was given odd jobs to do around the place. One day, as she was cleaning up after a large rally, she decided to shift a plaster bust of Chairman Mao from the right-hand side of the stage to the left. It was neither particularly large nor particularly heavy – even Wen Ju, feeble as she was, could have moved it on her own, or could at least have asked one of the men for help. She didn't call for anyone else; rather, she picked up the white plaster bust, which was neither particularly large nor particularly heavy, and carefully made her way across the stage. There was nothing in her way: the electrical cables did not snag her; the carpet did not trip her up; her arms didn't go out of their sockets; the soles of her shoes did not slip; still less did any strange, drugged feeling come over her. And yet somehow the statue fell from her arms to the boards of the stage, where it broke into pieces.

The crash resounded around the clubhouse, then was replaced by a deathly silence that spread instantly throughout the room, swallowing up even Wen Ju's cry of dismay. The other clubhouse workers froze where they were, like statues themselves, then turned to look at the stage, a captive audience, blank stares fixing upon Wen Ju from around the room. Wen Ju's wits returned, and in a trembling voice she asked the statues in the audience: 'Was that – Was it *me* who broke the statue of Chairman Mao?'

Nobody answered her. Statues can't talk.

The impromptu struggle session was already wrapping up by the time Sha Guangming came rushing in. There weren't many people at the struggle session, since it had been hastily convened: the clubhouse workers, still standing there like statues, and a handful of new arrivals standing up on the stage to restrain or criticize the accused. These were militia members who had arrived on the scene before Sha Guangming. On the big stage, Wen Ju and the guards and accusers standing around her looked like a scattering of coral reefs in the middle of the ocean. Wen Ju had blood on her forehead, and the ropes that bound her were all out of proportion to her fragile body. She was bent nearly double by the weight of an iron placard at her waist that said 'COUNTER-REVOLUTIONARY,' curling forward like a shrimp and hanging her head to reveal, in the middle of her black hair, a pale furrow of freshly shaved scalp. Sha Guangming rushed toward her, fists clenched. The militia men knew how dear his wife was to him; some of them had commissioned him to do off-the-books jobs for them before. They shifted awkwardly and tried to explain: 'It was a non-violent struggle session – nobody laid a finger on her. Those wounds on her forehead are from where she was hitting it against the wall to try to kill herself to escape punishment.' Sha Guangming ran to the foot of the stage. The two militia members restraining Wen Ju loosened their grips, even though they were carrying loaded rifles. But Sha Guangming was no longer the reckless young man who had thrown himself onto the point of a screwdriver. At the foot of the stage he stopped and meekly offered a suggestion: 'Let me take her place – let her go home and reflect on the wickedness of her counter-revolutionary crimes, and you can struggle against me…' This was out of the question, of course; class struggle was not a thing that could be bargained over. The militia men tightened their grip on Wen Ju and declared that Sha Guangming would not be allowed to take her place – not at that day's impromptu struggle session, not in the proper struggle sessions in the days to follow. However, as there had been no time to prepare a women's jail, Wen Ju would be permitted to return home for one night. The following day, once the new cell was ready, she was to take her belongings and present herself for investigation.

Sha Guangming climbed onto the stage and stood beside Wen Ju to be beaten along with her. He wore no placard or bonds.

The statement later given by Sha Guangming indicates that on their way to the clinic afterwards to have Wen Ju's wounds seen to, and then later on their way home, the two of them reached an agreement on how the rest of that night would go. Wen Ju initially had some reservations about half of the agreement, but Sha Guangming said, 'If I can't protect you then what point is there in going on?' After taking Wen Ju home, Sha Guangming took their daughters – Sha Sha and Sha Fei – to his mother's house on his bicycle. He returned home, where he and Wen Ju made dinner, had a drink, put their belongings in order, reminisced about the old days, wrote their wills, made love, and dressed themselves neatly. Then he took one of his finely crafted small-calibre pistols and fired it into Wen Ju's chest and his own. Before he fired, Wen Ju joked: 'Remember, my heart's on the left – don't miss.' He didn't: Sha Guangming pointed the barrel squarely at the left side of his wife's chest. When his own turn came, he aimed at the right side of his own chest, but something made his hand jerk at the last minute, throwing off his aim and sending the bullet into the left side. Maybe it was just too awkward to hold the gun in his right hand and aim at his right breast.

Sha Guangming didn't die; his heart continued beating

steadily. It was only later, after the gunshot wound in his left breast had healed, that he was executed for murder. When the time came, the residents of Unit 362 argued over where the firing squad would aim. The forehead? The mouth? The heart or the testicles? One busybody took it upon himself to remind the firing squad: 'The criminal has his heart on the right.'

Fingers

When we were little, my brothers and I used to eat our fingers. I don't mean we tried to chew them up like turnips and swallow them: we would put one finger – usually the thumb – into our mouths and suck on it like a popsicle or a piece of candy until we got every last bit of flavour out. Not that we really knew the taste of candy and popsicles back then. Turnips we did get occasionally, but never whole ones. Mama would always dice our limited supply of turnips up into small pieces and boil them, along with our even more limited volume of corn or sorghum or cornmeal, into a thick 'vegetable porridge'.

All children put their fingers in their mouths – something to do with the fact that people are mammals, perhaps – but my brothers and I kept on doing it until we were seven, nine, and eleven, and I'm afraid that this had more to do with the fact that we were hungry. Our family was as poor as most other ordinary people in China, never knowing when the next square meal would be, never keeping hunger away for more than a day at a time.

During the hardest period, the day's meal might be nothing more than water to fill the belly, and the previous day's meal a tiny saucer of rice gruel like you might feed a cat. Mama swelled up with dropsy, weak and fragile as a piece of thawed tofu, and she spent her days in bed, except for the time she spent outside gathering elm leaves to make 'dinners' that my brothers and I scarcely had the energy to eat. We could only huddle around her unsteadily with our thumbs in our mouths, on the point of death, like three river snakes stranded far from water. Mama tried to lull us to sleep, on the theory that we could survive as long as we conserved our energy and strength – but a person can only sleep so much, especially when their stomach is clenching and unclenching with hunger. And so we spent our time in bed mostly listening to Mama speaking to us listlessly. She thought this would work like a lullaby, or at least would distract us from our hunger. But hunger made her single-minded, and her murmuring never strayed far from the subject of food, and so we lay there listening, unable to fall asleep and growing ever more aware of our own hunger.

Mama liked talking about her father and grandfather: how they left Shandong during the famine and fled to the North-east, how they worked their way up from begging to full bellies. How they laboured and toiled, how they scrimped and saved, how they ate nothing but cabbage and tofu except at the new year, the one time they could bring themselves to slaughter a pig. How they would take the lead in the fields, working harder and faster than the hired hands, even after they became landowners themselves. How – criticising herself now – she didn't work hard enough, how she didn't save enough, and how our family was now paying the price. Though of course her father and grandfather had their flaws too. They kept to the old mentality, she said; their class-consciousness was low, and that was why they ran to the North-east instead of heading to the heartland and throwing their lot in with the Red Army. The Red Army had had it hard then – climbing snowy mountains and marching over grassland with nothing but grass and tree bark to eat – but they had the good life now, didn't they, with special ration books that let them buy pearl rice and white flour and pork and soybean oil. And it wasn't just them who benefited from the special treatment, it was their children and grandchildren too. 'If I was the daughter of a Red Army soldier,' Mama said dreamily, eyes fixed on the thumbs stuck in our mouths, 'it'd be mung-bean popsicles and milk candy in your mouths instead of your grubby little fingers…' We didn't understand anything about the 'special ration books' Mama talked about, but at the mention of popsicles and candy – mung-bean popsicles and milk candy, even – our mouths immediately began to water, and we wrapped ourselves up in our beautiful fantasies, and we sucked our fingers all the more loudly.

It was then that I heard my oldest brother whine: 'I wish fingers could fill your belly.'

Mama had never liked us sucking our fingers. She said it was how germs got into our tummies, and that it would stretch our fingers out long and thin. This time, though, she didn't scold us. 'Of course they can,' she said faintly, as if lost in her own dreams. 'But not your fingers – it should be Mama's fingers…' We looked at her in surprise, then looked at her ten fingers, which were so badly swollen they looked like pickled cucumbers. 'If there's ever a time when we don't have anything to eat,' she continued, 'if you're ever too hungry to go on, then you can eat Mama's fingers. Not your own, mind; never your own!' She raised her hands unsteadily and turned them over to appraise them. 'One finger a day for each of you,' she said. 'Mama's fingers will help you hold on for three more days – and maybe that will be long enough…'

'But what will you eat?' my other brother asked, worried.

'Me?' Mama could hardly keep her eyes open, and her voice was growing fainter and fainter. 'Mama isn't hungry,' she said. 'Mama's fingers are for her babies when they need them most…'

It looked as if she had drifted off to sleep, but I shook her. 'But you've got ten fingers, Ma – more than we can eat in three days.'

I was a clever little thing. I'd never been to school, but I already knew that if you took three threes from ten you'd have one left over, and I was sharp enough to hope that once I'd reminded Mama she would take my side, as she always had, and say 'You're the baby, so you can have the left-over finger too.' My older brothers would be so jealous, I thought – and with Mama's left-over finger, I'd be able to live an extra day, and I'd have an extra chance of a full belly or even popsicles and candy…

With a visible effort, Mama opened her eyes to take another look at her hands, as if she had only just realised that she had ten fingers. She forced a smile. 'You can all share it – or leave it for Mama…' She lifted the index finger of her right hand and waved it at us listlessly. 'Don't forget Mama's students – they need this too. When Mama goes to teach them, you can tie a piece of chalk to this finger so Mama can write on the blackboard.' Mama was the best maths teacher at the 362 middle school, and I had inherited her ability to do sums.

In the end, the three of us managed to survive without eating Mama's fingers, but I am sorry to say that her right index finger, the one she had planned to save for writing on the chalkboard, the one we weren't allowed to eat, was ultimately doomed. Several years later, when some of my mother's students were holding a struggle session against her, they took the sharpened steel drafting triangle from the maths classroom and chopped off her right index finger. Her students must have been as hungry as my brothers and me once, but they had enough to eat by then, and instead of eating her finger they nailed it to the blackboard and left it there for three days where everyone could see it.

Penis

The dead were 'departed' in Unit 362. A spell in prison was 'going inside.' Spouses were 'himself' or 'herself at home.' Such substitutions were more or less the same everywhere, I imagine; people in Yunnan or Gansu or Zhejiang would most likely be familiar with them. But we also referred to the penis as 'Number Two' in 362, and I'm not sure people in other places would understand the term. The penis was like the given names of leaders: best replaced with titles like 'head' or 'director,' being even less suitable for open discussion than death or prison or spouses. If someone were to conduct a nationwide survey, I'm sure they would uncover at least a hundred euphemisms for 'penis' – or at least they would have back then. Today *xiao didi*, 'Little Brother,' has swept the field as thoroughly as the conquering Qin army that first united China. There's nothing wrong with referring to the penis as one's Little Brother per se, but I find the 'Number Two' of my youth preferable to the cutesy softness of the latter: forceful, unambiguous, and to the point, with a stately touch of old-fashioned phallocentrism. But the battle has been fought and Little Brother has emerged victorious. The term has its origins in Hong Kong and Taiwan, like 'future outlook,' 'channels of communication,' and 'wellness'. But 362 was not Hong Kong or Taiwan.

But to get back to the story:

My eldest brother was curled up and rolling around on the floor, caroming between the corners of the chairs, the chest, and the bed. One of the corners set off the zip gun in his pocket with a sharp *bang* that froze my other brother and me on the spot and put a stop to our squabbling. Fortunately, the gun seemed to have been aimed at the foot of the wall rather than at any of us – otherwise we would have had some *real* excitement. Snapped back to attention, my brother and I took the gun away from my eldest brother, then turned our gaze to the wall, whose base was peppered with iron shot. We looked at this for a moment and then ran, as one, to the window and leaned out.

'Fuck – we've got to get someone,' my other brother said, then poked me. 'Get Mr Zhang!'

'*You* get someone,' I said, dodging to one side in case the pokes turned to blows. 'Get Mrs Zhao.'

Amid the crowd of neighbours returning home from work, Mr Zhang and Mrs Zhao went their separate ways, and my brother and I said nothing. Even if we did call out to them, we knew there was no guarantee that they would dare help us. People had generally left the three of us to ourselves ever since Dad 'departed' and Mama 'went inside.' It was under our eldest brother's feeble direction that we removed a door from its frame and used it to carry him to the clinic. On the way there we passed a few people we knew, but most of them only looked at us in surprise and then turned away. A few asked what was wrong, and my brother and I replied simply that our eldest brother's stomach hurt. The three of us were as careful to maintain our dignity as our parents had been.

Appendicitis. A common ailment, swiftly diagnosed by the doctor while we were still in the clinic corridor, but our eldest brother's pain was so great that if he didn't go into surgery immediately his life could be in danger. The doctors directed the nurse to give my brother a shot of anaesthetic. There were two doctors, a man and a woman roughly the same age as our parents, and two nurses, both women the same age as my eldest brother. They had us carry him into the emergency room and strip him while they prepped for surgery, as if we were medical workers too. We knew our surroundings well enough; it had been as busy as the social club over the past half-year, crowds of people coming and going, and when our father had 'turned his back on the people and on the Party' by killing himself, we had spent the night there. Our eldest brother calmed down as the painkiller took effect, and he motioned shyly for my brother and me to give him something to cover himself with. He was stark naked from the waist down. The doctor barked at him to stay still, and my brother and I turned our backs on him to fill out a form at a table in the corner.

The first thing was to pick a line from the *Quotations from Chairman Mao* to write on the form, but we couldn't agree on which line to use. Next was our brother's name, our parents' names, and the divisions in which they were employed. We were arguing over whether we should write our father's name when we heard one of the nurses at the operating table shriek, 'Pervert!' We turned around to see our eldest brother, face beet-red, arching his back, thrusting his buttocks off the table as hard as he could. His Number Two stood ramrod-straight in the middle of his body, bobbling up and down every time he moved. Thick leather straps criss-crossed his arms, legs, and chest, holding him to the operating table; otherwise he would have curled up or turned over or covered his Number Two with his hands. So *that* was why he wasn't lying still. My brother and I didn't feel right looking at our eldest brother's Number Two, so we turned to look at the nurse, who was off to one side, sobbing. *For goodness' sake*, we thought, silently reproving our brother: she was so ugly that it hardly seemed worth the bother.

'Oh, don't be a baby.' The male doctor chided the ugly nurse, smiling. He glanced at the form my brother and I had filled out. 'Hmm?' he said. 'His parents are –' and then our parents' names. The doctor walked back to the operating table. My eldest brother's Number Two had shrunk back down by this point. 'The son of a counter-revolutionary, and you think you can molest my nurses!' His tone was severe.

'I wasn't, I wasn't!' Our brother pleaded as loudly as he could, using whatever strength he had left after enduring so much pain.

The woman doctor came in to smooth things over. She urged the male doctor to calm down, soothed the ugly nurse, and directed the other nurse, the pretty one, to – Wait. The pretty nurse was holding a stainless steel razor, ready to shave off our brother's hair. He had a lot of it: fur covered his lower abdomen, and his Number Two lay concealed among his pubic hair like a withered tree branch fallen amid undergrowth. At least nobody would accuse him of molestation now. But it was not to last: just as my brother and I were sighing with relief, our eldest brother's Number Two rose again alongside the pretty nurse's hand – albeit with difficulty, like a soldier bent but not broken under enemy torture. The pretty nurse looked around at everyone else, then gave a little gasp. If she hadn't been the focus of attention for everybody in the room, I'm sure she would have been able to continue, provided that my brother's Number Two didn't get in the way of her razor. But now, with all eyes on her and my brother's misbehaving Number Two, she could only shriek to keep up appearances. The male doctor was the first to react. He ran over, pushed the pretty nurse out of the way, undid the strap holding down my brother's right arm, and tried to haul my brother to his feet.

'Dr. Liu,' the female doctor said, pushing my brother back down and placing herself between them. 'What are you doing?'

'A counter-revolutionary *and* a pervert,' the male doctor cried. 'Call a struggle session!'

'He's a patient, and he needs surgery immediately!'

'He's a counter-revolutionary and a pervert first! We must treat the mind before treating the body.'

'Come now, Dr. Liu. You're a man too, and you know perfectly well that this is an ordinary physiological response.'

'What are you trying to say, Dr. Chen? Are all men perverts? Are physiological responses exempt from the dictates of Marxism-Leninism and Mao Zedong Thought? That's a dangerous way to be talking, Dr. Chen, very dangerous– '

'I'm sorry, Dr. Liu, but the anaesthetic will wear off soon. Any further delay will *really* be dangerous. Now' – she turned to the pretty nurse. 'You prep the incision site, and' – to the ugly nurse – 'you prepare the sedative.'

The anaesthetic really must have been wearing off: beads of sweat covered my brother's face, and he clenched his eyes shut and bit his lip. I was more worried about his Number Two. Thanks be, the mischievous little bugger finally went soft and curled up limply in the gorse of his pubic hair. The pretty nurse picked the razor up and returned to the side of the operating table. Without warning, my brother's eyes snapped open and darted around; then his right hand, freed from the straps, shot out, caught the pretty nurse's hand as it lowered the razor towards his bellybutton, and snatched the razor away before it could touch his pubic hair. In the blink of an eye, he grabbed the handle of the razor, turned his wrist, and curled his arm back towards himself. He had always been a good fighter, ruthless and agile, but it was a pretty move even by his standards, as pretty as the nurse. What he did next wasn't pretty, though; it was cruel, though perhaps there was a beauty to the cruelty. He put his right hand back out, down, and up again in a glinting arc, and suddenly his dark pubic hair was all ablaze.

The razor was hard, his Number Two was soft, and the latter was no match for the former.

Toes

We didn't have the terms that we do now – 'hat trick,' 'banana ball,' 'flying tackle.' But that's not to say that we didn't have these things. You could always find them out on the pitch.

We didn't talk about 'golden left feet' then either, but nothing short of 'golden' would do justice to Hong Chunhao's miraculous left foot, which could put the ball anywhere it wanted. Hong Chunhao's left foot was best at direct free kicks from the 45-degree angles about 25 yards out. When he took a direct free kick, his run-up would be five paces or less, but he would charge the ball with such power that it would soar over the other team's defences and drop down perfectly into the goalie's blind spot. The reedy-voiced radio commentator always described his kicks as being like 'cannonball blasts.' Hong Chunhao was a member of the Unit 362 football team, and the reedy-voiced commentator's reference to cannonballs was a subtle allusion to the goods produced at 362. Even subtle allusions were no good: during the Cultural Revolution the reedy-voiced commentator was charged with revealing military secrets and ended up with a placard around his neck identifying him as a spy. But this came afterwards and has no bearing on our story, and so we will speak no more of it.

Our football team had won the national inter-factory cup, and they were the pride of Unit 362. When the twenty or thirty thousand plant employees and their families were going hungry, the football team still got two pieces of salt fish and three pieces of braised pork at every meal. We didn't begrudge them that. The salt fish and braised pork weren't just because of their status as champions: the team regularly took part in external affairs as friendship ambassadors between the Chinese people and the peoples of the world. You didn't want starved-looking ambassadors. They were responsible primarily for friendship with Albania and the Democratic People's Republic of Korea. (China stood proudly aloof at that time, extending the hand of friendship only to the DPRK, Albania, and a select few other countries.) As luck would have it, the DPRK and Albania were also fond of football, and so we conveyed our friendship via the feet. Unit 362 had no contact with any professional teams they might send to China, but whenever amateur teams visited, Hong Chunhao and the others would have their moment in the sun – and all the salt fish and braised pork they could eat for days on end.

The municipal radio station had a good relationship with the plant, and would record and relay broadcasts of all these 'world-class' matches. Those of us who enjoyed football – me, Jumbo, and the other kids – would happily listen to the reedy-voiced commentator calling the matches we had just watched. But we always turned the radio off in the final moments of the game. It wasn't that we already knew how the match would end; it was that the reedy-voiced commentator never reported the final score, so the broadcasts always ended in a disappointing tease. Being a football fan was about excitement, not disappointment. As the broadcasts drew to a close, the commentator would go from talking about the game to yammering about how the match had strengthened the friendship between our peoples in defiance of the forces of imperialism and revisionism, as if he didn't understand that even a nil-nil draw would be of interest to his listeners.

Jumbo's older brother, Big Jumbo, was the captain of the team, and Jumbo used to pass on the team's most closely guarded secrets to us, so we knew that the commentator's failure to report the final scores was a matter of foreign affairs, rather than simple omission. At almost every friendly match, the leaders dictated that if our team fell behind, they should do everything possible to equalise but they shouldn't take the lead, whereas if they did take the lead, they should allow the opposing team to draw level without being obvious about it. Draws were preferable, but even a loss was better than a win. As a result, the plant team was always victorious in domestic matches, for which there was no radio coverage, and had to draw or lose in the friendly matches that were broadcast. They did win sometimes. Winning meant mandatory self-criticisms, punishment, and deprivation of salt fish and braised pork. There was a skill to throwing matches, and the opposing team would be insulted if the miskicks and referee's decisions became too obvious. And there were times when our team made the mistake of scoring the first goal, or accidentally pulled ahead while trying to keep things even, or didn't have enough time to throw the match properly, or were pitted against a team so wretched they couldn't even put the ball in an open net; on these occasions the 362 team had no way of avoiding a diplomatic faux pas. Mostly, the 362 team spent its time hoping that the DPRK or Albania would send a professional team posing as amateurs. The home team might lose – it *would* lose – but at least they would have a chance to slip their fetters and play their best.

One day, when they were up against a team from the DPRK, Hong Chunhao put on the team captain's armband. Jumbo was the team captain, not Hong Chunhao, but any time we hosted a team from the DPRK, Hong Chunhao got to wear the armband. Big Jumbo was not happy about this, but the leaders explained that since Hong Chunhao's family was ethnically Korean, our friends from the DPRK would find a fellow Korean leading the opposing team to be a spur to friendly competition between our two nations. Usually, Hong Chunhao would liven up at the chance to wear the captain's armband, and his golden left foot would find a way to level the toughest match. On that day, however, he couldn't work up any enthusiasm: the leaders had explained that a draw would be unacceptable, and that the match would have to end in a loss – ideally, with the DPRK winning two-one. We had to score at least once, after all.

Hong Chunhao was a simple, stubborn sort, and he didn't like playing to lose – not as the captain, not even if you made him the coach. He didn't even want to go out on the pitch. Obviously this was not acceptable: the leaders expected him to deliver welcoming remarks to the other team in Korean.

The match began. It was a tough one. The two teams were evenly matched in the first half and played without holding back. Most games where the teams were evenly matched went this way: the fluffed passes and miskicks didn't appear until the second half. By the halftime break, Hong Chunhao had forgotten that he didn't want to be playing, and he began slapping palms and egging on his teammates. Seeing that he and his teammates were thinking about football rather than diplomacy, the leaders reminded everyone that they were supposed to throw the game. They specifically instructed Big Jumbo, denuded of his captain's armband, that the aim was to lose.

Eight minutes into the second half, before we could start throwing the game, the DPRK team scored the first goal of the match with a gorgeous header. Three minutes later, before we could mobilise an effective attack, they scored again after a beautiful break away. The boys on our side started to see red, and they began their counterattack, but the other team set up a Catenaccio defence, and we couldn't score no matter how perfect the build-up play. One of our defenders committed a foul in the penalty box 21 minutes into the half when he collided with one of their players. Never mind a penalty kick; it was a red card. We were losing three-nil, down to ten men, with only 24 minutes left of the game.

Hong Chunhao was getting worked up. Big Jumbo was getting worked up. All of our players were getting worked up. Losing was one thing, but three-nil was a whole different species of shame. No matter how we tried, though, we couldn't even get close to their goal. The DPRK team's defensive, physical strategy was crushing us left and right. Our team usually acted as a group in these friendly matches, rather than risk injury by having individual players charge forward on their own, but there was no room for cooperation now. Even if it meant sacrificing players, we were going to have to use the opponents' physical tactics to win some free kicks from key positions, so we could save face with Hong Chunhao's golden left foot. Thirty-one minutes into the second half, Big Jumbo set up a free kick from the right wing and Hong Chunhao came running over. He straightened out his captain's armband, squinted at the goal, then fired off one of his 'cannonballs.' Three-one. Thirty-seven minutes into the half, Hong Chunhao set up his own free kick, on terms more to his liking, from the left wing. Three-two. Face saved for the players on the pitch and the leaders off the pitch; gameplan achieved, both sides could now go home happy. But the DPRK players failed to read the Chinese gameplan, and began shaking in their boots at the thought of what the last eight minutes might bring. They saw the Korean-speaking captain of the Chinese team playing as if with divine assistance, and they knew that there was nothing stopping his golden left foot from scoring two more free kicks in those final eight minutes. Exhausted as they were, the only way they could preserve their victory was with aggressive play – and they targeted Hong Chunhao in particular, mobbing him and cursing at him in Korean. Hong Chunhao returned fire, though fortunately he retained enough political consciousness to answer them in Chinese and not Korean. He only got a yellow card for that. Then, with just two minutes to go, a perfect free kick opportunity opened up. The DPRK team was so stunned that they forgot to set up their wall – or maybe they thought it wouldn't do any good against Hong Chunhao's 'cannonballs'. Imagine their surprise when they saw an argument break out between two members of the Chinese team.

'Don't score, Chunhao!' This was Big Jumbo, who had run over to remind Hong Chunhao.

'I'll cut my fucking foot off if I don't put this away!'

'We're supposed to lose!'

'I know! Look, I'll score this and then we'll stop. There's still two minutes, we'll just stand where we are and let them win.'

'No way – too obvious. Let me take this!'

'Get fucked. Free kicks are my job.'

'I'm the captain and I'm taking it!'

'I'm the captain now, asshole!'

Hong Chunhao shoved Big Jumbo away, took a deep breath, and squinted at the DPRK team's defence and their goal. He ran up, swung his leg, lifted his foot, and – never touched the ball. His golden left foot flew down and forward, nothing between it and the ball but air and Big Jumbo's right foot. There was an almighty *crack*: the sound of Big Jumbo's right ankle snapping and three toes on Hong Chunhao's left foot shattering. The two of them were carried off the pitch.

Hong Chunhao could still play after that, but his left foot wasn't what it had been, and he had to switch to his right foot. The leaders encouraged him to serve the unity of the proletarian masses of the world by training up a golden right foot – not in so many words, but that was what they meant. He did train – but even at its best, his right foot was only a little bit better than mine or Jumbo's or any of the other kids'.

Metamorphosis

THERE ARE THOSE WHO would say that tales of the fantastic can come only from the time of Apuleius or Kafka. Nothing could be further from the truth. The truth is that no life, no matter how dull, ever wants for strange occurrences. Life treats every person in every age equally in this regard, and if the evidence of our eyes and ears should prove uninteresting then we have only our own diminished powers of observation and comprehension to blame. Fantastic tales are like romantic encounters: anyone with a mind to find them is bound to do so with some regularity.

It was my most recent such encounter that brought me the tale that I am about to relate.

It begins with Maomao and the old man who brought her into the city. Maomao was a cat, not a person; solidly built, with blue-green eyes and short, inky black fur. She could often be found skulking in out-of-the-way corners, busily washing her face with paw and tongue or sitting in quiet mannerly contemplation, the very image of a chaste and refined young lady. She was not a valuable cat, of course – her bloodline was nothing much to speak of – and the old man who brought her to the city with him had other reasons for doing so. But we shall come to these presently.

Maomao and the old man had lived together for many years. The old man had been the chief of a granary management station. His wife had been the deputy chief of the granary management station, and Maomao had been the granary manager. Maomao was a skilled mouser, victorious every time she moved against a target. By the time our tale begins, the old man's wife had already passed on to a better place, leaving the old man and Maomao with nobody but one another, and prompting the old man's son to send, once again, for the old man to come and live with him in the city. The son had been dutifully trying to get his father and mother to come and live with him ever since he first got his bearings in the city and converted his four-person dormitory room for a single-room apartment. But the old man had scorned the offer, saying, 'One bedroom's barely enough for a single person to snore in!' Later, after the son's one-bedroom apartment became a two-bedroom apartment and then a three-bedroom apartment, the old man had to fall back on other excuses: that he was too old, too set in his ways, too unused to city living. But now, with his wife gone and his son risen far enough through the ranks to merit four bedrooms and two living rooms, the old man no longer had any plausible reason to refuse. And the absence of anyone else around the house was a real consideration, now that his wife was gone. And so it was that the old man and Maomao said their farewells to the granary and rode to the city in the son's fine new Audi.

There were four people in the son's household already: the son, the son's wife, the old man's teenaged grandson, and a young housekeeper who was only a year or two older than the grandson. The young housekeeper had been brought in from the old man's hometown while the old man's wife was still alive. Under the highly ramified kinship system of their native countryside, she would ordinarily have addressed the old man as *Daye*, or Uncle; the son and his wife as *Dage* and *Dasao*, or Older Brother and Older Brother's Wife, and the grandson as *Zhizi*, or Nephew. As a mere housekeeper, however, she was careful not to forget her station, and since she was almost the same age as the grandson, she behaved like a member of his generation in addressing the son and his wife as *Shushu* and *Shenzi*, or Uncle and Uncle's Wife, and the old man as *Yeye*, or Grandpa.

The son, the son's wife, and the grandson were all smiles and deference when the old man arrived – but at Maomao they cast a more jaundiced eye. She was, as I have said, neither a dainty housecat nor a winsome young kitten, and though she may have been elegant in repose, graceful in action, and well-mannered at all times, she was still, after all, a fully-grown cat, and a large one at that. And perhaps it was natural enough for city people who rarely came into contact with animals to recoil at the sight of a majestic carnivore so large of paw, so sharp of tooth, so bright of eye. Still, the son, the son's wife, and the grandson kept their complaints to themselves: the son's earlier attempts to persuade his father not to bring Maomao had only upset the old man.

Before bringing him, the son had tried to explain that such large animals weren't allowed in the city, but the old man only said, 'You rank higher than a county boss now, don't you? Who else would dare say "no" to your old man?'

'I can get you a dog if you like,' the son said haplessly. 'A Pekingese or a Papillon or a poodle or a pug, but the cat...'

'Everything I own is worthless junk to you,' the old man raged. 'And now you'd have me get rid of a cat that's been like a daughter to me? You'd rather have me die of boredom there in the city, is that it? Oh, you say you're thinking about me, you're worrying about me – worrying I'll be a thorn in your side as long as I'm still drawing breath, more like! Better I should go there and twist in the breeze for a month or three, and then once I've given up the ghost you'll be rid of me!'

Nothing the son said could change the old man's mind, and in the end he could only call home on the drive into the city to tell his wife and son, 'The cat, Maomao, is very dear to my father, so you're not to say a word against her.' So they didn't – but the old man could read their faces easily enough. Fortunately, the young housekeeper from the countryside was very taken with Maomao, and her delight broke the tension in the room. The old man looked at the young housekeeper. 'She'll do,' he said.

Everything was fresh and exciting to the old man those first few days in the city. He passed the time chatting with the young housekeeper, asking about this or that, and to all appearances was perfectly content. But there was a change in him after those first few days: he grew restless, as if there was a great weight on his mind. When he was not sitting on his own and staring off into space, he was wandering around in a terrible temper. He held back with his son's family, and most of the time he had no target for his anger but the young housekeeper – but she was kinder to Maomao than anybody else in the household, and he could find nothing to fault her for. The old man had to keep his anger to himself, and it piled up on his face.

One day, while the housekeeper was out buying vegetables, the phone rang. The old man hesitated, but seeing that the phone had no intention of stopping, he picked up the receiver. A young lady's pleasant voice came from the speaker.

'Someone paged me?' the young lady said.

'Paid you?' said the old man. 'Paid you what?'

'Who is this?' the young lady said.

'None of your damned business,' the old man said. 'What do you want?'

'Well you don't have to get upset,' the young lady said. 'Who is this?'

'You're the one who called,' the old man said. 'Don't you know who you're calling?'

'Crazy old fool,' the young lady snapped. 'What the hell is your problem?' She slammed down the phone.

The old man sputtered with rage. After a moment's thought he picked up the receiver again, dialed a random number, and shouted down the line: 'I'm not paying you a *thing*, you little whore!'

Perhaps the old man took inspiration from this event: from then on, whenever he was in a bad mood, he would dial random numbers as soon as he was left alone in the apartment: 'I'm not paying you a *thing*, you little whore!' And whenever he bellowed this into the phone, his expression would soften a little.

The food was far better in the city than it had been in the countryside, of course, but the old man had no taste for it. It was less a question of how much or how little he ate than of his obvious inability to derive any pleasure or enjoyment from the food.

'Are you feeling all right?' his son asked.

'Is something wrong with our housekeeper's food?' the son's wife asked.

'Are you bored because I don't have any time to spend with you?' the grandson asked.

'No,' he said to all of these. 'No no no,' he said, 'It's fine. Everything is just fine.' The leftovers he fed to Maomao, who savoured every mouthful.

The old man's low spirits put Maomao, who was after all used to him, in low spirits as well. She had grown closely attuned to his moods, and was careful to observe his expression before doing anything. One night, hearing the flick of a cigarette lighter in the old man's room, she crept from her basket in a corner of the apartment's enclosed north balcony to the old man's door, which she pushed open. Inside, the old man was lying awake in the dark, smoking a cigarette and sighing to himself. He didn't hear Maomao enter, but he sensed something, and turned his head to see her sitting on the floor, looking up at him sadly. The old man started but made no other response; his eyes were turned in her direction, but he barely seemed to see her. After some time, he lifted his arm to wave at the space in the darkness where Maomao sat, shooing her away. The darkness had no effect on Maomao's ability to see the old man's face and the subtle changes in his expression. She left, dejectedly.

Instead of returning to her basket, however, Maomao slipped out the balcony window and descended by windowsill, planter, drainpipe, and gutterspout to the street, where she stretched and then broke into a run. She ran aimlessly at first, until a combination of experience and intuition gave her a bearing. She crouched, waiting, in a quiet corner of a grocer's store stockroom. She hunted by sound, by scent – and shortly before daybreak her patience was rewarded.

Victorious, Maomao ran happily back to the apartment and slipped into the old man's room just as the sky was turning a soft grey. The old man was ugly as he slept, and his ragged snores were unpleasant to listen to – but Maomao, unperturbed, jumped up to the head of the old man's bed and brushed her tail lightly against his face. The old man jerked awake and sat up to see Maomao and the fat grey mouse that dangled from her mouth. The dying mouse had stopped struggling and was now merely gazing around, wide-eyed, as if seeking some sort of communion or closure. The old man cheered up visibly at the sight.

As soon as the son and the son's wife and the grandson had left for work and school, and the housekeeper had gone out to run her errands, and only he and Maomao were left in the apartment, the old man sprang into action. He put a pot of water on the stove, got out the cutting board and a kitchen knife, and set about preparing the mouse. First he removed the fur with boiling water and a paring knife, then neatly sliced off the tail, which he tossed to Maomao. 'Sorry, Maomao,' he said as he cracked open the mouse's ribs, gutted it, and removed the head, 'But after all this time I think I'm going to need this one to myself. You'll have to make do with the head and tail for now.' Maomao slunk out of his way forlornly and watched the old man light the stove burner beneath the wok. The air filled with the scent of scallions, salt, MSG, pepper, and a small portion of mouse. A few moments later, with the extractor fan above the stove still whirring and the delicious smell still hanging in the air, the old man carried the mouse-meat out into the dining room and gobbled it down with a chaser of sorghum liquor. Maomao stayed alone in the kitchen, with the mouse's pointy head, thin tail, and a small, wet pile of fur in front of her. After investigating these with her nose and finding nothing of interest, she left the kitchen and returned to the balcony, where she buried her face in her own food dish. A lavish meal awaited her: fatty red-braised pork, pan-seared cutlassfish, and pig's trotters in sauce, as well as calcium tablets and capsules of Vitamins A and B. The old man carried his empty bowl back into the kitchen, where he was slightly put out to see that the mouse's head, tail, and fur were on the floor where he had left them. 'Now, Maomao,' he said, sticking his head into the enclosed balcony, 'You can't be stealing the food out of my mouth. They've made a gourmand out of you; isn't that enough?' Maomao stopped her careful chewing and leapt up onto the windowsill to lick the old man's face. The old man smiled. He belched contentedly, then wrapped the mouse's head, tail, and fur in a sheet of newspaper. He stuffed the little packet as far down in the kitchen trash can as it would go, then washed his hands and went into the living room to watch *Animal Planet* on television.

That night, Maomao again heard the flick of a cigarette lighter coming from the old man's room. Once again she padded silently to his door and pushed it open. The old man was lying awake in the dark, smoking a cigarette and humming to himself. He didn't hear Maomao enter, but he sensed something, and turned his head to see her sitting on the floor below, looking up at him amorously. The old man started, then quickly stubbed out his cigarette and waved at the space in the darkness where Maomao sat, beckoning her closer. The darkness in the room had no effect on Maomao's ability to see the old man's face and the subtle changes in his expression. She rose excitedly, went over to close the door, and then sprang up to the bed, where she nestled lightly into the old man's embrace...

Later that night, when the old man had settled into an exhausted, death-like sleep, Maomao sprang into action. Once again she slipped stealthily from the balcony and ran through the deserted streets raising her voice in long, full-throated yowls.

Once again, she slipped back to the stockroom of the grocery store; once again, she brought back a big, fat mouse.

As time went by, the two of them resumed some semblance of their old days at the granary management station. Their new environment was unfamiliar and less private than what they were accustomed to, but they had come to understand the rhythms of the household, and as long as they didn't get carried away or make any foolish moves, they wouldn't have to worry about disturbing the others. Their lives fell into a regular pattern: every few days, when the old man grew irritable and cooled in his affections, Maomao would dash out to the dark grocer's storeroom to provide a feast for his delectation. But some other things had changed, unnoticed. Once the old man stopped sharing his mouse-meat with Maomao – as he always had at the old grain depot – Maomao lost all interest in eating mice. Now, when the old man dropped the heads, tails, and skins onto the floor, Maomao no longer paid the slightest attention. One day when he was in a particularly charitable mood, the old man left a few large chunks of mouse in Maomao's food dish, on top of a pile of shrimp. He returned some time later to find that Maomao had eaten the shrimp and left the mouse untouched. 'Look at you,' the old man grumbled to her, 'Spoiled rotten. Picky as a human.'

As the old man's day-to-day mood improved, the moods of the other people in the household improved along with it. His son and his son's wife and his grandson even warmed to Maomao. The young housekeeper took Maomao on regular trips to the vegetable market. The grandson, always busy with schoolwork, would hold Maomao and play with her, occasionally reciting the poems and English vocabulary words he was busily memorising – and he taught her other skills besides. One time, for instance, he carried Maomao to the entrance of a little street and pointed to a boy who was reading a book at the far end. Maomao, understanding instantly, bared her teeth, unsheathed her claws, pounced like a tiger and left the face of the boy (who had recently unseated the grandson as head of their class) a mass of bloody ribbons. The son's wife had originally thought of Maomao as an extension of the old man, and her resentment of him naturally meant that she had resented Maomao from the moment she laid eyes on her. She was a crafty woman, though, and she softened toward Maomao after realising that it would hurt the old man all the more if she could come between Maomao and him. Whenever she had a free moment, she could be found holding Maomao close to her, endlessly brushing the vain Maomao's coat and dressing her up. She applied layer upon layer of her own cosmetics to Maomao's body and face, enveloping the beguiling Maomao in the scent of lipstick and eyeshadow and shampoo and hair cream and unguents. She even made a set of clothes – complete with vest, pants, shoes and stocking, and top hat – for Maomao, who followed her around at her beck and call. The son, meanwhile, not only changed his feelings toward Maomao but began to bring up the idea of breeding Maomao with a nice tom somewhere, on the strength of a single event. After dropping his wife off at work one day, the son found that Maomao was still there in his Audi, all dolled up. With no time to take Maomao home, he could only bring her in to work with him. A section chief under him happened to drop by his office to have sex with him that day, and they were in such a rush to get up against the desk that they neglected to lock the door. Another section chief, meanwhile, had chosen that particular moment to swing by to present a report. Sensing trouble, Maomao immediately ran to guard the door, where she yowled and spat at the section chief standing outside. In his eagerness to present his report, the man failed to take the hint – and severely underestimated Maomao's battle capabilities. It was a total rout. When the man worked up the courage to return, he found the son (who had pulled up his trousers in the interim) sitting imposingly behind his desk, reviewing official documents.

There were, of course, slip-ups, near-misses, moments when Maomao and the old man's secret nearly came to light. Several times, the young housekeeper returned from her errands just after the old man had finished his mousy repast, before the greasy smell of his cooking had completely vanished from the kitchen. When this happened, the young housekeeper would wrinkle her nose and narrow her eyes at the discovery of a sneaky eater in the household and adopt a tone of not-entirely-mock exasperation: 'Grandpa, I spend half my days going between the kitchen and the dining room. If there's anything you've got a hankering for, tell me and I'll make it for you and Uncle's Wife and the others won't have to find out about it.' The old man's face would alternately flush and blanch with an anger he could not express. He was not concerned about his son's wife finding out that he had been sneaking meals; what concerned him was what he would say if she wanted to know what he had been eating. 'No no no,' he answered the young housekeeper, unconvincingly, 'There's nothing I want to eat. No need to go to any trouble.' And then he would take the young housekeeper's hand and stuff two ten-yuan notes into it, saying, 'A young woman like you, you really ought to save up and get yourself some nice clothes, fix yourself up, you know, around the house and when you go out.' After a few of these near-misses, the old man and the discreet young housekeeper reached a sort of unspoken agreement – but still the old man felt that more precautions were in order. From then on, after he finished preparing his mice, he carefully wrapped up the head, tail, and fur as he lit the stove under the wok. Previously he had tried to entice Maomao with these, but by now he had stopped even showing them to her. To ensure that she wouldn't fish them out of the trash, the old man took to wrapping them in a packet of newspaper which he disposed of downstairs after his meal.

The young housekeeper was anything but empty-headed. Many times, on trips to the vegetable market with Maomao, she had complained, 'You're no housecat, any more than I'm a city girl. We were both just born to bad luck.' She spoke to Maomao as if Maomao were her closest confidante, and Maomao understood enough to look dejected and disheartened, leading the young housekeeper to praise her as being as understanding as a human. In fact, the housekeeper was not in the habit of sharing her thoughts with humans, no matter how understanding they appeared to be. She had never talked about her own business with the other housekeepers – but with Maomao she held nothing back. She told Maomao without the slightest trace of self-consciousness that she had enough dirt on Uncle and Uncle's Wife to make them promise to get city residence papers for her. Naturally she knew perfectly well that the old man was keeping something from her, and so she began to move more quickly through the errands that took her out of the home. The old man, meanwhile, understood what she was up to. He was enraged at being extorted and having his movements monitored – but it was no use. Every time he wanted to cook himself a meal, he had to swallow his pride and press ten or twenty kuai into the young housekeeper's hand, forcing a smile as he said, 'Why don't you go take in a movie?' That way he could ensure that she would be out of the apartment for at least two hours.

There came a day when the old man, knowing Maomao had caught an extra mouse the day before and had it stashed and ready his basket, was beside himself with anticipation all day long. But the young housekeeper broke her pattern. She saw the old man's excitement, and rather than wait patiently for her payoff, she went up to him and said, 'Grandpa, I'm going to go downtown and buy myself a pair of shoes at Zhong Jie. I might be back a little late, so make sure to look after things for me if I am.' Naturally the old man said, 'Of course, of course, by all means,' hoping to save himself a bit of money and thinking also that Zhong Jie was far away and that he would be able to enjoy his meal at his leisure for a change.

No sooner had the young housekeeper left than the old man flew to the north balcony and took the mouse out of

Maomao's basket. There was still some life in it, and the old man took his time, boiling the water and waving his knife around, like a cat playing with its catch. Uninterested in the old man's game, Maomao lay on the balcony and watched some young men playing football on the field outside, then bounded back into the bedroom with the vanity mirror, where she painted her eyebrows, did her mascara, and put her clothes and her hat on, humming a little tune all the while. Some time later, as she was strutting and posing like a model on a catwalk, she heard the old man calling her from outside. 'You ready yet, Lap Dancer?' he called. 'Lap Dancer' was the new, foreign name he had given Maomao after they moved to the city: the old man had grown used to some of the foreign ways of city people, and he enjoyed having Maomao there on his lap or in his arms as he drank his sorghum liquor and ate his mouse. Come on out here and make your old man happy, the old man said, 'Do a good job and there'll be a tip in it for you.' Maomao went obediently into the dining room, where there was a big bowl of mouse meat on the table and a pot of sorghum liquor warming beside it.

Just then there came a sound at the door – a key turning in the lock. The old man and Maomao jumped, but before they could react the door opened and the young housekeeper strode in, smiling widely. 'I'm back, Grandpa,' she said, coming to the dining room doorway and looking directly in at the mouse meat, the sorghum liquor, the old man on the chair and Maomao in his arms.

'Y– y– you – you –' the old man sputtered, unconsciously tightening his grip on Maomao until she yowled and leapt to the floor.

'What's that you're eating, Grandpa,' the young housekeeper said, drawing closer to the table and looking into the bowl. 'What meat is that? It doesn't look like anything I've ever seen.'

The old man snatched the bowl of mouse meat and arose, backing away to the other side of the table. 'It's not meat, it's – it's meat, but it's, it's artificial meat...'

The young housekeeper sat down in the old man's seat, taking her time. 'Do you know why I came back, Grandpa?' She reached back and took the old man's coat from the back of his chair, where he'd left it a moment before. 'I was thinking,' the young housekeeper said, 'that those shoes I wanted to buy are awfully expensive, and I don't have enough money. I was thinking I might need to ask for a little help.' She reached into the old man's coat pocket as she spoke and laid the contents on the dining room table: a wad of money and a small newspaper packet. She calmly and coolly peeled off two of the three hundred-kuai notes from the old man's pocket, then turned her attention to the newspaper packet. 'And what's *this*,' she asked brightly.

'D– don't, don't, don't –' the old man cried desperately. He lunged forward, but the young housekeeper held him off easily, and the bowl of mouse meat slipped from his hands and shattered on the floor, shocking him into silence. The young housekeeper froze as well – not at the sound of the shattering bowl, but at the newspaper packet, which had fallen open in front of her. The young housekeeper had grown up in the countryside, and she recognized the contents of the package at a glance: a small, pointy thing that was a mouse's head, a thin thing that was a mouse's tail, and a wet mass of silvery grey hair that was the mouse's fur.

'Grandpa, you're eating –' the young housekeeper's eyes were very wide and round, and she leapt up from her seat, allowing the two hundred-kuai notes in her hand to flutter to the floor. 'I – I heard about how the Cantonese...' She backed toward the dining room door as she spoke.

'You can't leave!' the old man yelled, lunging for the young housekeeper's hand. She darted aside, and the old man slipped on a piece of mouse-meat and fell to the floor. The young housekeeper stepped over him and was preparing to make good her escape when Maomao, who had been watching coolly from the sidelines, darted in front of her, blocking her way. Maomao advanced on the young housekeeper, pushing and feinting, until the young housekeeper slipped and fell next to the old man.

The old man rolled over on top of the young housekeeper and began cursing her between ragged breaths, 'You little whore, You dirty little slut, You nasty little thug, You thought you'd got your hooks in me...' He held the young housekeeper's head down with one hand and with the other hand picked up a shard of the bowl and slashed at her neck with it. 'That's right, you little whore, I'm an animal and I eat mice. What of it? Go and tell, tell the whole world, do your worst...'

The son and his wife were called home on the pretext of a major emergency. The old man had wanted to keep the affair from the grandson, but the grandson happened to leave school earlier than usual that day and walked in on the scene. Well, he was old enough, and now that he knew, he would have to help the family come up with a plan.

The body of the young housekeeper lay twisted and broken in the entrance to the dining room. The old man, the son, the son's wife and the grandson all sat outside the dining room doorway, staring up at the ceiling. Only Maomao remained in the dining room, where she was busily licking up the blood from the floor and the young housekeeper's body. Fragments of the bowl were all over the room, but of the chunks of mouse-meat and the contents of the newspaper packet there was not a trace. A jewelled ring lay in one corner. It looked, to all appearances, like an uncontaminated crime scene.

'What are we going to do,' the wife blubbed, tugging at her husband's sleeve. 'You've got to think of something we can do.'

'I don't see what the big deal is,' the old man said, glaring at the son's wife. 'So at worst we'll have to pay the family.' He was perfectly calm. 'It's not as if I wanted to kill her. It's a case of, what's it called?'

'Legitimate self-defence,' the grandson said.

'Right, legitimate self-defence,' said the old man. 'I caught her stealing my son's wife's ring, and she took a fright and started cursing at me, and then she tried to smash the bowl over my head. What was I supposed to do? She would have killed me. I fought back and I didn't know my own strength and I hurt her more than I meant to and she died. That's all there was to it.'

'A woman's dead,' the son said, 'whether you meant to kill her or not.'

'Those wounds,' the wife said. 'They'll know you kept going after she stopped resisting.'

'I saw something like this on TV,' the grandson said. 'The man got at least, like, 20 years...'

'Wh– what?' said the old man, a note of panic entering his voice. 'That can't – You're a big official, son. Can't you do something to help your old man?' Tears began streaming down his face.

'Calm down, Dad,' the son said. 'I'm thinking, aren't I?'

'See if you can find someone in the courts or the police,' the wife said. 'Pay them whatever they want. Maybe we can get a few years off the sentence.'

'Jail is jail,' the son said. 'Even a year in jail would be too much. What I'm thinking is, how do we make this look like a suicide? Even better – what if there were burglars who killed her to keep her quiet?'

'The way I see it, wouldn't it be better to take the body and bury it somewhere nobody will find it?' the old man said, haltingly.

'Did you ever read *The Deer and the Cauldron*?' the grandson asked, brightening suddenly. 'The hero in that had this powder that could completely dissolve corpses. If anyone got it in their blood or on themselves they just melted away without a trace, no matter if they were dead or alive. If we just had some of that, then we could put – oh, Maomao's licked up all the blood. So even if we *did*–'

'Rubbish,' the son said, cutting the boy off. 'What if the family comes looking?'

'Be realistic,' the son's wife said to the old man. 'How would we bury the body? *Where* would we bury it? Someone is bound to find it, no matter where.'

'Then what will I do?' the old man cried. 'What's to become of me?' He began to sob, a helpless innocent.

'Don't cry, Father,' the son said. 'I can't think when you–' But the son's voice broke before he could finish, and he had to stop and dab at his eyes. This proved infectious, and the son's wife and the grandson began to sniffle and sob as well. Seconds ticked by and the mood in the room grew heavier and heavier, until the old man crumpled to the floor, unable to stand anymore. Immediately the son, the son's wife, and the grandson fell to their knees to help him, surrounding him like a funeral wreath and sobbing 'Dad' and 'Grandpa' and 'Dad'.

None of them had noticed when Maomao slipped out of the dining room, and none of them noticed when, freshly brushed and washed and made up, she slipped back in. As their sobs died away, however, Maomao's voice rang out. 'That's quite enough of that,' she said. 'No more crying. Everybody get up.'

The three people jumped on hearing a new voice and looked up to see – 'Young housekeeper!' they cried as one.

'That's right,' Maomao said. 'I'll be the young housekeeper from now on. As for her – she nudged the body with her foot – You …well, there won't be any evidence left if you can eat her all up…'

And that's my tale. Some readers may remind me: Didn't you say something about a romantic encounter? True. I left that part out, and a few other things besides. I'm sure that there are bound to be a few romantics among my readers, and who's to say you won't make Maomao's acquaintance yourself some day, in the course of your own romantic encounters? If you do, I'm sure she will fill you in on all the parts I left out.

An Old-Fashioned Romance

THE DAY TIAN MIN first slept with me was the day she got her letter of acceptance to graduate school. I wouldn't say she was an old-fashioned girl, but it's true that she was not the type to jump the gun, either. The plan had been for us to get married as soon as she finished university – unless she passed her graduate school entrance exams. Now she had, which meant the wedding would have to wait until she got her master's degree. That was a long time, and I had no choice but to make a move.

'You're making me go against my principles,' Tian Min said. 'I wanted us to save our special moment for another three years from now.' She was still grumbling about it even after the lights were out and the clothes were off. 'It's all you men ever think about. I just don't understand.'

I'm honestly not one of the men who only ever think about 'it' – but I wasn't happy at the prospect of waiting another three years to do 'it' on our wedding night, either. Tian Min was a catch: soft-spoken, sweet-natured, and delicately beautiful, better-looking and better-educated than me. Small wonder if I felt like she was out of my league. I joked that I was just trying to mark my territory before someone else beat me to it, but of course I regretted the joke as soon as the words were out of my mouth. Tian Min was pure as the driven snow. Her understanding of love came entirely from soppy old Chiung Yao campus romances. She found jokes like the one I had just made crass, smutty. Her enthusiasm instantly vanished, predictably, and our first experience of what the old romances call 'the pleasures of clouds and rain' ended up feeling as uninspired and perfunctory as a meal of lukewarm, leftover rice.

So Tian Min continued her academic career, and I continued my bachelor life. She lived on campus, and I slept in my work unit dormitory; she had a heavy courseload – first and second foreign language requirements, optional and compulsory classes – and I had work dinners and office meetings and study sessions and business junkets at the taxpayer's expense. We were both busy. When I was in Shenyang, we would usually get together once a week for outings that fell into a predictable pattern: dinner; conversation; a movie; lovemaking, when conditions permitted. Tian Min's conditions for the latter were exacting, however, and more often than not all of my inducements and coercions resulted only in batted eyelashes and sweet smiles, rather than the unbridled passion I'd been aiming for. Women are funny creatures. They love to flirt, to seduce, to tempt, but then they refuse to carry these through to their logical end of carnal union. Do they really value their bodies so highly, or do they get so wrapped up in the mental pleasures of flirtation and seduction and temptation that they forget about their bodies entirely? I've never been able to decide.

It was around this time that I noticed something had changed between Tian Min and me. Before – back when we were still just ordinary sweethearts, before we'd had any physical connection – I'd always spent our time together talking and talking about nothing in particular. Now, though – now that we had become as one, now that I could have my way with Tian Min – I spent less energy on talking than on thinking of ways to make Tian Min cheerfully go to bed with me. It was Tian Min, not me, who led our conversations.

The first time Tian Min brought up her supervisor's story was a rainy weekend night. We were at a friend's home, a newly built apartment that hadn't yet been decorated and still retained the pleasant smell of construction materials. My friend's work unit was uncommonly generous: even unmarried workers got apartments. I'd managed to get rid of him and brought Tian Min over, thinking she'd like the ambience, and indeed she took an instant liking to my friend's apartment, and even formed a good impression of his work unit. She made a brisk circuit, kitchen to bathroom to balcony to bedroom, and remarked enviously that if the two of us could get a place like this in the future she'd be perfectly content. 'Unmarried people deserve respect too,' she said, concluding her praise of the apartment and turning her attention to the locked drawers of my friend's desk. 'Sometimes unmarried people have even more private business than married people.' I was standing behind Tian Min, agreeing with everything she said, 'yes yes yes yes,' and I began kissing and caressing her.

'But my supervisor…' she said, moving her lips away and murmuring to herself, oblivious to my petting. 'His room in the dormitory for unmarried teachers is like a tattered old shirt that leaves his frail old body half-exposed in front of all the young teachers.' Her face burned with moral indignation; her eyes were as blank as the clean white walls reflected in them. Her sudden shift in tone spoiled my mood, and I knew better than to push my luck.

'What do you mean?' I asked. 'Your supervisor doesn't have an apartment of his own?' I thought I had better play along and try to gradually shift the topic if I didn't want to be accused of never thinking of 'anything else'.

But Tian Min mistook this for interest. 'I only just found out too,' she said, the indignation spreading from her face to her voice. 'My supervisor still lives in the shabby old dormitory for unmarried faculty.' She freed herself from my embrace and stood up, glaring around at the apartment. 'The man's 50 years old. He hasn't got long left, and he doesn't even have a place to call his own.'

'How can that be? What's wrong with your school?'

'It's all because he never married.'

'Never married? 50 years old and still not married – is there something wrong with him?'

'You too!' Tian Min snapped. 'Everyone loves hearing about other people's private business, but none of you ever cares about how *they* feel, or about what's right. All I'm saying is, you shouldn't have to be married to have an apartment.'

I smiled hurriedly. 'Sure, sure, that's what I was saying. An old comrade in his fifties ought to have a place, married or no.'

'Anyone older than 18 ought to have a place of their own.'

'Of course, of course. I'm just so used to group living that it never occurred to me that other people wouldn't be.'

'Group living! Even the phrase is hateful.'

'So let's not talk about your supervisor.'

'No!'

'Go ahead and talk about it, then. I'll listen.'

'My supervisor – you'd never imagine.' Tian Min stood at the window and clasped her hands to her chest, gazing off into the distance like an actress delivering a monologue. 'He's a Romeo; a star-crossed lover; an old-fashioned true believer in the ability of Love to conquer all. For the sake of a woman he loved when he was young, he's never married or loved anyone else…'

'Oh really…' I cringed a little at the overblown, pretentious description of her supervisor. I'd seen characters fit this description in stories or movies, but there was something hard to believe about the idea of meeting one in real life. I was trying to decide whether admiration or mockery would be the correct response when I noted with some concern that for all the theatricality of her delivery, Tian Min was obviously sincerely moved. 'Your supervisor sounds like a real character,' I said lamely, sensing that I should keep my opinion to myself. 'There's got to be a story there – something must have happened between him and his old girlfriend.'

'That's for sure,' Tian Min said, her voice softening. She lowered her eyes and drew nearer to me. 'I just can't, can't, *can't* understand it – what could happen between two true lovers to lead to such a terrible lifelong regret?' She nestled into my embrace, lost deeply in her thoughts. 'My supervisor never talks about himself, of course – but I'm one of his favourite students, and his old girlfriend was from Zhangji too, like me, so he let a few words slip. Don't tell anyone.'

'Well, of course. I mean I don't even know him.' I paused for a moment, then reached out to stroke Tian Min's cheek. 'Don't be sad,' I murmured. 'These things are complicated. I'm sure your supervisor has his own reasons.'

'We'll never split up. We'll always be happy and content. Is that what you think?'

'That's right, Tian Min. We'll never split up, we'll be happy and content…'

She snuggled close, like a baby bird, and my heart swelled with love for her. As we approached climax, I thought of her lovelorn supervisor. Perhaps, in his own way, he had something to teach us about love. Tian Min and I shuddered together.

There was something between Tian Min and me that rainy night, something absolutely real.

Time flew by. Tian Min, future MA graduate, was always repeating her supervisor's words: knowledge is the only thing worth being proud of. She was working a lot harder than she had as an undergraduate, I noticed. School wasn't the only thing she talked about when we were together, but sooner or later, the topic always found its way back to her studies and her supervisor. One weekend she told me her supervisor's girlfriend had been a beauty, with the beautiful name of *Moli*, 'Jasmine'. Another weekend, she told me her supervisor and Moli had been the same ages as us – 25 and 23 – when they were together. Yet another weekend, she told me her supervisor and Moli had recently happened to bump into each other – I didn't want to let the romance of two total strangers govern our lives, but Tian Min seemed to be growing more and more obsessed. She couldn't get excited unless her supervisor and Moli were there between us. Of course, the stories she told me about her supervisor and Moli were fragmentary, with lots of missing pieces and suggestive gaps to whet the appetite. Discussing, analyzing, and trying to fill in the gaps in the stories became one of our chief pastimes together, despite my resistance.

One time I cut her off in the middle of a stream of effusive praise for her supervisor. 'You'd think *you* were the one in love with him.'

'Vulgar!' she said. 'I can't believe you'd say that.'

'Why not? What's wrong with saying that?' I'd only been teasing, but the look of scorn on her face stung me. 'If you can do it why shouldn't I say it?'

'If I can do what? What did I do?'

'You never talk about me the way you talk about that sad old geezer.'

'Not just vulgar,' Tian Min said, 'vulgar and petty.' She turned away disdainfully to look out the window at the crowds of pedestrians outside. 'First of all, he might not be in great shape physically, but he's not a "sad old geezer". He's a gifted, romantic man in the prime of life. Second of all, the only thing you know how to do is drag a girl into bed with you and then treat her like your property and control her with nasty, jealous little comments. Not much to praise there, is there? Besides, you–' Her voice was unusually cool, but it made my hair stand on end.

'Bullshit!' I said, slapping the table angrily. It was all I could do to keep from slapping her across the face. Tian Min had just finished her junior year of university when we first met. She was as pure as water back then, and blushed every time I looked at her. Then I got her into bed, and I became her rock, her everything. But now, not even a year into her master's, she'd become a sharp, caustic woman. I'd thought it was a good thing when she set aside her old Chiung Yao romances, but that decrepit old recluse of a supervisor was even more dangerous.

But I loved Tian Min. And I knew Tian Min loved me.

All I could do was accompany her for the rest of the weekend in the ongoing story of her supervisor and Moli. The two had been truly, deeply in love, but had agreed to go their separate ways. Neither Tian Min nor I could guess what had made them do it. Not family pressure: both of them came from families of minor intellectuals, and their parents had been all in favour of their union. Nor was it for health reasons – neither had had any serious illnesses, and Moli had since become a mother of two. It wasn't about personal history: this was first love for both of them, and neither had discovered or indeed even imagined any distancing or disloyalty on the part of the other during their time together. It hadn't been politics: both of them were politically insignificant, needless to say, and even though they had lived in a time when people were expected to take public stances and join groups on any number of issues, they remained uninvolved and apolitical. It couldn't have been geographical: they were university classmates, and both had been assigned to work in Zhangji after graduation. Tian Min's supervisor hadn't been transferred to Shenyang until after Moli had married another man. Try though we might, we couldn't think of anything that could make two plighted lovers part ways.

'A joke, maybe.'

'Perhaps a misunderstanding.'

'It could have been…'

'Or….'

Even 20 years on, Tian Min's supervisor said that there was nothing that could make him go back to Zhangji. It wasn't that he didn't miss the place; he was just afraid that being in the same city as his beloved would tear open old wounds. And yet a twist of fate brought him face to face with Moli. The day he heard that Tian Min was from Zhangji too, something stirred in that quiet heart of his. Back in his shabby dormitory room that afternoon, he took down a thick photo album that Moli had given him years earlier – he always convened his mandatory classes in Moli-appreciation late at night. The lonely old man must have paged through that photo album 7,000 times over the past 20 years, and every one of those times the lovely Moli had been silent. But on that day, the day Tian Min from Zhangji walked into his life, something was different. On that day, he heard the distant voice of his old lover. What she said was: she missed him. Before that moment, this solitary man had known only that he missed Moli. He assumed that she missed him too, but had no way of proving as much, and so had never even thought of doing anything to disturb Moli's peaceful life. Now he had received unexpected confirmation: more than 20 years later, Moli still missed him. Putting the photo album away, the old bachelor ran, not even stopping to eat dinner, to catch the next train to Zhangji, where he spent a restless night. At daybreak the next morning, he set out for the place where Moli had lived, and then for her old work unit. At both places he was disappointed: Moli's former residence had long since been replaced by an amusement park that promised visitors all manner of enjoyable diversions. Her old work unit had moved several times, and nobody at the old building, from the leaders down to the elderly gatekeeper, knew anything about a woman named Moli from more than two decades before. The ridiculousness of his search began to dawn upon him, and he began the heavy-hearted trudge back toward the train station. Just then, as he was preparing to leave Zhangji in despair, he heard a woman in the crowd excitedly calling his name. He turned to look. He saw Moli.

For the nearly four years that Tian Min and I had been together, we knew – even if we didn't see each other – that we were both somewhere within the borders of the city of Shenyang. Sometimes I had to travel for work – three to five days at a time mostly, sometimes a fortnight or the best part of a month. The longest was a 37-day trip with our outgoing director and his wife to various picturesque locations in Sichuan and Yunnan. It had always been me leaving and Tian Min staying. She had never left me. Even the winter and summer breaks, when she went back to Zhangji, were some of our closest times together. I had a good relationship with everyone at my work unit, so when Tian Min went home to visit her parents, I would find some way to get sent to meetings or research exchanges in Zhangji. 'I can't bear to have you leave me,' I would tell her. But now Tian Min was in her third year of graduate school, and I was going to have to bear it. Now Tian Min had to spend time away from me and from Shenyang. About 45 days – longer even than my record.

Tian Min was in the last year of her master's programme, and her main task for the year was to work on her thesis. According to the course of study her supervisor had drawn up for her, Tian Min would have to make a tour of the provinces, municipalities, and autonomous regions under his direction – this was called 'field work' – before she ever set pen to paper on her thesis. With that many destinations, there was no way I could be assigned to the same places, no matter how many strings I pulled at work. I couldn't even if I covered the expenses.

'Field work? More like sight-seeing,' I said unhappily. 'And your school's footing the bill, with funds as tight as they are. It's a terrible waste, is what it is.'

'Short-sighted and narrow-minded,' Tian Min said. The last two years of studying had sharpened her teeth and tongue. 'We're going to visit specialists and colleagues. It's a fact-finding tour. Unlike the taxpayer-funded trips your work unit sends you and your family members on.'

'My work unit has the money. Your school doesn't.'

'So they shouldn't be doing research or training scholars until they get more money?'

'Listen, Tian Min – don't go. Please? Any materials you need to write your thesis, I'll get them for you. No matter what, no matter where. Just stay.'

'Don't be such an old woman. How could any materials replace the experts I'm going to be talking to?'

'I just don't want to be away from you.'

'I'll write you.'

'It's not the same. I won't see you.'

'You can look at my pictures.'

'Hmf.' At the mention of photographs, I felt my anger grow. Did that cold-blooded old supervisor of hers think everyone else was just as alone and friendless as he was? 'We can't all get by on pictures.'

'I'm warning you, don't start talking about things you don't know anything about.' Her face grew stern. 'I'll tell you – my supervisor is going to have to go without seeing Moli for a month and a half.'

'Wh– what? Seeing Moli–?'

That was the first I heard of it. Ever since Tian Min's supervisor had run into Moli, the two of them had been like me and Tian Min, at it like young lovers. After a week of class preparations, writing and teaching, her advisor would take the Saturday morning bus to Zhangji every weekend. He and Moli would have a meal in a fancy restaurant and spend two or three hours in quiet adoration of one another.

'What does your saint think he's doing,' I sneered. 'The woman's married and the mother of two children, no?'

'Never you mind that,' Tian Min said, a faraway gleam coming into her eyes. 'They have a truly pure relationship. They have a love that's weathered the years unscathed. You don't think that's beautiful?'

'Beautiful? You think Mr Moli would think it was beautiful?'

'He should admire them. Everyone should.'

'Is something wrong, Tian Min?'

'Just the opposite. I feel like I'm learning more and more about what life and love really *mean*.'

What was I supposed to say to that? I realised that under the influence of her supervisor, Tian Min had become a fearsome creature. During the time she was away from Shenyang, I became obsessive, paranoid, delusional. Tian Min and I were still caring and affectionate toward each other, I thought miserably; we had indulged in physical pleasures at countless times and places of Tian Min's choosing – but our original love for each other had faded almost completely away without our noticing it. What was once an unconditional physical and spiritual need for one another had become a backdrop in front of which we acted out our passions; our every move, every gesture, every expression stiff and lifeless. How I longed for the days when we could simply ad-lib, without any thought of what we were supposed to do, what we were supposed to be.

Tian Min was a reasonable woman, after all, and our arguments were only ordinary friction: we talked and argued, but when the arguments were over, they were over. She knew how much I loved her. She teased me about not being manly in my romantic feelings for her, but for the whole month and a half she was away from Shenyang, whenever she was going to be somewhere for more than four days, she would send me a telegram with a phone number. Before she left, we agreed that whenever she sent me a phone number, it meant I could call her from my office phone at 10pm. There were times when I could call Tian Min at the same place for a few days in a row, so all in all we had twelve long-distance phone calls over the course of the month, double the number of times we would have seen each other in Shenyang during the same amount of time.

'But I can't touch you.' Sometimes, as Tian Min was singing the praises of the fast-growing telecommunications industry, I would viciously curse the distance between us. 'I can't make love to you!' Originally I'd only said it to set the mood, but every time the words came out of my mouth I felt the ground fall out from beneath me.

'Do you still love me, Tian Min?' I asked. It had always been her asking me that before.

'Oh, would you listen to yourself. Of course I do…' She always soothed me as if I was a child, whether there were other people in the room with her or not.

She came back to Shenyang a little thinner, a little more tanned, and I felt that there was something unfamiliar about her. She seemed preoccupied all throughout the writing of her thesis, and when she went to bed with me her heart wasn't in it. When I asked what was wrong, she always said, 'Nothing.' She didn't even bring up the story of her supervisor and Moli. One time, when I wouldn't drop it, she asked if I didn't have anything better to worry about. 'All you ever think about is the pleasures of the flesh,' she said. 'But love is so much more than that.' I had no idea what I could do to restore happiness to Tian Min's heart. All I could think was:

Oh, Tian Min, Tian Min. Hurry up and graduate.
We'll get married and have a baby and spend the rest of
our days together, and all of your ridiculous nonsense
about 'the true meaning of love' will melt away.

But my understanding of Tian Min was far too simple. I realised later that by the time she came back from that trip, by the time she stopped talking about her supervisor and Moli's love story, she must already have made her decision.

The last time we made love was the day Tian Min finished her thesis. I was preparing a big feast at my parents' apartment to celebrate what was effectively the end of her master's course. I arranged a plate of cold appetisers and sat at the window to watch for her to appear at the end of the street so I could start the stir-fry in time for her arrival. My attention was beginning to wander when I caught sight of the familiar form of Tian Min cycling home. She seemed to be in a hurry. I leaned out the window to call to her: 'Hey, slow down! No hurry - I haven't started cooking yet!' I was about to go back in to light the stove when I saw her waving her arms: 'Don't bother, don't bother…'

Tian Min came into the apartment and, without so much as pausing to wipe the sweat from her face, she dodged my parents and pulled me into my room.

'I can't eat. I have to get back to Zhangji right away.'

'What's wrong – did something happen at home?'

'No–' She calmed slightly. 'It's my supervisor. I have to deliver a message for him.'

'He – a message for Moli?'

'Yes–' Seeing my expression, Tian Min fished out a folded piece of white paper and handed it to me. It was a thick, heavy sheet of photocopy paper. I unfolded it carefully and saw that half the paper was covered with a letter an elegant cursive hand:

> *Moli: I have been unwell this week and fear I shall have to cancel my visit to Zhangji tomorrow. Please forgive me. You need not worry on my account: I promise that I will appear, hale and hearty, at our usual place next Sunday. My student Tian Min will tell you more about recent developments.*

Beneath was the ambiguous signature: 'You Know Who.' The bottom half of the sheet was given over to two sets of addresses. One was clearly a home address; the other, the name and address of a work unit. I felt the hairs on the back of my neck stand up as I read and re-read the letter until every Chinese character and Arabic numeral was burned into my memory. Then I looked up.

'He can't just call her?'

'Moli hasn't got a phone at her home, and the phone at her office has been shut off because of unpaid bills,' Tian Min said.

'I don't like this one bit.'

'I'm sorry.'

'I don't think your supervisor is the introverted, lonely romantic you think he is.'

'What do you mean?'

'To be just laying himself bare in front of a student – a female student?'

'Are you–'

'I'm not trying to hurt you, Tian Min. But is it really right for a grown young woman like you to be passing messages back and forth between a couple?'

'I'm–'

We were both about to erupt. I had no idea what to say or do. The two middle-aged strangers and their romantic entanglements had made it impossible for me to think. Any more of this and I would surely go mad, I thought. Just then the phone rang, and I slipped around Tian Min to answer it, grateful for the distraction. A deep voice greeted me by name. Before I could ask who was calling, the voice asked for Tian Min, and I knew, without having to ask, who was on the other end of the phone. I thrust the handset into Tian Min's hand and hurried into the kitchen before I could do anything I would regret later. After a while, Tian Min came in and stood beside me, watching as I placed the chicken, the fish, the pork, the eggs back into the refrigerator. Suddenly she ran up and hugged me from behind.

'Don't be upset. I won't go. Let's make dinner together.' Her warmth spread instantly from my back to my heart, and I melted.

'Not going? Change of orders?'

'My supervisor, he – he wants to go to Zhangji tomorrow anyway, sick as he is.'

'Will he be all right?' I actually felt a little sorry for the lovelorn old man.

'He said –' Tian Min's voice caught in her throat – 'He said nothing but death could stand in the way of true love…'

A year later I married a girl named Yu. The first time we made love, when we were first dating, I repeated what I had said to Tian Min the first time her and I made love – deliberately or not, I don't remember. I told her I wanted to mark my territory before anyone else did. She was like Tian Min – soft-spoken, sweet-hearted, delicately beautiful – but she was enthusiastic in bed, too, and the joke didn't faze her at all. 'This is prime land,' she said cheerfully. 'You could spend the whole rest of your life ploughing it.'

She was from the same town as Tian Min, as it happened, and her parents still lived there. We split our honeymoon between Shenyang and Zhangji. As we were preparing to go back to Shenyang, I turned to my new bride and said, 'I want to look for someone – can you keep me company?' Putting things together quickly, she said: 'A woman, is it?' I said it was. 'An old lover?' I smiled, but didn't say anything. There was a vague tension in the air as we got dressed and prepared to go out, and without a further word to each other we walked arm in arm, making our way to the two unfamiliar addresses that were deeply imprinted upon my brain. There were no apartments at the first address, or anything else either, and a group of old men playing cards said it had been a park ever since the Japs occupied Zhangji in the '30s. At the second address there was no work unit of any name or description: there was nothing but a group of high school students kicking a football around on a bare, uneven expanse of mud who told me there had been talk of building a stadium there once, but no construction crews ever turned up.

As we left to go back to Shenyang, my new wife asked me, in mock-jealousy, 'Are you disappointed you didn't get to see your old girlfriend?' For a moment I didn't know what to say, and then I hugged her tightly. My tears spattered onto her shoulder, but she didn't see.

Squatting

SUMMER IS HIGH SEASON for criminal offences, particularly at night.

I'm not just referring to crimes of a sexual nature.

That sexual assault is more prevalent during the summer months, and especially on summer nights, is a fact in need of little explanation. Indeed, summer nights facilitate many other forms of crime, as may also go without saying.

Brawling, for example. On summer nights, when the heat lifts a little and a light breeze blows, when outdoor barbecue stands line both sides of the street and fill the air with the aroma of roasting meat, even people who have already eaten dinner will take the chance to slip away from their stifling homes and sit out on the benches by the barbecue stands, drinking beer and husking boiled peanuts or brined flatbeans, nibbling at skewers of roast chicken or slices of kidney or grilled fish, gossiping with friends, playing drinking games, growing louder and rowdier as the night wears on. The combination of strangers in close quarters, alcohol fanning the flames, and a conversational milieu consisting largely of idle chatter, boasts, and swagger is ripe for disagreements, for conflict, for violence, for incidents leading to injury or even grievous bodily harm.

Or robbery. It is considerably harder to rob someone's person in the winter, when layers of heavy clothing pile up so thickly that no sooner has one shoved the victim into a narrow alleyway or a grove of trees or a tight corner, than one has to rifle through a dozen pockets in different layers of clothes – tissues in this pocket, handkerchief in that one, nothing at all in that one over there – and there's no guarantee one will even find the money before a patrolman comes running. Much more straightforward in the summer, when people only have a couple of places to store things on their person and the pickings are easier by far.

Breaking and entering likewise. Doors and windows are shut tight in the wintertime but left quite agape in the summer. Many individuals who might be merely satisfying their own vulgar curiosity by peeking through other people's windows will find, after discovering the ease of egress and the convenient placement of mobile phones on tables and wallets in handbags, that one thing simply leads to another, a problem of morality becoming a problem for the courts.

Or homicide. Chinese people don't possess guns, or at any rate don't generally have access to them, so most murder weapons are improvised – clubs, hammers, axes, screwdrivers and whatnot. The padded jackets and insulated hats of winter wrap their wearers so thickly that an attacker using insufficient or improperly applied force will find that even with a perfectly timed attack, these improvised weapons will let them down almost every time. They may manage to tear a hole in the victim's cotton-stuffed vest or down jacket, or to knock the victim's cotton or leather or woollen cap out of shape, but the victim will remain physically unharmed, possibly reeling for an instant before understanding the situation. Whereupon most people will bolt like startled rabbits. But from time to time a victim made of tougher stuff will respond by rearing up like a horse and pouncing like a tiger, and then there's no telling who will end up killing whom. Summer homicides are a different matter altogether, and a malefactor of sufficient strength and accuracy will be able to effect the expiration of their victim with nothing more than a single well-placed blow.

SQUATTING

Summer is beautiful, and summer nights more beautiful still, but in our city it was a deadly beauty.

The above shouldn't be taken to reflect the primary characteristics of summer nights in our city – merely a single aspect, incidental, a footnote to a greater whole. In principle, I believe, the overall mainstream big picture situation of our city at the macro level is hardly different from Paris or Warsaw, Pyongyang or London, Tokyo or Beijing, Baghdad or Port-au-Prince, Canberra or Kabul, Sarajevo or Caracas, Addis Ababa or Buenos Aires. Not that I've been to any of these cities – but insofar as issues of public security are concerned I am confident, going by common sense, deductive reasoning, and what I've seen in books and television, that the problem of increased crime during summer months is by no means limited to the city in which I live. That it is a general phenomenon by whose very commonness we may see that conflicts will arise anywhere people are gathered, and that promoting public morality and social progress is not as simple a matter as, say, acquiring a new production line for the manufacture of televisions or refrigerators or washing machines. Far from it. The road to a better world, as the poet said, is a long and winding one. My colleagues and I therefore composed a delicately couched, politely worded, mildly phrased letter along these lines to the highest-ranking municipal administrator – not to criticise or assign blame or complain or bellyache or grumble; merely an earnest, sincere, humble, written reminder that summer was nearly upon us and, with it, peak season for crimes, and that we hoped the highest-ranking municipal administrator and the relevant departments would find the time to note the passing of the seasons and make such preparations as might be needful.

We sent the letter in the middle of April, when the air was cool and crisp.

Every year summer comes to our city a few days earlier than the year before, owing supposedly to the greenhouse effect. Meteorological authorities had already said it would be another veritable scorcher: even our far-northern city would be running into temperatures of 25 degrees Celsius or higher by the start of May, and authorities couldn't – or wouldn't, or at least couldn't honestly – say how hot it would be come July and August. Indeed, by the beginning of the May Day holiday week anyone setting foot outside was instantly inspired to change into shorts and undershirts; meanwhile air conditioners, fans, window-screens, and cool bamboo sleeping mats sold out overnight. During those first few days of the May Day holiday, all of our city's media outlets – the 'three mouthpieces' of newspapers, radio, and television – began replacing front page and prime time coverage of tourism revenues with reports on a new regulation from the municipal Counter-Criminal Crackdown Command Office, stipulating that starting after the May Day holiday week, all public buses, motorcycles, bicycles, and other human-powered vehicles would be barred from city streets between the hours of 8pm and 5am.

There was a public outcry, in response to which 'CrackCom' issued a full explanation of the new regulation.

The explanation was faithfully transmitted by all news outlets. Through a barrage of interviews, special features, opinion pieces, letters from the editor, recorded lectures, public service announcements, televised exposés, and topical artistic performances, newspapers and radio and television stations informed the masses that while the new regulation would, most certainly, result in minor public inconvenience, any honest comparison against the major public inconvenience of rampant nocturnal criminality would conclude that the restrictions on the 'three categories of vehicles' were merely a small inconvenience. The brilliance of the new regulation, in other words, lay in using a minor inconvenience to the public to utterly eliminate the major inconvenience of criminal activity; in employing a minor curtailing of the public's ability to do its business in order to allow the authorities to discharge their duty of wiping out criminal elements; in engineering a beneficial trade-off between inconvenience and convenience.

The logic behind the regulation was straightforward. Having buses, motorcycles, and bicycles on the roads at night contributed to crime: some vehicles, such as buses, were sites of criminal activity; some, such as motorcycles and bicycles, were implements of crime; some, such again as motorcycles and bicycles, were targets of crime. There were pickpockets and hooligans on buses by day, but at night they ran rampant; likewise, there were daytime thefts of motorcycles and bicycles, and thieves who snatched at people's wallets, necklaces, and mobile phones from moving bicycles and motorcycles during the daytime, but under cover of night the snatching and thievery became downright brazen. If, during the dark hours from 8pm to 5am, these three categories of vehicle were barred from city streets, then the problems might be resolved, and the ability of criminal elements to commit crimes effectively restricted. Gesturing with his hands as he addressed the television cameras, a CrackCom spokesman said: 'Ladies and gentlemen, citizens of our fair city, we have every reason to expect a sharp drop in crime rates this summer.'

The residents of our city are understanding, law-abiding sorts – except for the criminals – and after an initial period of stunned silence the public came to appreciate the municipal government's concern, and took to the media to express its full support for CrackCom's new regulation. Public support or no, however, the new regulation undeniably gave rise to more than a few new problems – most obvious of which, and anticipated by CrackCom, was the massive inconvenience caused to the work and everyday life of people throughout the city.

The inconvenience to people who began or ended their work shifts at night may be imagined. Even for those who didn't, the inconvenience will be readily apparent. People couldn't just barricade themselves indoors talking or making love or watching TV or playing mahjong as soon as the sky began to darken. Many enjoyed taking evening strolls in the city's parks or commercial districts – but how, once outside, were these ordinary citizens to get there without buses or motorcycles or bicycles or other everyday means of transport? More troublesome still: if, at 8pm, a bus or a motorcycle or a bicycle or a cargo tricycle was out on the roads, it would be compelled to stop where it was by the sight of a police car zooming by on its rounds, or by the deafening blast of sirens that signalled the beginning of the curfew. This was no problem for people who were within sight of their homes – they could simply get off and walk, or gun the throttle a couple of times and slip in under the wire – but what about those left stranded between work and home? Unable to afford taxi fare, bus passengers would have to disembark and contemplate the long road ahead of them; riders of bicycles, motorcycles, and tricycles faced the additional question of what to do with their vehicles. The regulation banned even pushing a bicycle between the hours of 8pm and 5am, since any moving motorcycles, bicycles, or even tricycles would place patrolling officers in a position of having to ascertain whether the people pushing the vehicles were thieves or the vehicles' rightful owners.

And then there were secondary issues not to be overlooked. In one instance, the sudden blast of the curfew alert startled an old lady so severely as to affect her heart. Some drivers, lacking proper respect for CrackCom's new regulation, would gleefully follow the curfew alert by leaning on their horns, resulting in a blast of urban noise pollution in excess of the regulated three minutes. A young boy on a bicycle forgot what the 8pm alert was for and kept pedalling through the streets while other cyclists throughout the city stopped in their tracks – presenting a problem for the patrolling officer who caught him, since detention or fines would be inappropriate given the boy's status as a minor. An old scrap collector pedalling back to the little shack he rented was so startled by the alert that he overturned his cargo tricycle, scattering rubbish all over the roadway and bringing the remaining legitimate traffic to a halt for 15 minutes, infuriating the motorists on the scene. One woman chained her scooter to a sapling by the side of the street; upon returning to retrieve it in a car two hours later, she and her husband found that the scooter and the newly planted tree it had been chained to were both gone, leaving only a shallow pit.

Though by no means common, such problems could only lead to greater problems in the future if they continued to go unaddressed. After spending nights compiling a list of such cases, my colleagues and I wrote an urgent letter to the highest-ranking municipal administrator, which we passed to one of his secretaries through the secretary's wife in order to ensure prompt delivery. It was our hope that the highest-ranking municipal administrator would receive our report on recent conditions from his secretary the following morning.

(It should be noted that one of our number had attended university with the wife of one of the highest-ranking municipal administrator's secretaries, and had for some years been romantically involved with her).

My colleagues and I weren't People's Congress delegates or People's Political Consultative Committee members, nor indeed were we employees of any governmental authority. We were writers of reportage, teachers of history, players of oboes, designers of computer software, extractors of teeth, translators of foreign languages, creators of advertisements, students of calculus, researchers of pharmaceutical compounds. We'd all gone to university and taken at least undergraduate degrees, and if forced to give an account of ourselves we would shyly admit to being intellectuals. Engaged in different lines of work, living in different neighbourhoods, of different ages and genders, we shared nonetheless a common concern for the development and growth of our city, and wrote regular letters to a succession of highest-ranking municipal administrators addressing the strengths and shortcomings of our city and the strengths and shortcomings of municipal policy in the hopes that our suggestions would aid them in the performance of their duties. Our efforts were motivated not by a desire for official recognition or pecuniary reward, but by a sense of righteousness and justice, of responsibility, of social morality, and of love for our fellow man.

Our little group had its roots in a happy coincidence some years before.

While other parts of our city had prospered, the west side was at the time still a desolate swathe of brick shacks, linked together by a few secondary roads, that stared out uncomfortably at the rest of the city. Any attempt to change the fortunes of the west-side slums was bound to be an uphill battle – but, we felt, a battle well worth fighting! Leaving aside more complex issues like housing and employment for the time being, we felt that the simpler issue of transportation could be readily addressed through public transit links between the west side and the rest of the city, and that the remaining problems might not seem so insoluble once this had been accomplished. In virtually every other part of the city, even the unimportant roads were immaculately paved, bordered by gleaming sidewalks lined with emerald trees stretching as far as the eye could see, punctuated at intervals by red and green lights merrily a-twinkle. But on the west side of the city, even arterial roads like Huashan Road or Qishan Road or Buyunshan Road were little better than the dirt roads of the wild North-west: on clear days, they were covered in thick clouds of dust; on rainy days, water pooled waist-deep; and they were so pitted and rutted, rain or shine, that even any senior cadres driving over them would find their sedans being tossed to and fro like boats on a choppy sea. Not that senior cadres took these roads – their residences and offices weren't in the area. Even when municipal inspection teams visited our city from the Central Committee, and foreign guests and overseas compatriots came, saying that they wanted to see every nook and cranny of the city, nobody ever visited that part of town. But we felt that a lack of visits from officials and foreign friends shouldn't mean that the west side never got to see brighter days. A city is a single organism. Allowing one part of an organism to wither away while the rest of the organism develops might seem to have no effect in the short term – other than a possible saving in development expenditures – but if matters continued as they had been, the imbalance could potentially cause incalculable damage to the appearance, structure, and overall progress of the whole. Consider a family in which the majority of members never touch tobacco or strong drink, but one member becomes addicted to drugs. The addict's cash-flow and health problems may not initially affect the other members of the family, but as his money runs low and his health begins to fail, he becomes progressively likelier to drag all the others down with him. Seeing the condition of the west side of our city and its key roads in much the same light, we wrote down our observations in letters which we sent to the official then serving as the highest-ranking municipal administrator, humbly requesting that he consider the west side of town and its pitiful roads.

None of us had ever met any of the others at the time, I hasten to add. Each of us was perfectly unaware of the others' existence. We were making our proposals as individuals, and so naturally our letters went out separately.

The letters' common addressee was nonplussed, as you may imagine, to receive so many letters containing roughly the same content at more or less the same time. His bemusement gave way to nervousness and suspicion, and he turned the letters over to the Public Security Bureau. Someone who was with him at the time told us later that he had suspected us of being American spies or Russian special agents before deciding that we were working with a political rival, or were at the very least plants hired to stir up the waters and force him to resign. After analysing the letters, the Public Security Bureau agreed that the evidence suggested a conspiracy. The cover story – that a group of people from disparate backgrounds had written letters for purposes other than pleading their own cases, complaining about their own mistreatment, or making personal demands – was transparently flimsy, and yet the PSB had no idea what to make of letters from authors scattered all around the city – except for the west side, where none of them lived – on the subject of roads on the west side of the city that had nothing to do with them. The more the PSB analyzed the letters, the more serious the situation grew: they raised the municipal security alert level and deployed officers on the west side of town, particularly around Huashan, Qishan, and Buyunshan Roads, while also employing every available method of detection to investigate the senders of the letters and conduct round-the-clock surveillance and tracking operations. Fortunately none of us had sent our letters anonymously, and fortunately we were all cleaner than a fresh sheet of paper and purer than water. The PSB realised soon enough that it had blown matters out of proportion, and reported to the highest-ranking municipal administrator that we posed no threat whatsoever. In its report, the PSB attributed the coincidence of our letters to the fact that we were a bunch of intellectuals who minded other people's business for fun instead of playing mahjong or going out with friends or getting massages or singing karaoke. Embarrassed at his own over-reaction, and perhaps eager to create an impression of being open to good advice, the highest-ranking municipal administrator actually did take our suggestions to heart. In addition to repairing Huashan, Qishan, and Buyunshan Roads, he drafted an urban rejuvenation plan for the west side of the city with the stirring slogan of 'One Small Step in One Year, One Medium Step in Two Years, and One Big Step in Three Years.'

His successors must have heard the story, because subsequent letters were not forwarded to the PSB, and the urban rejuvenation plan ultimately did make the transition from paper to reality. Like anywhere else in this changing city of ours, the west side today is full of bright lights and all the trappings of healthy prosperity, of families living together in peace and loving kindness in the high-rises that dot the area, and citizens co-existing in amicable fraternity on the streets outside. The public order and strong governance our city enjoys today is due in no small measure to the way the west side was reunited with the rest of the city. Despite improvements, crime rates are admittedly still higher than average – especially during summer, and most especially on summer nights – but this is merely a small bump in the road, the brief darkness before the dawn. I will extend the analogy I laid out earlier: the addict's family has successfully prevailed upon him to change his ways, and he finally understands the importance of just saying 'no' – but he can hardly be expected to quit cold turkey.

But of this, no more. I still have to say how my colleagues and I found one another.

During the PSB's distressing investigation of us, we'd had to submit evidence proving ignorance of one another, lack of organisational structure, freedom from external control, and absence of malicious intent. But there was an unexpected benefit – namely, discovering that there were others out there who shared our goals and our sensibilities. The woman who did computers and the man who did ads were the first to meet each other after the investigation wrapped up, and they promptly fell in love. Using the list of names the PSB had compiled, they contacted us one by one and brought the whole group together. From then on, acting as a loose collective of friends sharing a mutual concern for the public welfare, we resumed offering advice to the highest-ranking municipal administrators with renewed vigour and enthusiasm. We never received any response from the relevant departments, other than the investigation; nor did we come in for any praise or criticism. But we believed that many of our suggestions had been taken seriously by a succession of highest-ranking municipal administrators and the relevant departments, meaning that at least a tiny smidgen of the credit for the continued prosperity, rejuvenation, modernisation, and growing cultural sophistication of our city belonged to us – or rather, to our letters.

We wrote letters beyond counting in the years that followed, and countless numbers of people joined or left our loose collective as their interests changed or their passions shifted. Throughout all of this, whether our ranks were swollen or depleted, we continued not to form a civilian organisation or even to admit that we were an organisation of any description. We had no name, no program, no charter, no stated goal. Every letter we sent to the highest-ranking municipal administrators of our city was a personal letter: if it was written by one person, then one person would sign; if by three people, then three people would sign; if by seven, then seven would sign. If there were disagreements on an issue, but people felt that the issue needed to be aired, then we would each write our own letters, or one faction would write a letter expressing its views and another group would write its own letter. Our members exercised the strictest self-discipline: never once did anybody attempt to seek personal gain by means of their 'public service letters.'

Never before had we seen such a rapid response!

Three days after we sent off our letter, CrackCom published a set of supplementary recommendations that rendered the new regulation instantly more humane. Firstly: the sudden three-minute siren at 8pm was to be replaced with three snippets of classical music, each one minute long, starting at 7:50pm. Specifically: at 7:50pm, there would be a minute of the Czerny études; at 7:54pm, a minute of the allegro from Chopin's 'Les Sylphides'; at 7:59pm another minute, this time of the famous Fate-knocking-at-the-door motif from Beethoven's Fifth. In this way citizens would be reminded and given advance warning before the curfew, and instead of harsh sirens, the alerts would promote high art in a clear case of killing two birds with one stone. Secondly: the city had recruited 10,000 migrant workers on short notice, and set them working around the clock to put up simple shelters anywhere around the city there was sufficient empty space. These were to be used by cyclists as 8pm drew near for the free storage of their motorcycles, bicycles, and cargo tricycles, to which end CrackCom and the Urban Law Enforcement Bureau had also hired, at no small expense, a crop of strapping young unemployed men – priority given to those with martial arts training – to act as night-watchmen for the bicycles. Finally: people who were caught on buses at 8:00, or who locked their motorcycles or bikes in a shed far from home or work, would be eligible for partial reimbursement of taxi fare. Anyone who could present a taxi receipt time-stamped after 8pm, marked with the starting point, destination, and circumstances of the cab ride, and stamped with the official seal of their work unit or the residential committee where they lived, would be eligible for reimbursement of two-thirds of the fare by CrackCom. At the discretion of representatives of the person's work unit or residential committee, two-thirds of the remaining one-third of the fare could also be reimbursed, with a full report of expenses incurred in the reimbursement thereof to be presented to CrackCom by the applicable work unit or residential committee at the end of the month.

Once the new recommendations were announced, what little public resentment there had been simply evaporated, and people went happily back to their everyday work and life routines with relatively minor changes. No less happily, my colleagues and I discussed writing a letter of thanks in the form of a poem expressing our gratitude at having city fathers and mothers who cared for us more deeply than our own parents had. The person drafting the letter likened the city leaders to 'father and mother' and 'dad and mum,' and cast us and our fellow citizens as 'children' and 'sons and daughters,' a rhetorical flourish that set our little group of thin-skinned intellectuals squabbling. The war of words ended with a decision to leave the phrasing in, even though it did betray a rather serf-like mentality, if only because the government leaders' solicitous concern for their citizens really did reflect nothing so much as parental love.

We mailed our encomium with a long sigh of contentment in the knowledge that at long last, our city's public security problems had been solved, and promptly split into separate groups to apply our minds – there were nine of us at this point – to other pressing issues that required our attention. Two of us conducted an investigation; three of us engaged in research; the other four sank into wild cogitation. But just as our three groups began drafting letters based on the fruits of our investigations, research, and cogitation, and as our three groups began to draft our three letters of advice, we found that the state of law enforcement in the city remained grim.

We knew, of course, that the size and scope of the problems facing municipal law enforcement meant that they might never be completely resolved. Naive – not to say childlike – we may have been, but we still lived in the same society as everybody else, and we knew enough to be sceptical of utopias and panaceas. Still, the negligible effect of the new CrackCom order on night-time crime rates came as a shock to us. Statistics showed a nearly vertical drop-off in crimes related to the 'three vehicles' – buses, motorbikes, and bicycles – but a nearly vertical increase in unrelated crimes, as if the miscreants who'd been committing vehicle-related crimes had suddenly all decided to move into new lines of criminality.

First among these was an upswing in brawls: at roadside kebab stands, in street-side parks, at night market stalls, outside the entrances of internet cafes – anywhere crowds of people gathered for fun, shoving would turn to arguments, would turn to shouting, would turn to cursing, would turn to bloodshed. Second was an increase in rape. Not all the women on the streets after 8pm were able to take cabs, or might not find it so easy to get that second two-thirds reimbursed, and a lack of transportation meant more women spending more time in dangerous areas, which meant more targets for sex offenders. Breaking and entering was up: without transportation, many people didn't get home from work until late in the evening, providing a window of opportunity for criminal elements to climb onto balconies, squeeze through windows, pry doors off the hinges, drill locks, and strip homes bare – in some cases arranging for moving trucks to haul away their takings. Following the promulgation of the CrackCom order, overall crime was down from the previous summer by one-fifth but brawls, rapes, and robberies had increased by one-fifth, three-fifths of a fifth, and five-tenths of a fifth, respectively.

The nine of us reconvened: what to do? Social order was the most pressing issue of the day, and we devoted all of our free time to thought on this new front. This resulted in a new letter, and upon learning that our city's highest-ranking municipal administrator would attend a ribbon-cutting ceremony for a new bathhouse, we took collective, concealed, coordinated action. One of us darted forward, lightning-fast, delivering the letter directly and vanishing back into the crowd before the highest-ranking municipal administrator's three bodyguards and three secretaries could stop him. In addition to our usual report on on-the-ground conditions, this letter put forth several suggestions, including cancelling restrictions on the 'three vehicles,' removing the current ineffectual head of CrackCom and appointing a new CrackCom leader who might be more effective, and expanding the police force to guarantee no fewer than three patrolmen per square kilometre. We had twelve suggestions in all, several of them eminently practicable.

Not all of these were the product of unanimous

agreement. The nine of us had originally planned to write separate letters, as usual, with different groups signing their names to letters representing their own viewpoints. The circumstances of this letter, however, seemed clearly to require an exception. Even if we got past the secretaries and bodyguards, we could hardly expect the highest-ranking municipal administrator to stand there next to the young female compère, holding his oversized pair of golden scissors, celebratory firecrackers going off on all sides, while we each submitted our own letter – and presenting a united front with a joint letter might underscore the importance of the letter and convince the highest-ranking municipal administrator to take it more seriously. And so, in an unprecedented turn of events, we composed a joint letter without unanimous agreement on its content. Our disagreements were on points of principle, naturally, rather than on fundamental issues. Democratically minded intellectuals that we were, we took pains to indicate at the end of the letter which signatories agreed with which suggestions.

This time we saw no immediate effect. Days passed, and CrackCom continued to implement the original regulation. The office's revised recommendations made the regulation more palatable to the general public, but did nothing to address the newly created problems of social order. Brawling, rape, and robbery continued to fill the nights with terror and besmirch the civility and social harmony of our city.

Our minds raced. We had never worried too much about the letters that we'd sent out before, since any misgivings we might have could be explained by the possibility that the highest-ranking municipal administrator had never received the letter. After all, he worked night and day with the pressures of a thousand weighty matters bearing down upon him; where would he find the time to read a letter from a group of nobodies? This time we knew to a moral certainty that he had received the letter himself – so why, when he had always responded to us through real-world policy changes in the past, was there now only silence? Some among us suggested that we write another letter, something more strongly worded than the last, but most of us were against this – indeed, one of us suggested worriedly that we not get ideas above our stations. After careful reflection, we decided unanimously that the highest-ranking municipal administrator had read our letter and chosen not to take any of our suggestions – possibly out of annoyance at us, and quite possibly out of annoyance at the way we had delivered the letter. We guessed, also, that the CrackCom director we had judged ineffectual might keep his position and could retaliate against us at any time – his background was something of an open secret, and his backers outranked those of the highest-ranking municipal administrator. And after all, we weren't as young as we had been. Our passions had cooled, our impulsiveness given way to rationality. Memories of our time as the focus of the municipal PSB's attentions elicited a twinge or two of retrospective terror. In the end, the people who had advocated writing another letter abandoned the idea owing to a lack of support and a shortage of new suggestions.

At the same time, of course, we reproached ourselves for our timidity and selfish hesitation. As patriotic intellectuals concerned for our country and our fellow citizens, we felt, we lacked the craft and courage of our literati forebears, who staked their lives on their words. For a while, our loosely knit collective threatened to fall apart in a storm of recriminations. Our manners may have been the only thing that kept us together – all of us were too embarrassed to make the first move to disband the group, secretly hoping it would happen through a gradual distancing and cooling, a shifting of the subject, a slow disassociation.

It was just at this time that CrackCom issued a new regulation, which the three mouthpieces of state media promptly broadcast at full volume, and at once we were back to our old selves again, like balloons re-inflating. Regardless of the content of the regulation, our letter had produced at least one visible effect: the new CrackCom regulation bore a new signature. We couldn't help but blame ourselves once again, this time for our lack of faith. As for the original director of CrackCom, there was a sense of concern that we might have ended his career with our focus on his shortcomings. Not until we heard that he had taken up a new position – a minor promotion, albeit to a post without many of the perks of his former job – did our sense of guilt lessen slightly. We debated whether or not to write another letter to the highest-ranking municipal administrator expressing our thanks in the form of a poem, but our new found caution convinced us not to write.

The new regulation was: in addition to strict enforcement of the previous regulation, all individuals engaged in outdoor activity between the hours of 8pm and 5am would be required to do so while squatting.

…To do so while squatting? How were people supposed to do everything squatting? *Why* were people supposed to do everything squatting? Wasn't the ability to rise from a squat to a stand the very trait that separated men from apes? The broad masses of the public didn't understand or accept the new regulation, and expressed their discontent through murmurs and grumbles and other means of silent protest. Being more incisive thinkers, however – I'm sorry, but we really are just a bit smarter than most – the nine of us instantly understood the reasoning behind the new requirement, which was precisely the same as that offered by the mass media.

First, the drawbacks. There are two major drawbacks to doing things while squatting: how much slower it renders all movement, and the numb legs and aching joints that result from protracted squatting. The negative aspects of squatting are familiar to everyone and will require no further description – unlike the positives, which merit further enumeration. The positive aspects of squatting are complementary to the negative aspects: slow movement, numb legs, and sore joints are objectively positive factors in preventing criminal elements from committing crimes. A group of drunks looking for a fight, for instance, will shortly ascertain that a persistent squatting position renders one unable to move with any physical strength. Even if armed with knives, they will find that the sudden motion of attacking meets with painful protest from their numbed, cramping legs, causing them to drop their knife hands reflexively to maintain balance, and nipping neatly in the bud what might have otherwise been a bloody incident. Imagine a rapist squat-rushing at a woman in short, mincing steps, backing her into a corner, and then – but how would sexual relations occur between two squatting people? Of course, the rapist could throw the woman to the ground and throw himself on top of her, but even ignoring the effects of protracted squatting on the human sex drive and sexual performance, how intimidating could a lowlife be, so close to the ground? Especially when the woman could resist by simply standing up – an option open to her, but not him, under the same legal principle permitting violence in the cause of legitimate self-defence? Even if he dared stand up, patrolmen would descend upon him for violating the regulation before circulation ever returned to his legs, and our would-be rapist would end up worse off than when he had started. Imagine a group of thieves planning to rob the empty home of a wealthy man. They have done reconnaissance, planned their escape route, prepared a car to transport their takings and a full set of pliers, screwdrivers, crowbars, scissors, and other implements of crime; they have waited for just the right moment, and now – but how are they to get up onto the balcony? How will they squeeze through the window? Their sole option will be to enter the building and attempt to pry the iron anti-theft door off its frame, a time-consuming and difficult proposition. Any ideas of climbing onto a balcony or squeezing through the window are doomed to failure: either of these would require them to stand up straight while outdoors, a move that would instantly mark them as thieves to any law-abiding citizen or police officer within the vicinity. Clearly, evil-doers of all varieties would find their ambitions thwarted, were squatting to be generally enforced.

It took only a week for the results of the new regulation to become clear in the form of a pronounced improvement in the state of public security in our city. Criminals of all kinds had simply scattered in all directions and vanished without a trace, like cockroaches after the light comes on. It appeared that squatting was a true panacea for crime. Some of the more arrogant criminals, lacking a full appreciation for the seriousness of squatting, continued in their wanton behaviour, but no sooner had they made their move – which is to say, before they had left the scene of the crime and in some cases before the crime had even been committed – than they were caught red-handed by patrolmen. Some would even manage to flee the scene, but the act of standing, even under cover of darkness, caused them to be noticed and promptly reported by law-abiding members of the public, and in the end all were caught up in the sweeping nets of justice. As you can imagine, all eyes will instantly lock onto a man who stands while everyone else is squatting, and he will be left with nowhere to hide.

But after our initial excitement had abated and we had reflected upon our individual experiences, we came to feel that there was a major flaw in the new squatting regulation. For the majority of the public that had no criminal designs, the matter of numb legs and sore joints was a minor one, and easily addressed with a bit of rest, a slap or two with the hands, some rubbing and stretching – but the slowness the squatting caused was an intolerable inconvenience. An example. When a girlfriend came to visit me at my home one night, the security guard at the gate of my residential compound refused to allow her cab to enter the development. Her only option was to disembark and enter the gate at the northwest corner of the compound, squat down, and proceed towards Building 23, where I lived. Building 23 was in the south-east corner of the compound. She had walked there from the north-west corner of the compound before. While large, the compound could be traversed in three to five minutes. But this time, she had to do it in a squat, simultaneously contending with high heels, a long dress, long hair that kept spilling down over her face, and a handbag that kept slipping off her shoulder no matter how she carried it, all of which contributed to her bursting into tears halfway across the compound. It was a full 20 minutes before she arrived inside the gateway of my building and was able to stand up straight again. I asked her why she hadn't called for me to go down and get her, and she replied, still sobbing: 'Wha- what g-good would th- that do when you d-don't have a c-car? You'd j-just be keeping me c-company...'

She referred to squat-walking as 'crawling.' She crawled over to my bed and started crying her heart out, and wouldn't let me wipe her tears away. We only got to spend the night together once every couple of weeks, and all she did that night was cry.

After compiling together many such reports, we wrote another letter to the highest-ranking municipal administrator to express our firm opposition to the squatting regulation. In heated tones, we said that preventing crime by forcing citizens to squat-walk was a modern variation on the fable of the man who swore off food for fear of choking, or of the policy that would kill 3,000 innocent men to prevent a single guilty man from escaping, and that continuing to enforce the regulation would hold back the development of our society and inhibit the growth of our city.

But when I say 'we' here, I am being imprecise: it still refers to our group of nine, but although we were by and large of the same mind, there was such disagreement over how to express our sentiments that only one or two of us were willing to co-sign letters. The majority of us opted to write our own letters, and three of us decided that although they supported our views, they would not write any more letters – that is, that they would leave our loose collective.

We knew they must have heard the news – all of us had, though we didn't say anything about it. A few days earlier, the highest-ranking municipal administrator had invited a famous singer to a banquet in our city. She complimented him on the progress our city had made, and joked that the sight of all the people squat-walking under the starry, moonlit night sky made her feel as if she were watching a colossal work of performance art. She called our highest-ranking municipal administrator one of the great postmodern artists of our time. Recognizing a kindred spirit, the highest-ranking municipal administrator replied unhappily that he had worn himself out in the cause of promoting good and repressing evil, of protecting the land and securing the common people. But still there were people who, being given an inch and taking a mile, being given a bit of face and taking a whole nose, being insufferably given to picking nits and finding fault wherever they could, were in the habit of constantly writing negative letters. 'I envy you your stalkers,' the highest-ranking municipal administrator sighed to his guest. At least they understood love and loyalty. If only the people of his city could be more like them.

The news filled us with a sense of foreboding, but still – times were changing and society was progressing, and if the involvement of the PSB years before hadn't made us fall apart, then we could hardly allow a bit of back-alley gossip to scare us into silence now. On the other hand, since there was strength in numbers and we didn't want to be accused of attempting to sow discontent by sending separate letters, we stuffed the four letters that the remaining six of us had written into a single large envelope and sent them out as one communiqué. As we mailed the letters off, another two members of our group told us this would be their last letter to the highest-ranking municipal administrator.

Our sense of foreboding was basically correct. As I said, we are more incisive thinkers than most. Two weeks went by without any sign that the highest-ranking municipal administrator had considered our views – but on the other hand we didn't see any signs of a new investigation into us, either. There were only four of us left, and two were married to each other. Many evenings we gathered together in a high building that overlooked the streets, and gazed out to see, under the shimmering lights, parallel to the streams of vehicles, on the streets that stretched out as far as the eyes could see, the ever more familiar sight of crowds of men and women, young and old, shifting their weight from side to side and rocking backward and forward as they squat-walked to and fro. It was a funny sight, but we weren't laughing. We knew that if we needed to go out to work or visit friends or family, and we couldn't catch a ride with a friend or put together money for a cab, then we would join the freaks squat-walking outside. Even as we stood inside, looking out from the air-conditioned comfort of the apartment, we might already be among them. It was a chilling, gloomy realisation.

We wrote another letter, a joint missive signed by the four of us. We expressed our firm moral convictions by means of heated, even confrontational language – phrases like 'human dignity,' 'the difference between man and beast,' 'no different from mindless tortoises,' 'slowness equals death,' and 'adapting to numbness is a sign of a tacit acceptance of atrophy and regression.' We even wrote that 'an even surer way to protect the streets might be to keep the entire populace as house pets, or to declare martial law outright.' But after finishing, we looked at each other and decided we didn't have the courage to mail off anything so fiery. After a long silence, the wife in the husband and wife couple – our group's only female member, the bright young computing prodigy who had joined us all those years before – burst into tears.

'Why don't we just play mahjong?' she said. 'We've got the right number of people.'

And so we began to enliven our otherwise dull night lives with our new found hobby of mahjong – no wonder so many people found it addictive. Hunting under the sofa for a dropped tile one evening, we found the letter that we had written but never sent out. After re-reading it, we all agreed that despite a certain elegance and moral force, it was undeniably a work of juvenilia – trite, ill-considered, focusing on details at the expense of the big picture.

As we played round after happy round of mahjong one evening, two of our old comrades – the two who had sent out the last letter with us – called to say they'd heard we were all together, and to ask if they could drop by. We'd missed them since their departure, we said, but it was already 10pm, and to get to where we were gathered there was a stretch of road that cabs were barred from, meaning they'd have to cover the distance in a squat. Our mahjong club usually got together before 8pm so that we could avoid squat-walking. Never mind that, they said. Just wait for us.

We assumed they wouldn't arrive before 11, but at 10:17 there they were – driving, each in his own car! They grinned wildly as they parked their cars beside our building so that they only had to squat-walk for ten or twenty metres before stepping inside and stretching their limbs to stand back up in front of us. They had become members of the driving classes, and night-time excursions no longer presented any inconvenience to them.

We were by no means poor, intellectuals that we were, but neither were we politicians or big shots. Though tempted to join the growing number of private car owners, we had decided to wait and learn to drive first, and to date this was as far as any of us had allowed ourselves to go. Partly this was out of a desire to wait until prices fell; partly it was because new expenses kept cropping up – new houses to replace old work-unit housing, private school tuition for children, savings to help parents enjoy a comfortable retirement – and none of us felt particularly wealthy. So how had these two become big spenders?

They sat down across from us and explained how they had come to buy the cars. Big spending didn't enter into it, they said: their new luxury cars had been practically free, thanks to special vouchers they'd been given by the director of CrackCom. This flummoxed us – what did cars have to do with CrackCom, and why would they have vouchers from CrackCom anyway?

They squirmed a little at the question.

'Maybe the letter?' one of them said.

The last letter we wrote to the highest-ranking municipal administrator? we said. But we wrote to him too, we said. How come we didn't get anything?

Their new car-owning self-assurance returned, and they began to look amused.

'You want to join the driving classes too, is that it?'

But before we could accuse them of having forgotten who their friends were, they leaned forward earnestly.

'After all the years we've known each other, after all we've done together,' said the one who was the lover of the highest-ranking municipal administrator's secretary's wife, 'what's ours is yours. We were just worried that you were going to say we'd sold out, or that we'd just driven over here to lord it over you. You know the saying about the bravest person in human history being the first man to eat a crab? That's us – we tried the bourgeois crab first so you wouldn't have to.'

As he spoke, he pulled out four vouchers authorizing low-cost car purchases and slapped them down on the mahjong table, where we could see the red seal of CrackCom and the signature of the CrackCom director on each.

The secretary's wife's lover explained that a few days earlier he had received a call from the secretary asking him to come in for a chat. Naturally he found this unsettling, but the secretary's wife assured him that he had nothing to worry about – her husband knew they were old classmates, but had no clue that they were sleeping together. So he went and sat down with the husband of his lover, the secretary of the highest-ranking municipal administrator, in an office just across from the administrator's own. After a prodigious amount of small talk and conversation filler, the secretary finally brought up the topic of the squatting regulation.

'I understand that you intellectuals may have a hard time getting used to the regulation,' he said. 'The leaders don't have to squat, because they have cars; the big shots don't have to squat, because they have cars; the labouring classes mostly don't mind squatting because they've got strong knees and waists, but you intellectuals... CrackCom has made an internal decision to periodically offer batches of high-quality cars to select intellectuals at borderline suicidal discounts – so what do you say? If you're interested, I'll get the director of CrackCom to write you out a voucher right now.'

'Not interested,' our comrade nobly replied without giving the offer even a moment's thought. 'There are plenty of intellectuals out there like me, and if they have to squat, then I'll squat along with them.'

'You're a stand-up guy,' the secretary/husband laughed. 'No wonder my wife is always saying good things about you. How about this: there are five cars in the first batch. I'll get CrackCom to give them all to you, and if five's not enough then you can have the second and third batches too. How about that? Any problems with that arrangement?'

Our comrade immediately called the other comrade who had left our group with him, and they went to CrackCom to get their vouchers. Instead of startling us with the sudden news, the two decided that they would each take a car home first. After 8pm they took their new cars out for a long spin around the city. Then they called us.

The four of us rushed forward to shake their hands. Tears filled our eyes as emotion overwhelmed us.

Our sole female member broke the silence some moments later, her eyes sparkling as she stroked one of the vouchers with a fingertip.

'Even if he' – she meant the secretary/husband – 'didn't mention the letter, it's obviously what all this is about. But' – she laid a hand gently on her husband's chest – 'how on Earth could he have known that two of the six authors were married to each other? And that no matter how cheap the cars were, the married couple would only be able to afford one?'

She spoke seriously, but we all laughed, including her husband. Sometimes being a little naive, a little silly, a little dumb, just makes women more lovable. Even if they're former computer geniuses.

In no time at all, we became members of the car-owning classes. The five of us would go out for drives together, enjoying our new status. When we got together in the evenings, we could drive wherever and whenever we wanted, without having to concern ourselves with being unable to take a cab down this street, or having to squat-walk down that street. So far as squat-walking was concerned, I had it better than the others: there were times when they couldn't avoid squat-walking – like when the two of us who had first received cars had come to visit: they'd still had to hunker down and squat-walk the ten or twenty metres from their cars to the doorway. It was a short distance, and it was inside the residential compound, but not squatting was still against the rules. I, on the other hand, had simply hired a chauffeur, since I'd never learned to drive. When I came or went, the chauffeur would drive to the front of my building. The burden of squat-walking to and from the parked car was his, and I never had to squat down again – one long stride would be sufficient to carry me from my building into the car, or from the car back into the building.

My comrades joked that I was acting like a leader or a big shot. They were right – leaders and big shots had chauffeurs and people to do the squatting for them, too.

'Never mind leaders and big shots,' our sole female member said. 'Why not just say he's acting like me?'

We laughed, after a moment of surprised silence. That was our former computer genius – an analytical thinker. She was right, I was like her. Her husband was her chauffeur, and any place or any time she didn't feel like it, she didn't have to squat down either.

Imagining the Possibilities

1

THEY WERE ALL THRILLED when they brought my son home – my mother, my wife, my younger brother – but I just couldn't manage to get excited about it. I don't know what the problem was.

I had been able to get excited – before they brought my wife and son back from the hospital. I joined in the excitement with my mother and younger brother as we fixed our apartment up. We shifted all the furniture two feet to the west, moved my desk into my brother's room, and strung up a steel wire across a third of the newly enlarged space. On this we hung a big white curtain that encircled our queen size bed and made the brightly coloured bedspread look rather drab and lonely. My younger brother was uncharacteristically enthusiastic and hardworking throughout, I noticed, not complaining once. Something about it didn't feel right, and I found myself glancing over at him every now and then. A funny expression spread across his face after he caught me looking.

'You must be happy with all this, for your wife and son?' he asked with an air of forced cheer.

'Why shouldn't I be?' I replied, slightly taken aback.

Our mother had always talked to him like that, asking if he was happy with things or not. Subsequently my brother was always asking my wife if she was happy with things or not. As far as I can remember, no one ever asked me whether or not I was happy with things. Things were what they were, anyway, whether I was happy about them or not.

And so, happy or not, my wife and my son came back home from the hospital.

It was my first time seeing my son, and my first time seeing a newborn baby. He might only have been a few days old, but my son was bright-eyed, rosy-cheeked, and full-throated, a strapping young fellow to all appearances. Not bad at all, you would think – but something about it didn't sit right with me. I would have preferred that my son take after me in some ways: a vaguely distracted gaze, say; a somewhat husky voice; a slightly frail body. But he was nothing like me. I couldn't help feeling that it was a bit of a shame. Of course, I knew perfectly well that this was a cruel thing to wish on a boy and, of course, I hoped that the child – my own flesh and blood, after all – would grow up to be a beautiful boy.

He was, at that moment, being held in the arms of my mother. She walked carefully, on tip-toe almost, as if she were carrying a soap bubble. 'Oh, he's a *solid* little treasure,' I heard her coo. 'Just like his mother.'

I turned unconsciously to look at his mother – my wife. I saw her sturdy body, her thick arms and legs, her fleshy face and big ears. She lay on top of the blankets, panting, like a caged she-bear with nothing to do but sun itself.

My vision blurred. 'He does look like you,' I said to my wife.

Her fleshy face broke into a blurry smile, exhausted but content.

2

My wife was 30. We had been married for seven years before we had our son, and it hadn't been easy. My mother had been married seven years by the time she had me, too. I don't know whether or not she and my late father took all the fertility drugs we did. I don't remember ever seeing them take anything, anyway, and they had me and my brother – who is eight years younger than me – without any problem. Though of course it's not as if they would've told me if they had been taking anything, no matter how mature I was.

My wife's milk was good, and was so abundant that the shirt covering her ample chest always had two wet spots in front. This I didn't mind so much – it saved me from being sent out for milk at all hours – and it's not as if there are many women who manage to look good while lactating. My son was a powerful little pisser: it came bursting out of him strong enough to soak through his nappy and leave the brand-new quilt beneath sopping wet. This I did mind, but there was nothing to be done about it, and at least I could sleep on the fold-out cot on the far side of the bed. My wife would be resting in bed for the next month as she recovered from the birth, but with my mother there to take care of all the household chores, I had almost nothing to worry about. The way things were, the only real difference between new fatherhood and my days as merely a husband was that I couldn't lie down on top of my wife once or twice a day. I had nothing but free time on my hands after work, and I spent most of it playing *go* with my brother.

I was the one who taught my brother to play *go*. But he was a quick learner and a hard worker, and by this point he was as good as me if not better. It was embarrassing to lose to a former student, and I hated having to concede to him. It wasn't about the natural order of things or anything so serious; it was just a hang-up on my part. Even though I'd never been a competitive person.

There was a major flaw in my brother's game, though: he kept taking moves back. I doubt he did this as much when he played other people – bad form, the general rule being *you lay it, you play it*. If you get a reputation for retracting moves, soon nobody will want to play you. Against me, though, my younger brother was always taking moves back – and he was pushy about it, without offering any word of explanation. Eventually I realised he only ever did it when I was winning – it was a sneaky *go*-shark trick, playing dumb. Being a fair-minded person myself, I couldn't stand playing an opponent who resorted to constant mind games. Maybe the problem was all in my head: time after time, I'd found that whenever an opponent took back a move it completely threw me, ruined my concentration, and made me start making dumb moves that got worse and worse as I went on. I'd called him out on it plenty of times, but he just smiled brightly and kept on doing it. He had a sly side to him. He knew what he was doing, and he knew I didn't have anything to counter with. He knew I liked playing *go* but was lousy at making friends, and that there were only two people I regularly played with, and he was one of them. Even if I stomped out in a huff, swearing never to play him again, he knew perfectly well I'd be back in no time, asking for another game.

In those few days, though, he barely took back any moves, and when he did it didn't seem as if he was doing it just to shake me. I could tell that his mind wasn't on our games. He lost most of them, but the wins didn't seem to go to his head and he didn't seem to take the losses to heart. He just sat there, uncharacteristically calm and collected. Like a sponge, it sucked all the fun out of the game.

'What's with you?' I asked him when I finally couldn't take it anymore. Actually I had a pretty good idea of what the problem was.

'I'm just bored, is all,' he said unconvincingly, rolling a tile between his fingers. 'No big deal.'

3

One day, as we were playing and I was trying to think of a way to make the game more appealing to him, I hit upon the idea of exploiting the gambler mentality. They say eating, drinking, whoring, gambling, and smoking are the five deadly sins – from a certain perspective. Hoping to pique his interest with gambling, I asked, 'What do you say we make this more interesting? Two kuai fifty a round, or five. Your call.'

'Five,' he replied without the slightest hesitation. 'But from now on I'll only give you one game a day.'

'Give me? One game? What, you don't like it or something?'

'I'm not fussed,' he said coolly, picking up a *go* tile. 'Guess which hand to see who'll make the first move?'

'Of course,' I said limply. A few sentences, and already he had seen right through my plan.

I picked black, so I went first. I opened with a three star-points gambit, which he promptly matched. I hated his petty cleverness, but there was something else bothering me too, something bigger. I glared at the *go* board.

My brother loomed across from me, his shadow covering me. His playing style was quick and sharp, each move coming as if by divine inspiration. He cut a striking figure, and it occurred to me that perhaps my son would end up looking like him. When I paused to light a cigarette, my brother got up and went over to our mother. They had a brief whispered exchange, glancing over at me as they spoke, and both stifled a laugh. My mother was in the middle of making dinner for my wife.

I called my brother back to the game, but our mother put out a hand to stop him. She handed him a bowl of piping-hot poached eggs in broth for my wife. I turned my attention back to the board. My mother kept ordering my brother around to help take care of my wife during her month of bed rest. I would have been happy to help, if our mother had asked me – she was my wife, after all. The cigarette in my hand burned all the way down to the filter without my noticing it, and my brother still hadn't returned. I had come up with five possible plans of attack for the next move. I rose, stubbed out the cigarette, and wandered over to my wife's room, where I pushed the door open loudly. I walked in and opened the curtain around the bed to see my wife, reclining against the folded quilt, blowing the steam off the bowl of eggs. My brother was bent over at the side of the bed, his rear end sticking up in the air, and driving my son into paroxysms of laughter with big wet kisses. A glance – several glances – passed between them at the sight of me, quickly followed by seemingly well-rehearsed expressions of calm. I fixed my gaze on my younger brother's shapely rear end, which strained solidly against the seat of his jeans. 'Finish the game first,' I said. 'You can play with him after.' The past few days he'd been running in here whenever he could to chat with my wife about child-rearing, and to play with my son. But I knew that my son was too small for anything but crying, nursing, and sleeping.

Back at the *go* board, before he even touched the tiles, my brother turned back. 'Mind you don't eat too fast,' he called. 'You don't want to scald yourself. I meant to remind you.'

'I know,' my wife replied sweetly from inside the room.

'Don't disturb my boy,' I hissed at them both.

They laughed.

I picked up a shiny black *go* tile and slammed it down hard inside a formation my brother had been setting up. 'Break!' I crowed.

'You still haven't picked out a name for the baby,' my brother said.

'Not your problem,' I said. 'Your move.'

He laid his tile down without bothering to look at the state of the board. 'You have to call him *something*,' he said. 'I could suggest a name if you're having a hard time coming up with one.'

I tapped a *go* tile against my cheek. This was not a move I'd foreseen. Maybe he didn't have his game all planned out after all; maybe he wasn't putting up a smokescreen. 'What's that?' I mumbled distractedly, my eyes still on the board.

'A name,' my brother said. 'What about Diao Min? Something cheeky like that – there won't be many other children called "Rascal".'

After a moment's hesitation, I countered with a large right-angle formation. The game was starting to turn in my favour. 'Excellent,' I said.

My brother turned around excitedly and called out, 'My brother likes the idea of Diao Min!'

'Great,' I heard her reply happily. 'That's your contribution to this family.'

So my son was 'Diao Min' from then on.

4

Diao Min was always crying. He cried so much I couldn't sleep at night. I suggested to my wife that we could take him to the hospital to see if there was anything wrong with him. 'Better we should find out now and start treatment than to wait,' I said, perfectly reasonably. 'And if he's got something that can't be treated, then at least we'll have more time to decide what to do.' But my mother, wife, and brother were all against the idea. I was a jinx, they said, thinking that way; that was no way to talk about their child. 'He's not just your child,' they said, 'he's ours too. Don't you go jinxing our Precious. Babies cry and that's all there is to it.' They said, 'It's the babies who are always crying that go on to make something of themselves when they grow up.' There was someone from our block who was the same age as me, they said, made section chief by the time he was 30. They described to me, as if seeing it happen, how that certain someone used to always be crying. 'Louder and louder the later it got,' they said. 'Cried himself into conniptions a couple of times. Just kept howling and howling until his mother wanted to get rid of him altogether... And do you know what happened in the end?' At this point they would pause for a beat before brightening and lifting their voices as if they themselves were the mother of the baby.

'In the end–' they clasped their hands to their chests and looked straight through me, eyes gleaming, at something in the distance, something on the other side of the wall. 'Wouldn't you know it, he just got brighter and brighter, better and better, top of the class in looks, brains, personality, and luck.'

I had my suspicions. The story was full of holes, and I couldn't see any causal relationship between crying and professional success. But what really puzzled me was, how were they all so familiar with the details of that person's story? I had no interest in pursuing the matter any further, though: they had assigned me a task, and I thought I had better go and do it.

As I said, for some days now I had been a new father in name only, having done not a single thing for my newborn son. Diao Min was being completely taken care of by my wife, mother, and brother. The task described below fell to me only through a series of coincidences.

While on her way out the door that morning, my mother had charged my brother with the task of going to the local police station to add Diao Min to the family's household registration booklet. This my brother had agreed to do. However, after getting the household registration booklet from my wife, he had a sudden and irrevocable change of heart. He started complaining that his head hurt and his vision was blurry – and since he couldn't possibly leave the apartment, he began prevailing upon my mother to reassign the task to me. 'No need for that,' my mother said. She would go herself in the afternoon. I could see clearly that it didn't make any difference to her. But my brother and my wife stood their ground, insisting that it had to be me that went. They said there would be people at the station in the morning, but in the afternoon everyone would be away for a political 'study session'. The two of them seemed determined, eager almost, to get me out the door. My mother seemed to detect this – she even winked at my brother when she thought I wasn't looking. Her expression grew unreadable, mysterious. It didn't belong on a 60-year old woman's face. 'Then you go,' she said, 'if that's all right.' 'Sure,' I said, seeing that I had no choice in the matter, 'I'll go.' I knew that it was the way of the world for fathers to do things for their sons, and Diao Min was my son. And so I went with my mother. We talked idly about the weather and the best way to the police station as we walked, each of us occupied with other concerns. When we had walked a few yards from the apartment building, something made me look back, and I saw my brother's face pressed up against the window like a big lump of dough: pale, flat, and utterly false.

That strange face stayed with me all the way to the police station. The household registration counter was staffed by a chatty, middle-aged woman who had a passing familiarity with our apartment block. She greeted me by asking cheerily if it was true that Mr Zhang had died.

I had no idea, but rather than say as much I asked which Mr Zhang she meant.

'The man from the meat-pie stand,' she said.

I still wasn't sure who she meant, or even where there might be a meat-pie stand, but put on an air of sudden recognition rather than disappoint her: 'Oh, *that* Mr Zhang! Right, right, yes, so he did.' I handed over the household registration booklet and birth certificate.

She said, 'Make sure you remind his family to come do the –' but stopped as she looked at the household registration booklet, then guffawed like a man. She held her stomach and shook her head: 'Oh dear, oh dear.'

I looked across the counter at the booklet and the birth certificate. 'What's wrong?' I asked, hesitantly.

She laughed louder. 'Not you,' she said. 'My mistake, about Mr Zhang. He's not on your block. It's always good news from your block – all births, no deaths. And now you've got a bouncing baby boy at home, eh? Your little brother's a new father? And you didn't even bring me any candy to celebrate.'

'Right,' I said, with an embarrassed smile, and then '–No. It's me who's the father. My brother isn't even married.'

Her smile disappeared as I spoke. She regarded me suspiciously for a moment, then looked back down at the booklet and the birth certificate. 'You? I thought they said it was the younger – no, here it is. You.' She finished registering Diao Min without any further banter.

Sensing from this little interlude that I had some catching up to do, I stopped at a toy store on the way home and bought a toy car for Diao Min. It was monstrously expensive, top quality, sky blue, about half the size of a chessboard, and (with the installation of a D-cell battery) capable of zooming around, siren blaring. I was pleased with it, and I thought my son would be too.

Sure enough, Diao Min could hardly contain himself when I demonstrated it for him at home. He settled comfortably into my embrace with his arms and legs splayed out and a big smile crinkling his eyes into tiny little slits, his chubby head flopping around. He was my boy, after all, I thought, perfectly lovable when he wasn't crying or kicking up a fuss. A wave of emotion swept over me. 'My boy,' I called him, over and over again, 'my boy.' I was bending my head down to kiss his face when I heard my wife's voice pierce the bed-curtain like a wolf's howl, a tiger's growl, a lion's snarl, startling both Diao Min and me.

'Don't kiss him! You'll give him germs! Quick, give him back here – what do you want to hold him for?'

I was so startled by her sudden, unreasonable intrusion that it took me a moment to react. 'You'd think I was crawling with germs,' I said angrily. 'Just let me play with him a little longer.'

'I thought you didn't want anything to do with him!' my wife said. 'After all the time it took him to settle, you'll just go and upset him again. You don't like Precious and Precious doesn't like you.'

'Don't you go trying to make trouble between us menfolk,' I said, cooing at Diao Min. 'I bought him a car, and he likes it, and now he likes me. And I like–' but before I could finish, Diao Min started crying in my arms, twisting his tiny face up into an ugly little pustule of rage and squirming in the direction of my wife.

My wife poked her head out from behind the curtain. 'Quick, give him here. He was doing just fine without you...'

I thrust Diao Min back at my wife, my good mood evaporating. My mother and brother burst in, I suppose at the sound of Diao Min's wailing. My brother kicked the new toy car out of his way. The three of them poked their heads in through the curtain that surrounded my wife's bed, cooing at the baby to soothe him, leaving me, the father, out in the cold. Diao Min's cries grew fainter and fainter, and eventually turned into gurgling chuckles. The sound of four laughing voices rang in my ears, blending into a chorus that made me shiver even though it wasn't cold.

5

To all outward appearances, nothing had changed. My mother bustled about taking care of the cooking and cleaning and anything else that needed doing; my wife watched the baby and rested up, growing ever stronger; my brother and I played one game of *go* a day like clockwork, our games declining sharply in quality; Diao Min changed from day to day, growing steadily and healthily.

The apartment was all abuzz on the day of Diao Min's one-month birthday. Friends and relatives came bearing loads of gifts, which they heaped on my folding cot. Diao Min roved amidst the presents, lord of all he saw, as happy as a miser in his treasure room, and you could see from his responses to different gifts that he could tell instantly what every one was worth – what it had cost. The guests were lavish in their praise of the boy's genius in this matter. A regular *go* partner of mine – the one who wasn't my younger brother – came to offer his congratulations. He was a young guy, unmarried. He shrank into a corner, and after a long silence blurted, as if experiencing a sudden epiphany, 'No wonder everyone wants a boy; no wonder everyone envies people with baby boys; no wonder the presents for boys are so big – boys are just natural-born... *boys!*'

I was proud at this. Of all the boys deserving of endless praise, I knew that my son was the finest, most flawless specimen of them all. A flood of thoughts washed over me. I remembered how years before, I too had been a boy; how I had grown into a man, thereby ceasing to be a boy; and how my son had come along just in time to take over for me, allowing me to see another side of myself as a boy. The fact of his gender was a reminder that he had been created by *me*, proof that I was still, myself, a precious boy. The feelings went beyond anything I could put into words. I thanked my *go* partner silently for opening the eyes of this slow-witted father – and I felt a pang of regret at not having been able to invite more people I knew to the celebration.

Most of the guests were friends of my younger brother's, and all of them were as jubilant as if they were celebrating a holiday. They seemed to be well acquainted with my wife as well, and she formed a part of their chuckling, laughing mass. They passed my son from person to person like a baton in a relay race, much to his consternation. I tried several times to stop them, but every time my wife stepped in to stop me. It was some time before Diao Min reached my hands.

My wife got a strange look on her face when she saw me take Diao Min. 'What do you want him for? Here, give him to me.'

'I want to show him to my *go* partner,' I said happily.

'What do you want to do that for?' she said.

'My brother's friends got to see the boy,' I said. 'Why can't mine?'

'He doesn't even like *you*,' my wife said. 'What are the odds he'll like your friend?'

'He's starting to like me,' I said.

'Fine,' she said, 'Fine. Just don't make him cry, not with all these people around.'

I said, 'Why would—'

But Diao Min started bawling before I could finish, as if he'd received a secret signal from my wife. My brother happened to be passing by and took Diao Min into his arms; immediately, Diao Min stopped crying and started playing contentedly with my brother's earlobes.

'They're all sitting down,' my brother said to my wife. 'Why don't you and Diao Min go over and make a toast.'

From this I knew that my boy's one-month birthday dinner had begun.

My wife slid herself off the bed and straightened her clothes in the mirror. 'You take the boy,' she said to my brother. 'Don't want him getting my clothes rumpled again.'

Their party didn't break up until very late that night.

6

My younger brother's work unit was sending him on a business trip, and he wasn't happy about it. He said it was his boss trying to stick it to him. My wife and mother tried to calm him down. 'What a nice trip,' they said, 'Practically as good as a trip abroad. Plenty of people who'd love to be going, but your boss never gave them the chance. He's taken notice of you, is what it is.' My brother was sitting down on the floor holding Diao Min and rocking peevishly back and forth while my mother and wife packed his bags for him. I was off to one side, leafing through a book of *go* strategies.

'It's nice that he's taken notice of me,' my brother said. 'But it'll be far away and I'll be all on my own with no one else to talk to.'

I couldn't help myself. I didn't often interrupt when they were talking about their own affairs, but this time I found myself saying, 'Worried you won't have any playmates to keep you company? Or worried you'll miss this family?' I didn't ordinarily talk to people like that. At that moment, though, I felt a certain spiteful pleasure.

'What's that supposed to mean?' my brother said.

I patted the *go* book. 'Nothing, nothing. I just mean I'm sure you'll miss our daily *go* games.'

He didn't have anything to say to that. My mother told me to come out with her to get the groceries.

I was in high spirits that evening, bustling around and feeling like a prisoner on early release. My *go* partner came round to the house to invite me over for a game, but after a moment's hesitation I lied that I had something to do at home that evening.

I realised after seeing him off at the door that I actually did have something to be doing at home that evening, or at any rate had long been hoping I would. At that, I forgave myself for lying to him.

There really is a difference between having nothing to do and having something to do. It was exciting to have a clear end in mind, and I was on my best behaviour all evening. Not only did I wash my face before bed – with soap – but I even brought a basin of hot water into the toilet to wash the other parts of me as well. After all the preparation I was like I had been on my wedding night, a mess of emotions and excitement. Night had fallen outside, and the light inside the room was dim and soft, and the sight of a full-figured woman lying on the bed stirred the passions. My wife lay on her side, lying diagonally across the bed beneath the thin terrycloth coverlet and gazing contently at Diao Min, her face serene and her eyes full of love. Diao Min, beside her, was off in dreamland. He breathed delicately through his nose; his skin was as smooth and flawless as a jade figurine. I trembled all over with waves of happiness as I looked on, feeling – strongly now – the warmth of being alive. I shut and locked the door behind me, careful not to make a sound, carefully made my way over to the big bed from which I had been so long exiled, and asked my wife, by way of a conversation starter, whether Diao Min was sound asleep.

'Sound as can be,' she said. 'The way he sleeps and eats, he's bound to grow up big and strong like his uncle.'

I hadn't thought until then of my younger brother, who at this very moment was tossing and turning on the hard bunk of a sleeper car. 'Oh yes,' I said, playing along, 'Yes.' I knew I had to play the biggest idiot in the world.

I allowed my nerves to relax slightly as I lay face-down next to my wife and draped my arm innocently across her shoulder. Her broad, round shoulder peeked out from under the coverlet like a water cooler jug laid on its side: smooth, soft, pleasant to the touch. I could feel my heart clenching again and again, my body preparing itself for battle. My hands began to roam over a wider area now, and I pressed my lips against my wife's fleshy face. 'Come here, love,' I said. 'I missed you so much. We left the equipment idling for months, but now it's time to start up production again.'

But my wife did not answer my summons. She was knitting her brows, and there was a look on her face that I couldn't read — whether it was fear, revulsion, happiness, or something else. It spoiled the mood somewhat, but I had to rally my spirits. 'I'm dying for it,' I said. 'I need it.'

My wife must have needed it too – she had loved it back before we had Diao Min, could never get enough – but now she was shrinking away from me.

'Let's wait a while longer,' she said. 'I don't want to get sick.'

'It's fine, I looked it up. There shouldn't be any problem after this long.'

'I just don't want to wake the baby up. He'll start crying again.'

'I'll go easy,' I said. 'We wanted a child who could fill our lives with joy, but there are other joys, after all – we can't overlook those.'

'But...'

'Come on – we could have another Diao Min, if it wasn't for the family planning.'

'That's easy for you to say,' she said. 'I was the one who had Diao Min, not you.'

'I did my part. It takes two.'

'Oh, come off it. Your "part" didn't amount to much.'

'What kind of way is that to talk?'

'I keep track of these things,' she said. 'That's all.'

Our voices rose, and our physical passions cooled. In the end, I retreated to the fold-up bed under my wife's cold and scornful gaze.

7

It occurred to me later that it might not have been so unbearable if the pressure had only been at home, but the combination of problems at home and outside caused things to take a rapid turn for the worse.

My brother and I grew even more distant after he returned from his business trip. He was almost always playing with Diao Min, and he had no time for our daily games of *go*. I didn't feel like begging him – you can't just beg people to play games with you – and besides I had a growing sense that I was underfoot in my own household. I was surplus to requirements. Better just to stay out of everybody's way, I thought, so I went to play against my other *go* partner.

He lived two buildings over in the same compound as us. His family knew me well, since I was often over there to play. It used to be that nothing could bother me when I was over there playing: we would sit in the living room, and no matter how loudly other people in the room were talking or laughing or blasting the TV, we would always play silently, paying the others no heed, an island of quiet amidst the noise. But lately things had been different: people kept dropping by the apartment while we were playing, uninvited and for no apparent reason. They were shifty, sneaky, up to something, not there on any legitimate business – it looked like they were there just to see me. They came and went back and forth around me, whispering and pointing, questioning my *go* partner's parents in low murmurs. I could feel their stares pricking into my back like thorns, and it made me fidgety and uneasy. 'What are these people doing?' I finally asked my *go* partner one night. 'What are they saying about me?' His answer was rambling and evasive. I could tell that those people and their comings and goings were as much of a torment for him as they were for me – but he was clear-eyed, and I was confused.

A middle-aged woman came by my *go* partner's apartment while we were playing that evening. She stood behind him and stared at me fixedly until I was thoroughly unsettled. 'Are you going to play a game of *go* or what,' I asked her, as venomously as I could.

'Oh no,' she stammered. 'Never learned how.' She followed my friend's mother into the other room, and I heard her clucking: 'Yes, that's him, our neighbour. I know all *about* their family...'

That evening, like the many evenings before it, I was badly off my game.

When I got home that night, I heard gusts of laughter coming from my bedroom: my wife, my brother, and Diao Min. When I closed the front door loudly behind me, however, the sound stopped abruptly. Even Diao Min fell silent. The last thing I heard was my brother saying, 'He's looking more and more like me every day.' I turned and went into my mother's room.

My mother was watching the television, which was showing some atrocious soap opera about a woman who found a baby girl on the streets and raised her as her own. I watched, dully, as the actors cycled from tears to laughter and back again, and my mother's eyes darted back and forth between the television and me. Just then my younger brother walked in and sat down next to my mother affectionately, casting a quick look at me out of the corner of his eye before turning back to smile at her. My mother smiled back at him.

I stood up, glaring at them. 'You two are awfully close,' I said. 'Anyone would think you were his mother.'

My mother's face stiffened. 'What's that supposed to mean?'

My brother drew nearer to her. 'She *is* my mother.'

'But you never let *me* do that,' I said to my mother. 'Obviously I'm not family enough for you.'

My mother said 'What—'

'He's crazy,' my brother said.

Back in the bedroom, my wife and Diao Min were already asleep. I lay restlessly on the folding cot and smoked two cigarettes one after the other in the dark, all kinds of strange thoughts running through my head. After I finished the cigarettes and began preparing to sleep, an urge began to take root in my mind: I wanted to see if my wife was sound asleep or not; I couldn't take any more of this endless separation. I turned on the lamp and shifted my gaze to the big bed, where my wife was indeed sleeping, breathing deep and low, and drooling slightly from the corner of her mouth. To my surprise, however, Diao Min wasn't asleep at all: he was looking straight at me, wide-eyed and scornful. His gaze was simultaneously scathing and impassive, and it was clear that he had been staring at me in the dark for some time. I felt the hairs stand up on the back of my neck. Anyone would feel the same, I think, to be stared at that way by a baby not even a hundred days old yet. I composed myself, and did my best to wink and smile at Diao Min. Unmoved, he broke eye contact and shifted his gaze sideways to the bare wall behind me. Still, I could see that not a single move I made escaped his attention. I was at a loss, unable to make any rational appeal that would end his hostile attention. No son, I thought, probably no son would ever look at his own father like that. Not unless his father wasn't his father.

I heard the quiet coming from my mother's room and my brother's room. All around me was still and silent. I saw that there was not even the slightest resemblance between me and Diao Min, and the realisation filled me with revulsion. I balled up one hand into a fist and shook it at him, baring my teeth, but he paid it no heed. I was left flustered and frustrated. Moving suddenly, I hopped down to the floor and stepped closer to the bed, my expression growing cruel and ugly. As I drew closer, Diao Min raised himself from his reclining position to meet my bluster with a mocking, sneering gaze. It was a challenge, no doubt about it: he left me no choice. A tiny little baby like him could sleep or not sleep, eat or not eat, play or not play, could even torment and degrade people with tantrums or illness or other sudden, irrational behaviour – but a baby could absolutely not act the way he was acting. I unclenched my fist slightly, leaving my hand curled into a loose semicircular grip. It occurred to me that the shape would fit snugly around Diao Min's bare neck, like a machine part snapping tightly into place, and that what I should do at that moment was to gently but firmly squeeze and tighten.

And so, with Diao Min watching me coldly, my hands began their cruel work around his little neck. Gently, but firmly, squeezing, harder and harder…

8

What happened after that is another story.

117

The Last Shot

WHEN THE ORDERS COME I have already been sitting at my desk for some time, concentrating hard in preparation for the work that I'm about to begin.

Whenever I'm getting ready to work, I spend a half-hour or so sitting at my desk with my senses withdrawn and my mind a perfect blank. It seems to make the work go better. My desk is as big as a bed, and just being near it is enough to fill my head with warm, happy thoughts. It has a desktop finished in chestnut brown, commodious drawers, and thick legs that give an overall sense of weight and solidity. At the back, where the desk meets the wall, is an old dual-deck cassette player of Japanese manufacture. A stack of blank writing paper and a black fountain pen sit on one side, near the front; my feet rest on the other side. My eyes are half closed, my whole body is sunk into the brown swivel chair, and my feet, in dark patterned socks, are comfortably propped up. My foam slippers lie on the floor where I kicked them off.

This is when the orders arrive.

Two rows of red lights are flickering back and forth at the top left corner of the cassette player. I watch them dully, two bloody swords stabbing and retracting in tandem. The machine is playing a Cui Jian album, and as I listen to the music I contemplate the last thing I saw before I closed my eyes: the grey album cover with its headshot of Cui Jian, his face as round and flat as a target. Two words hang above his head and to the left in large, deathly pale type: 'The Fix', the final diagonal of the 'X' slashing down toward Cui Jian's right temple like a bullet. It strikes me as a curiously inauspicious choice of cover design. The lyrics are almost completely unintelligible. I'd strained at first, trying to make out what Cui Jian was singing, before realising that he didn't want to be understood. One of the songs is just two or three lines repeated over and over. The words don't matter, I think, as long as you can lose yourself in what the music means. I recently began listening to music I find meaningful before I start writing, songs like 'I Love Tiananmen Square' and 'Sabres Out, Forward March.' A friend told me it would be a way for me to get some culture. Though it's my first time listening to Cui Jian.

But my orders are here now – no time to be thinking about either Cui Jian or writing. My only thought is that it's time to turn away from the personal project I've been preparing to do and start doing the job laid out in my orders.

The orders are complex and detailed, with diagrams, instructions, specific requirements, and explanatory footnotes. Most people wouldn't be able to make head nor tail of them, but a seasoned professional like myself, who often receives orders of this sort, can quickly grasp the substance – which is actually quite simple. Someone is a problem, and I'm to go 'fix' them.

I'm an outstanding civil servant. I never cavil or complain, let alone ask questions about the whys and wherefores. Carrying out orders is what I was born to do; that's the only thing I need to know. Any value I add to the process comes solely from my ability to serve as a tool. It's no different from my fountain pen, whose value comes from its utility as a writing implement, or my weapons, whose value, when I'm carrying out orders, comes from their utility as implements of killing.

Taking a rough appraisal in the mirror, I see a face that is firm, resolute, and perfectly expressionless, straight out of an American cowboy movie. This is satisfactory: exactly the sort of face called for when carrying out orders. I set off at a brisk pace, checking my invisible gun as I walk out of the apartment. An extraordinarily deadly weapon: not complicated to manufacture, supposedly, but it'll never go out of date and it'll never let you down. In the time it takes me to check it and put it away again, my body carries me down three flights of steps and out into the sunlight.

It's a good time of year for sunlight – warm and pleasant, neither too cold nor too hot. Though really there's no bad time of year for sunlight, and no real difference between this time of the year and any other. Even if there were, it wouldn't make any difference to me. It isn't the sunlight that's compelling me to go 'fix' someone; it's my orders.

I walk briskly, like a clockwork figure with the spring wound as tight as it will go. A broad, spotless asphalt road comes into view, stretching out as far as the eye can see in either direction. The graceful parabolae of electric tramlines glint and sway in the sun above it. Brightly coloured cars of all sizes drive by from time to time, their horns singing as sweetly as birds in a forest. The profusion of these little details at the outset is soothing, and I take it as a sign that my task will go smoothly. I decide to keep following the road. Quick in, quick out, I think, and maybe it will even make the writing go better once I got back. Pleased with the thought, I start humming 'To Sail the Seas, You Need a Helmsman.' But in my complacency I allow my mind to wander, and before I know it I've turned onto an unevenly lit side street tucked in between buildings. I don't even notice my change in course; by the time I realise that I'm in a bustling, noisy commercial district, my footsteps have already begun to slow of their own accord. I pause, hesitating. Was I supposed to pass this way, or have I taken a wrong turn somewhere? But no – my orders said I would have to pass through a busy commercial district. I'm relieved not to have made a mistake, though it seems a pity to be unable to keep following the wide, straight road.

But it's not up to me. It could be a war zone before me

instead of a bustling shopping district, and I'd still have to keep going unquestioningly forward.

As with every other time I've ever walked through a commercial district, I am subjected to frequent obstructions and inquiries, as if everyone around me is a dear friend. I am invited to examine imported brand-name suits at discount prices, asked whether I have any interest in piping-hot pig's-head meat, and informed – by a fellow who plops a fedora on my head and claims to be from Xinjiang – that a hat like that would make me look as steely and suave as a hitman in a Hollywood movie. I'm briefly tempted to reply that I already am a hitman, and an uncommonly good one, but I smile and say nothing, politely declining all the obstructions, questions, and compliments that came my way. I've always been somewhat cold – I don't usually have feelings for people, which is what comes of spending so long in such a bloody line of work. But a sudden and unaccustomed rush of empathy makes me look more sympathetically at the men and women around me. I realise later that this never would have happened if I hadn't slowed my pace; I suppose physical speed is inversely proportional to the speed of one's thoughts. At this moment, my thoughts are occupied with wondering what all these people hope to achieve, scurrying around like ants, day in and day out. The ones bustling to and fro in front of me, for instance, are cheerfully going about earning money or buying things – but who's to say that someday, unbeknownst to them, they might not end up in my orders, as problems for me to fix? Their grieving relatives can burn their money and bury their purchases along with them – they won't be good for anything else. The way of the world, I suppose. People talk about seizing their destiny, but all this destiny-seizing is nothing more than a masturbatory grab at self-comfort.

And so I walk along, thinking unusually compassionate thoughts – and what happens next demonstrates that God, in his infinite justice, looks compassionately upon the compassionate. Usually I keep moving forward, eyes ahead, focused on the task at hand, whether I'm in the middle of a crowd or the middle of nowhere. But this unusual spell of compassion is making me place myself on the same level as all God's other creatures. As I walk along, lost in thought, I cast a thoughtful eye on the people around me – and on myself. This is how, in the course of my observations, my eyes alight upon the man skulking in the middle of the crowd as he gets ready to make a move against me. Did God allow me to discover Him because of my newfound feeling for my fellow man? Or has He been quietly pushing me towards developing the compassion and fellow-feeling that led me to spot the man?

A jolt of fear runs through me at the realisation that I've become the object of someone else's plans. My first reaction to this is shock – shock that even a crafty old hand like myself is still capable of fear. My next thought is that I should keep calm. I'm an excellent assassin. I'm going to win. I'm not going to be meat for anyone's pot.

I consider the situation coolly for about five seconds; then, taking cover behind a drunk whose friends are walking him unsteadily through the crowd, I duck into a clothing shop and take up a position in front of a full-length mirror that lets me observe the scene behind me. I see my tail looking around stupidly – thrown, I suppose, by the sudden loss of his target. He's a middle-aged man, pushing 50, flabby and poorly dressed. His face appears slightly twisted – I don't know whether it's a flaw in the mirror or whether he's just anxious. Maintaining my composure, I ask the shop girl to show me a white suit, and I take my time holding it up against myself in the mirror, front and back, so that the girl has to dart back and forth around me. Maybe the additional visual distraction will confuse my tail even further. My tradecraft fails me here, unfortunately: the idiot smartens up somehow, and after a brief but intense search he finds me again.

He comes to a halt outside the door of the shop, no more than ten metres away from me. There's a dull satisfaction in his eyes, a sure sign that he doesn't realise I've made him.

New to the game, evidently, despite his age. He half-raises his invisible gun, trembling. Other people might not spot the motion, but it doesn't escape me. I snort at his reflection in the mirror and draw my own weapon, keeping my face expressionless. A weariness comes over me. I don't want to hurt him, I think, not really. I could even let him go, if he doesn't take this any further. I shake the white suit I was holding, hard, hoping its reflection in the mirror will interfere with his vision, that he'll realise he's dealing with a pro and quit before it's too late. But the poor idiot doesn't wise up, doesn't take the chance – much less show any gratitude for it. People new to this line of work must find something about fixing people incredibly seductive. The inevitable disappointment comes a moment later when the man makes the amateur mistake of pulling the trigger with the glare of the white suit still in his eyes. The shop girl goes limp beside me and slumps against the counter next to the mirror, a red flower blooming at her ample chest. That was over the line – you don't kill innocent bystanders. I raise my hand and pull the trigger without a second thought. Thanks to years of practice in the field, my technique is flawless. Under ordinary circumstances I wouldn't dream of taking a life unless my orders said to, but since the man was planning to murder me I have no choice but to respond in kind. I fire – once – and the incompetent staggers out of the store like a drunk and falls in a heap outside.

I feel a pang of regret after I fix the middle-aged man. Not at having taken another life – as I said, my attention to carrying out orders makes me an exemplary civil servant. I'd take every life in this world if my orders told me to. I'd do my job as tirelessly as a mechanical reaper, working my way pitilessly back and forth until every last man standing was left lying horizontal. No – I regret not leaving the man alive. I should have captured him and found out why he was trying to harm a man he'd never met. Now that that's no longer an option, I can only walk out of the blood-spattered clothing store with a bellyful of questions. My compassionate mood is long gone by now, and I feel myself starting to despise the bustling markets and the crowds jostling around me.

Leaving the commercial district behind, I come to a vast, empty stretch of ground. I brighten a little to see the bare expanse lying exposed to the sunlight. There is nothing unfamiliar about it; indeed, I feel certain that this is where I come every night on my evening strolls. There used to be raised flowerbeds here, with flowers planted in pretty geometrical designs that bloomed and withered with the seasons. But the wooden railings around the flowerbeds rotted, and the plants died off, and now this empty patch of earth is all that's left. The granite benches beside the planters have managed to survive and maintain their positions, the only decoration that remains in this place. My orders come to mind again: if I recall correctly, my target is in the residential block on the other side of this expanse.

My good mood is back, and by the time I begin crossing the barren expanse, I have put the distressing incident in the commercial district out of my mind completely. I'm no stranger to violence, as I have said. A certain breadth of mind, an ability to not dwell on things too long, is one of the hallmarks of a mature talent in my profession. My attention is focused on happier matters at the moment: the orders that occupy my thoughts, and also the pretty woman just now coming into view.

I'm about 15 metres away from one of the granite benches when I see her sitting on it. The afternoon sun gently caresses every bit of the 15 metres of hardpan between me and the bench – between me and the woman – and it feels almost as if the silent air is trying to convey some secret message, as if it has taken on a consciousness of its own. For no clear reason, I feel a swell of emotion. I really shouldn't be paying attention to anyone else while I'm carrying out my orders, much less attempting anything in the category of thought – emotion, for instance – but something about me is off today.

I don't know what it is, but something is keeping me from focusing my thoughts, no matter how hard I try. But I don't want to beat myself up about it – you can't be too hard on yourself while you're on a mission, can't do anything that might interfere with the natural, unforced composure that the job requires. Instead I try telling myself that perhaps what I need is to ease up a little, to go wherever my desires take me. It might even help me carry out my orders. The thought relaxes me considerably.

I'm happy to stroll past a pretty young woman, naturally – but more importantly, my route really does require me to walk past her bench. It's nice to have the bench – and the young woman on it – as points of reference as I walk, though it's a pity about the vast 15-metre gap that separates us. I can see, indistinctly, that she's not so young – I'd put her somewhere between young woman and young housewife. She sits straight and proper, her outfit perfectly suited to her, her posture recalling a piece of elegant statuary. She's reading a book. Her head is tilted slightly toward me. At the sound of my footsteps she gives a start and looks up at me with a motion that doesn't seem quite natural. She hugs her book to her chest, still open to her page, and looks at the ground under my feet, her eyes scanning shiftily back and forth. Her left hand cradles the spine of the book, and her right hand is concealed behind it at an unnatural angle. Just nerves, I think. I could go up and chat or flirt a little, if I weren't on the job. But an instant later I see that something's not right, something about the way she's watching me out of the corner of her eyes. As a man, it's nice to have a pretty girl looking at you – but not with the kind of hostile, knowing gaze that she has trained on me. The incident in the shopping district – the attempted fix and the counter-fix – flashes into my mind, and I immediately become alert.

But I'm a moment too late. The gap between us has shrunk to a metre or so, without my noticing it – close enough for us to reach out and touch each other. By the time

I notice the discordant changes flitting across her pretty face, she's already pulled her right hand out from behind the book and pointed it straight at my chest. The invisible gun in the pretty young woman's delicate hand – so grimy I can almost see it – goes off with a silent bang.

So this is it, I think in that split second. I'll be like a master sailor, a veteran of ocean voyages, running aground in the pitiful little ditch this young woman dug for me. Sadder and more distressing still is the way she went from pretty young thing to stone-faced killer in the blink of an eye.

In that same split second, I feel a rush of gratitude for all the orders I've been given over the years. They gave me the experience that made me the outstanding killer I am, and the training that makes me confident even now that anyone trying to fix me will not only have their work cut out for them, but will be in mortal peril of getting fixed themselves.

Subsequent developments bear out this confidence. Instead of falling dead at the young hitwoman's feet, I have her like an ant in the palm of my hand. Just as she is drawing a bead on me, I leap at her. An instinctual move, driven by instinctual fearlessness and the instinct to survive. Those instincts protect me like talismans. Instead of hitting me in the chest, the bullet that comes screaming out of the invisible gun's chamber tears a scorching rent in my left shoulder. I feel the wound, but there's no time to think about the pain. By the time I notice it, I've already grabbed the young woman and sat down heavily beside her on the cold, bright bench, my shoulder next to hers, snuggling up close as if we were lovers.

I'm sitting on the hitwoman's right, with her fine-fingered delicate hand beneath me. I sit on it as hard as I can. Thanks to my years as a writer, my buttocks are as hard as millstones and covered in calluses. I can hear bones shattering under me: a lovely sound, like young timber popping in a furnace. I imagine the woman's pale, jade-like hand and the invisible pistol it held being ground slowly into a fine powder. I can hear something else, too: blood-curdling cries and pleas from vocal cords strained to breaking point. With my left hand, I reach around behind the nape of the hitwoman's neck and grab her left hand, which still holds her book of spells. With my left shoulder wedged in under her right cheek, the wound on my shoulder looks like a bow in her hair, a gaily coloured patch of pain that goes all the way down to the marrow.

'I can't take it,' the hitwoman cries hoarsely. 'Mercy! Just kill me!' Pale beads of sweat stream down her pale face.

I tilt my head forward and lock eyes with her, as if I were inhaling her fragrance. I have what I'm pretty sure is a mild, tender expression on my face. 'Tell me why you tried to kill me. I want to know everything.'

'I got the wrong person – I…'

I sit down harder, and I hear bones popping like fire-crackers on New Year's Eve.

'Aiiieeeeeee, I can't take it! I can't –'

I bear down harder.

'I'll talk! I – I don't know who you are, I don't know anything about you. It was just an order… a complex, detailed order, telling me… telling me to fix you at this time and this place…'

'An order?' My mind goes blank. 'Really? An order?' I can feel every muscle in my body clenching. The hitwoman struggles to breathe.

'You – I was telling – the truth… please…'

'It was an order? Another order?' I barely understand the words; I can only repeat them loudly, again and again, paying no mind to the woman beside me: 'An order? Another order?'

After a while I relax my grip on the whimpering hitwoman, get to my feet, and start making my way shakily toward the residential block ahead of me. I came here to carry out an order. There's someone to fix. I can't stay here and keep delaying things. I tear a strip of cloth from the front of my checked shirt as I walk, and use it to bind the painful wound on my shoulder.

Evening is approaching, and the sun is beating a slow downward retreat through the gaps between buildings. The residential block is warm and homey, with sweet scenes of everyday life everywhere I look. Men and women pass in and out of the doorways, carrying shopping baskets. There's a group of boys kicking a ball around the patch of ground in front of the buildings, and a group of girls skipping rope. Parked randomly in front of the entrances to the buildings are bicycles of all ages, makes, and colours. Nobody pays me any attention, and I have no interest in paying attention to anybody else.

I make straight for Building 13, certain that nothing can go wrong now. The building houses four separate blocks of apartments; my target is in the second. I know Unit 2 well enough to describe it with my eyes closed. There's a cargo tricycle parked in front of the doorway, a mobile sales counter for the neighbour who started a business selling tangerines on the street. Behind it, the battered door to Unit 2 testifies to battles lost to the cargo tricycle. The retired worker who lives on the second floor reinforced it with beige sheet metal. Bolted to the wall just inside the door is a ludicrously oversized green mailbox, its slot big enough to admit a child's hand. On the front is a name and the number of an apartment on the third floor of the building. Evidently it belongs to a writer. Someone's stuck a palm-sized piece of paper to the wall next to it, a reminder for the family on the fourth floor to take their child in for vaccinations. It's been there for a month. Beneath the mailbox and the reminder is the brightly coloured German racing bicycle that the young guy on the fifth floor uses when he wants people to see how young and vigorous he is. It leans against the door to the small storage space that was added under the stairs; this is the perquisite of the old lady on the sixth floor, who was the building's first occupant. Above the sixth floor is the roof; above the roof is the sky – I know it all like the back of my hand. I feel pleased with myself: my orders were complex and detailed, but they didn't go into anything like this level of detail.

I pause in front of the German racing bike to gather my thoughts and re-check my invisible gun. I prick up my ears cautiously, listen to my surroundings, and look back outside. Once I'm 90% certain that all is as it should be, I start creeping quietly up the stairs.

My steps are light; my eyes are sharp. On the landing between the first and second floors, I note two tattered burlap sacks next to a basket, and a few scribbled obscenities on the wall above them. Continuing upwards, I arrive at the landing between the second and third floors, which is cleaner by far: nothing but cardboard boxes, neatly stacked. I step back against these and look up until the third floor comes into view – and with it, my target.

At the third floor I pause. My orders said that the door on the third floor would be sky blue, and indeed the door is sky blue. I take out my keys, unlock the door, and step inside. My orders said that the first thing I would see would be the bathroom, just inside the front door on the left. This was also correct: there's a bathroom on my left, with a shower in it. I pass through the foyer and come to a halt outside the study. My orders told me I would find an armchair, a tea table, and four overflowing bookshelves there – 100% correct, as I could have confirmed without having to look. I am looking, though, eyes fixed straight ahead, at –

The first thing I see is a writing desk with a chestnut-brown desktop, commodious drawers, and thick legs that gave an overall sense of weight and solidity. It's as big as a bed, and looks as if it could inspire plenty of warm, happy thoughts. At the back, where the desk meets the wall, is an old dual-deck cassette player that appears to be of Japanese manufacture, on which two rows of red lights flicker back and forth like two bloody swords stabbing and retracting in tandem. At one side of the front of the desk sits a stack of pages, covered in writing, and a black fountain pen. At the other side are two feet, clad in dark patterned socks. As I track back from the feet with my eyes, I realise that there's someone else in the room. His body is sunk deep into the brown swivel chair in front of the desk, the back of the chair providing comfortable cover that hides his head and body from view. I blink, hard, trying to make out what sort of person this silent figure might be, but the back of the chair conceals everything but a left shoulder, bound with a scrap of checked shirt, and the two feet in their dark patterned socks. Gradually, I remember my orders, and realise that I can't let myself be distracted any longer. I cast another look at the feet propped up on the desk in their dark patterned socks. Whoever this is, he knows how to take it easy. *Bad luck, friend*, I think – not unkindly. *You just stay where you are, and you'll go right on being comfortable after I fix you.* I raise my invisible gun slowly and point it at where his right temple must be, knowing that the invisible bullet, barely even there at all, will trace a deadly diagonal through the air, the final stroke of a letter–

And a silent bullet explodes in my mind with a roar and a bang, and a shockingly mild change comes over the room. I feel like an autumn leaf adrift on the wind as I sway, an orderly shambles, and begin, with a senseless logic, to fall to the floor. A breeze rises around me, gentle as fog, as my body continues collapsing, and softly blows a few sheets of paper off the desk. The last thing I remember is seeing the first of those insubstantial pages fluttering to the floor, like a faded flag, covering a pair of foam slippers lying where someone kicked them off, and written on it I can just make out the curious title –

THE LAST SHOT

Going to Zhangji

1

I'M A PROFESSIONAL FICTION writer. I enjoy making things up; I like being able to pick up my pen and create anything that strikes my fancy. I've written a few dozen stories over the years – the numbers are still coming in – and invented a number of characters that's approaching the triple digits. Because of my lack of knowledge and my limited experience, I have a habit – once I get a flow going – of passing off complete nonsense as if it were gospel truth. I'll talk about the flowers of the steppe creeper or describe the effects of alpzolonomine pills with a completely straight face, as if these were as common as peonies and cough syrup, when in fact they're completely made up and would fall apart the minute you looked at them too closely.

And yet for some reason the places that crop up in my stories are almost all real – Shenyang, Dalian, Beijing, Guangzhou, all genuine articles. I'm even scrupulous about the little details – the North Market, Tiger Beach, the Haidian District Library, the Tianhe Sports Centre – which is more than I can say for certain authors who only ever set their stories in, say, the city of S— in L— Province. Reflecting on my own penchant for fabrication, there are times when I'm bemused, even a little self-critical, sensing that I haven't gone far enough with my untruths, the authorial equivalent of running out of steam halfway through sex. The first case is an affront to the art of fiction; the second is an affront to the woman who gives me pleasure and receives pleasure from me. But fortunately, now that I reflect on my own work, I find that the place names aren't monotonously factual after all. In some of my stories – more than a few – you'll find Zhangji, a city without any basis in reality whatsoever.

I've got Zhangji. There's always that.

I've written more than a few stories, but that's not to say I understand literary theory. Are stories about completely true things really not good stories? If there's a real-world basis for everything in a story – the names, the places, the plants and the medicines – is it mere reportage, rather than fiction distilled from experience? I don't know. I don't think you can make hard and fast rules like that. Still, the realisation that I had a made-up place of my own came as a relief, a slight lessening of the literary pressure exerted on me by the weight of Macondo and Yoknapatawpha County.

I had never thought much about what my creation, Zhangji, meant to me. My fiction deals mainly with contemporary urban life, and most of my stories take place in Shenyang, where I've lived ever since I was born, since it's the most readily usable setting for me. But fiction isn't like official propaganda: it can't always sing happy songs, and even a work in a major key can't avoid the occasional note of complaint or criticism. I have no quarrel with anybody, or with the world in general; I only write fiction because it's the game that my sort of intelligence is best suited to. I don't want to write something incautious and offend anybody – especially not here in Shenyang: a peaceful life is more important than fiction, after all. And so I invented another city, Zhangji, that I could use for misdirection and to avoid stirring up trouble when it seemed best not to use Shenyang.

I've gone on too long already, but now that I've got this far I might as well add a few more sentences – it's not against the rules for a writer to take his time getting to the point. I invented my toy city of Zhangji on a whim, nothing more. I was working for a magazine at the time. There were two other editors at the magazine, a man named Zhang Xiaowei and a woman named Zhang Ying, and we always got along well – our shared responsibility made us brothers (and sister) in arms. I got the idea of writing a story as a token of my friendship for the two Zhangs, and found in the process that I needed a fictional place name. Without much thought, I wrote down 'Zhangji' – 'a group of Zhangs' – since the two friends with whom I had the most contact could be grouped together under the surname Zhang. I tend to be picky about names, and with more time and more thought I'm sure I would have come up with something as unusual and odd-sounding as my pen name, 'Diao Dou.' There's a city in Xinjiang called 'Hammy,' for instance, and a place in Shandong called 'Geemow'. In Guizhou they have a town called 'Peachy,' and there's a place named 'Byeso' down in Guangxi. I've never been to any of these places, and I don't know the stories behind the names, but just reading or writing them – Hammy, Geemow, Peachy, Byeso – is enough to give me a little rush. Which is to say that given my tastes, names like these belong in my personal dictionary of toponyms more than 'Zhangji' does. Unfortunately I'd already used 'Zhangji,' and have since used it for long enough to be familiar with it and to have a certain soft spot for it, so I keep it around. But to be perfectly honest, I've never paid it enough attention. I've treated it the way a mother treats a foster child – with caring and concern and even love, but more out of a sense of obligation toward a guest than the natural love she would show to her own offspring. So when Mary asked if I could go to Zhangji with her, I never noticed the way she stressed the name, or thought that the 'Zhangji' she meant was the one in my stories. I fell all over myself to accommodate her: 'No problem,' I said. 'Anywhere you like – all the way south to Sanya, all the way north to Mohe; just say the word.' I wasn't thinking clearly at the time. My brain was so overwhelmed, as if I were drunk on wine or women, that I completely forgot that I had written a city called Zhangji into existence.

Incidentally, if the names Hammy or Geemow or Peachy or Byeso had been my own creations, I don't think any amount of wine or women would be sufficient to make me forget that they're not to be found on any maps of China. But the name Zhangji is completely unremarkable, as ordinary and everyday as Shenyang or Dalian or Beijing or Guangzhou.

2

Mary and I met in Lhasa, at Gonggar Airport.

I had just walked into the departures hall, and was looking around for the check-in when I heard someone calling my name. I could hardly believe my ears – who could know me in such a remote place? But turning toward the voice, I saw right away who it was. A man in a Western-style suit and leather shoes stepped out of a group of fashionably dressed men and women and strode toward me. Our expressions were not dissimilar: he looked pleasantly surprised; I just looked surprised.

'Diao Dou! Imagine seeing you here – what are the chances?'

'Y– James?'

James cheerfully made the introductions, and that was how I got to know Mary and the rest of the group – well, no; I never really got to know any of the others, just Mary.

'Hey everybody, this is my good friend Diao Dou. Diao Dou's a celebrity – a big-name writer – here, let me introduce everyone. These are my co-workers – our company sent the mid-level staff to Lhasa for a "conference". (It's mostly just an excuse for a trip.) This is Philip – and Roth – and Mary – and Helene – and Frick…'

Don't picture James as an English gentleman, or Mary as an American beauty. They were yellow-skinned, black-eyed Chinese, as were the rest of their foreign-named co-workers – they just worked for a multinational. Nor were James and I particularly good friends: we'd met somehow or other on one of my visits to Beijing, and our interactions had been limited to me using his car twice. If we really had been good friends, I would at least have known what his Chinese name was – if he had one, that is. At James's friendly invitation, I joined him and his fellow young professionals as we checked in and got our boarding passes, went through security, sat in the waiting room, and discussed football, Saddam Hussein, film adaptation rights for novels, Harry Potter, Snoopy, and the storybooks of Jimmy Liao, then made our way onto the plane. When we boarded, I found that my seat was next to Mary's. In Row 60, at the centre of the plane, just in front of the toilets, Mary had seat C, I had seat B, and James had seat A, which is to say that Mary had the aisle seat to my right, James had the window seat to my left, and I was sandwiched between the two of them.

I didn't care much one way or the other about running into James at Gonggar Airport, but I was quite willing to see the hand of Providence in being seated next to Mary on the aeroplane – even if nothing had come of it afterwards, I'd still prefer to think of things that way. Out of all the young professionals in James's group, and out of his five or six female co-workers, it was Mary I'd taken a liking to from the first time I saw her. Of course, I'm not saying that if I like someone then anything will necessarily come of it, or that anyone I like is bound to tremble with delight and take a liking to me too. I'm not that far gone. All I mean is that it was nicer to spend a dull trip in a crowded aeroplane sitting next to a pretty woman, even if she had no interest in me at all, than sitting next to someone boring or unattractive. In point of fact, for nearly two hours, from the time I joined their group of young professionals to more than 40 minutes into the flight, Mary and I never said a word to each other. Even during the second half of the flight, after cheerful James had fallen asleep, my interactions with Mary were extremely limited. Our verbal interactions, at least. There was an unspoken understanding between us, a silent communion, from the time our eyes first met. Mary was not a bubbly woman; she was on the introverted side, and tended toward fits of shyness. Oh – also, when I said I liked her from the first time I saw her, it wasn't because of anything distinctive about the way she looked, any sort of extraordinary beauty or sex appeal. No; she was perfectly ordinary: educated, in her early 30s, calm and low-key; no worse-looking than the other five or six women in their group, but certainly not any prettier either. Her introversion and shyness probably had something to do with why I liked her; women like that tend to give men the urge to take care of them. And when she and I exchanged glances, I saw that her eyes were artless, confident, pure, and moderate, with none of the shallowness, coldness, sharpness, or arrogance you see in fashionable women's eyes these days.

Our ocular communication began the moment James introduced us. Most of the polite young professionals were friendly enough during the introductions, particularly the ones who had heard of me. They chatted with me briefly, and later on I was able to talk to them about various topics, quickly forming a sort of bond with the ones who had heard of me (and had even read my stories, in some cases). Even if some of them didn't consider me worth paying attention to, their regard for James and the Western-style manners their company had instilled in them meant that when I greeted them they greeted me back. Mary alone kept me guessing whether she was one of the warm and friendly ones or one of the cool sophisticates. She seemed distracted when I said hello to her, and her nod and smile were somewhat perfunctory. She didn't say hello back. An instant later, it seemed to occur to her that she should be more polite to her co-worker's friend, and she favoured me with another nod and smile to make up for her distraction, though both were rather awkward.

But then again two nods and two smiles, issued in quick succession in these busy surroundings to such a brief acquaintance as myself, seemed out of place, and she paused for a moment and knit her eyebrows, as if she was trying to take back the redundant nod and smile. This was impossible, obviously: a nodded head is a nodded head, and even a shake of the head can't cancel out the nod. Likewise, a scowl or a frown isn't enough to wipe out a preceding smile. But Mary apparently thought otherwise, and so she tried – though her way of retracting the second nod and smile was to toss another nod and smile my way. This all took place in an extremely brief span of time during which Mary nodded and smiled at me three times in quick succession. I didn't understand at first, but after quickly carrying out the above analysis I smiled back at her, shooting her a look that said I understood it all, from her initial distraction to her attempt to retract the second nod and smile, before I turned away to be introduced to her co-workers. Thus ended our first communication. The sign that it had ended was an expression of thanks for my understanding, which she executed by favouring me with a fourth nod and smile. That time she did it just right.

She didn't join in when I was chatting with her co-workers, not even when the men and women who hadn't originally considered me worth their attention took an interest in the idle conversation with me at the centre. She stayed slightly apart from the rest of us, looking quietly out the window toward the landing strip. At times her lips twitched unconsciously into smiles that were clearly not unconnected to our conversation. I was certain that she could hear us – could hear me – talking. Our gazes only met two or three times, but every time she quickly broke eye contact, as if there were some secret between us that she didn't want revealed. That was when I started to like her. I started glancing at her out of the corner of my eye, and soon I was thinking of her as the sole audience for my bloviation, turning up the charm and doing my best to display what I considered to be my intelligence and sense of humour. My intuition told me that she really was listening to me – not to us, to me – and whenever I saw her eyes shift ever so slightly in our direction, I was certain that I was the main object of her gaze. Though I allowed for the possibility that I was flattering myself.

At long last, more than 40 minutes into our flight, when people had eaten their in-flight meals and drunk their in-flight beverages and gone to sleep, James, who had been discussing the matter of religion with me, went to sleep as well. I drained the half-finished cola in front of me, took a deep breath, and turned my head to the right, toward Mary, with the intention of saying something to her. She had the in-flight CAAC magazine open in front of her, and I couldn't tell from her expression and body language whether she was paying attention to it or not.

3

'What are you reading?' An awkward opening, but it was all I had.

Mary only smiled – one of those slightly shy, slightly mocking smiles. She didn't look at me or hold up the magazine to show me the cover, and my conversational gambit hung in the air between us. I hung there along with it, unsure of how to continue.

But a moment later, while I was still drawing a mental blank, Mary stood up. 'Let's switch seats,' she said, almost in a whisper, glancing up at me briefly. After a moment's hesitation, I stood, crab-walked out of the row of seats, and let her take my seat before I sat down in hers. I didn't ask why; taking orders from her just seemed natural. It was only after I sat back down that she offered an explanation: 'You've got long legs – that middle seat must be cramped.'

So that was it. 'Thank you,' I said, sincerely grateful. I liked her even more now. I liked her low-key considerateness, even toward strangers.

'A noble sacrifice on my part, in the spirit of Lei Feng[1]. The middle seat's cramped for me too – but I wanted to do something to thank you.'

'Thank me? What for?'

'For your stories, you engineer of the human soul, you. I like your stories – I've read a bunch of them.' Mary blushed. She seemed even more shy now and avoided looking at me. She glanced over at James, said it must be nice to sleep so soundly, and then leaned a little closer to me, her voice a little calmer now. 'I thought I must have heard wrong when James introduced you – I never imagined he knew you…'

'So *that's* why–' I remembered how distracted she'd been when I greeted her. I suppose she must have thought of it, too.

We started chatting, our lowered voices making the conversation feel intimate. Of course it was mostly me talking and her listening. I encouraged her to talk more, but she shook her head and said she wan't much for talking, and anyway she didn't have anything to say.

'Well let me know if I get annoying and I'll shut up,' I said.

'No,' she said, 'go on. I like listening. Now I know why you write so well. It was really interesting when you were talking with them back there.'

She spoke very sincerely, and it warmed my heart right up. Seeing that things were going well, I expressed the hope that we could stay in touch in the future. I wrote out my mobile phone number, home phone number, e-mail address, and work address for her. She looked closely at the scrap of paper.

'Your handwriting isn't anything special,' she said.

I pressed a ballpoint pen and another scrap of paper into

---

1. Lei Feng (1940-1962) was a People's Liberation Army soldier whose mythical tirelessness, generosity, and selfless devotion to Chairman Mao made him the centrepiece of 'Be Like Lei Feng' propaganda campaigns starting in 1963 and reoccurring periodically to the present day.

her hand, but she made no move to write anything.

'Go on,' I said. 'There won't be time once we land.'

She smiled, but she didn't write anything. I couldn't very well force her; the only thing I could do was go on talking. I didn't know her at all, didn't know what interested her, so there wasn't much I could say. But I had to keep talking, as if I could catch hold of her that way, as if she would cease to exist if I stopped speaking. And I wanted more and more for her to go on existing – at least to go on existing here, next to me, 10,000 metres off the ground. So I did my best to talk about things that had some sort of connection to her.

'Isn't it funny how they translate names,' I said. 'Like "James". From the pronunciation you'd think it would be *jian-mu-si* in Chinese, or even *jia-mu-si*, but instead it's always written as *zhan-mu-si*. If James were a foreigner, and I called him "Zhanmusi", do you think he'd understand that I was talking to him? Or "Mary", like your name. *Ma-rui* would work well – you'd have your choice of three or four different ruis – or *Mai-rui*, but whenever it's written down it has to be *Ma-li. Mai* and *Ma* sound close enough, but there's about a million miles of difference between *rui* and *li*.'

'Why do they do that?' I was still trying to get Mary to speak.

'Did you have a good rest, James?' Mary spoke – but she had already turned to face James, as if we hadn't just been speaking intimately.

The plane landed. We had arrived in Beijing.

4

James, Mary, and the others had to wait for the company minibus to take them back to their office at Dabeiyao, on the east side of the city, and I was planning to take the airport shuttle over to my sister's place at Weigongcun, on the west side of town. The two were far enough apart that even James wasn't so overly polite as to invite me to catch a ride with them. He just said he hoped I could stay in Beijing a few days longer, that he'd take me skiing. 'Sure,' I said, 'sure. Definitely.' I waved goodbye to him and his foreign-named young professional colleagues. I kept looking back at Mary as we parted ways, but even when she caught me looking at her she remained expressionless. She tagged along behind her colleagues, looking pale and distracted, as if something was wrong. I was a little concerned, but of course I couldn't go over and say anything. And maybe she didn't need my concern. Maybe I was over-thinking it.

But I often get strange ideas, and sometimes I do things even I can't explain. After I got on the airport shuttle and paid for my ticket, I saw James and Mary and the others standing by the side of the road off in the distance. Obviously the company minibus hadn't come yet. I got up from my seat, put on my backpack, and squeezed out the door. The shuttle driver called out that he was getting ready to leave, but I ignored him and made straight for James and Mary and the others. Naturally I stayed in the shadows to avoid being noticed as I drew nearer and watched them – not that it was them I was drawing nearer to or watching: I was drawing near to Mary, watching Mary, even though she stood there with all the others.

Actually, that's not right. Mary wasn't standing with James and the others anymore: she was inching away from them stealthily. If James and the others formed a scattered, irregular circle, then Mary was the farthest-scattered, most irregular outlier, a breaking point. She still had that strange expression on her face, I saw, and she kept looking down at the mobile phone in her hand, until finally she seemed to reach a decision. She lifted the phone to her ear.

That was when their minibus arrived.

That was when my phone rang.

The display showed an unfamiliar number, and I decided to ignore it – I'd call back after Mary had gotten into the minibus and vanished from sight. James and the others started loading their things onto the bus. Mary stayed where she was. My phone rang insistently. I gave in and raised it to my ear.

'Hello?'

'Diao Dou? This is Mary –'

'Mary? Hey, how – how've you been?'

'.....'

'How come you're not on the bus?'

'.....'

'Well? They're waiting for you!'

'I've still got your pen –'

'Ha! You keep it as a souvenir. Go on now, get on the bus –'

'No – I wasn't calling about the pen...'

'What was it, then? Or look, how about I call you back once I'm in town? They're calling you.'

'I don't want to go back to the office with them. Can you come get me? I was wondering if we could go to Zhangji? Together?'

'Oh, is that it? No problem, Mary – anywhere you like. All the way south to Sanya, all the way north to Mohe; just say the word. But even if you're not going back to the office, surely you should go home first?'

'Don't worry about me – I'm at –'

'I know where you are.'

Mary walked back over to the minibus. I don't know what explanation she gave James and the others, but sure enough, the bus drove away and left her there. A moment later, just as my phone showed another incoming call from her, I emerged from behind my column. I picked up the red suitcase at Mary's feet without her noticing, then laughed aloud.

'No need to phone, miss. If you've got instructions, best to give them to me face to face.'

Mary was startled, but she had other things to worry about. 'It's a bit much of me, isn't it?' She tried unsuccessfully to laugh. She looked tired, helpless, somehow hard done-by. 'I must be losing my mind...'

5

Finally I realised that the Zhangji Mary wanted us to go to was the Zhangji from my stories. She said she'd wanted to go there ever since she read my stories, but that the idea had only been a fleeting one until she met a guide who specialised in taking people on trips there. That was me. And now – even though she'd only just met me – she had my contact information, and she could book a trip with me if she ever wanted to go to Zhangji. But she didn't know if she would still want to go later on, or whether she'd still be able to make another appointment with me if she did. And how would she explain it to her husband? How would I explain it to my wife? Added complications, for sure. No – the time to ask me to go to Zhangji with her was right then: she had her business trip as an excuse, and I was far from Shenyang. All we had to do was prolong our trips a little. Call it going full steam ahead.

It was a good plan for going full steam ahead, and if the destination had been anywhere else – Hammy or Geemow or Peachy or Byeso – it would have been trivially easy to go there. But Zhangji–

'Mary, I think you might have misunderstood – Zhangji is a city I made up.'

'I didn't misunderstand. I know that. Why else would I have asked you to go with me? I'm not as helpless as you think, you know – I went to Chicago and Melbourne all by myself. I've probably been to more places than you…'

'But Chicago and Melbourne are on the map – they exist, they're far away, but they're places you can go to. Zhangji is only in my head, in my stories –'

'And it's in my head too.'

'Yes, because of my stories, it's in your head too now. But it's not in the world, and it's not on the map.'

'Is that all? You don't have to look at an atlas to know there's such a place as Chicago. You don't have to go to Melbourne to know there's a Melbourne. They exist first in people's heads too. Where do you think everywhere on earth came from? How do you know that they didn't start with an author who wrote a Chicago, wrote a Melbourne, stirred his readers' curiosity, and when his readers asked him where Chicago was, where Melbourne was, he led them to Chicago and said, "This is Chicago," led them to Melbourne and said, "This is Melbourne," and from then on there was a Chicago and a Melbourne. Why can't it be the same for Zhangji?'

'Can you explain why we never see God, Mary? People are creatures with all kinds of strange needs, and sometimes they need to create things that don't exist to fill the voids in their spirits. But anything that doesn't exist in the physical world, whether it's a person or a place, can only be fictional, imaginary.'

'But the imagination exists. The imagination is real…'

Mary wasn't just arguing for the sake of arguing, I saw, let alone trying to have a laugh at my expense. Her earnestness and sincerity – and even her confusion and frustration – were written on her face. She must have been frustrated at being unable to make herself clear. What she was trying to say was that 'something' is born of 'nothing,' that 'nothing' gives birth to 'something' – '*cogito ergo sum*,' extended to the nth degree. Since neither of us knew where our next step would take us, we had by this point gone back inside the airport and sat down on the hard plastic seats. We watched as people who knew where they were going came and went, and we listened to the PA system calling out other people's destinations: Hong Kong, Seoul, Tokyo, Shanghai, Chongqing, Xi'an…

'Have you ever read Descartes?'

'What's it about? I don't really read very much – Jin Yong is my favourite. Work's always too busy for me to read. Oh – I like your books too, of course…'

'Do you read philosophy? Descartes was a French philosopher.'

'I'm not one of your colleagues, Diao Dou, just one of

your readers. I read to pass the time. Sartre is the only French philosopher I know – we read about him in college. He said hell was other people, right? So don't try to beat me over the head with your philosophy books.'

'That's not what I meant – what I mean is, yes, from a philosophical point of view, Zhangji does exist…'

'Great! Then pick up your philosophy books and let's go there.'

'We can't.'

'Why not?'

I reached out to stroke Mary's face with the back of my hand. I brushed aside her shoulder-length hair and continued, stroking her neck with the back of my hand, resting it on her cheek. She stiffened, but didn't push my hand away. I moved it to the other side, pressing my palm against her other cheek and slowly drawing her face closer to mine. I kissed her. Her hair first, her cheeks, her eyes, then her lips. She didn't kiss me back.

'You think this is just about *that*?' Her body stayed in my embrace after her lips left mine.

'There's nothing wrong with *that*,' I said. 'Why not make it about *that*?'

'I thought about it – but I want to wait until we get to Zhangji.'

'Then what if I told you that another name for Beijing is Zhangji?'

6

This minor bit of cleverness did not deter Mary. She was, after all, a widely travelled woman, a woman who had managed to find her bearings in the harshly competitive work environment of a foreign multinational – which is to say not at all like the romantic girls one finds in university literature departments. She disagreed with my assertion that Beijing was Zhangji.

'If you went to Chicago,' she asked, 'would you call it

Melbourne? Once a name's established in common usage, you can't just swap it for another name – you could only call Chicago Melbourne if Melbourne didn't exist.'

But hard and soft alternated in Mary's nature, and she agreed at least to give me a little longer to consider the nature of Zhangji's existence. So it was that she followed me to a hotel near the Forbidden City, where we got a room together. The sky had just begun to darken, and I indicated that we could shower and go to bed before we went out for dinner. But she said. 'I need more time too. Of course, I know it's not a big deal, I'm mentally prepared to sleep with a man I like, but I still need a little more time to think it over – even if I'm not sure exactly what it is I'm thinking over. Can you understand that?' She looked very solemn. I said I could, though I couldn't really. I'm a man; I'll never be able to understand why women always bring so many nonsexual considerations to purely sexual behaviour. It seems to me that women are always finding things to worry about where sex is concerned, always adding self-imposed constraints. But of course I have to respect them, have to allow them to do as they will, have to say, insincerely: *I understand.* I don't think that counts as lying.

In the interest of convenience I suggested that we eat at the hotel restaurant. It was quiet and dimly lit, with soft music piped in. Mary and I sat in a corner, allowing for moderate petting. I kept nudging the conversation toward the topic of sex, toward men and women, toward Mary and me – but Mary couldn't get her mind off of Zhangji. She asked me how big Zhangji was, how wealthy; she asked what sort of people lived there and what their lives were like. When I couldn't answer, or gave perfunctory answers, she even helped me redesign and improve Zhangji, as if the two of us had the power to plan out a new city. I had no choice but to spend most of the meal with her taking in the sights and sounds of a paradise apart from the world, called Zhangji. I did bring up (showing off more than a little) Thomas More's *Utopia* and

Tommaso Campanella's *La città del Sole*. Not, I emphasized, that Zhangji was Campanella's City of the Sun or More's Utopia: there were no such places in the world, and Zhangji was no different from any other city as far as beauty and ugliness or goodness and wickedness were concerned – no different from Shenyang or Dalian, Beijing or Guangzhou, Melbourne or Chicago... We had eaten and drunk our fill by this point, and all my talk of sex had long since yielded completely to the topic of Zhangji. Suddenly, to my surprise, Mary flushed a deep scarlet and tightened the arm she had draped around me, pulling me closer and closer, until my ribs started to hurt.

I shifted to return her embrace and put her face against mine. 'What's wrong, Mary?' I realised what a stupid question this was as soon as I said it, and I called hurriedly for the bill. 'Come on. Let's go back to the room.'

Mary and I hardly slept at all that night. We talked a lot, but neither of us mentioned Zhangji again. We didn't close our eyes until the next morning, and when hunger woke us around midday we darted downstairs for a quick meal at the restaurant, went to a convenience store for instant noodles, tinned ham, and some tangerines and bananas, then went back to the room and stayed there. We didn't even let the cleaning staff in. We ate when we were hungry, slept when we were tired, and when we weren't eating or sleeping we were talking and making love, making love and talking. We did everything together – eating, sleeping, making love, and talking. We didn't even separate to go to the bathroom. The only thing we separated for was the phone: when I called my wife, Mary got out of the way, and when she called her husband I made myself scarce. We stayed at that hotel near the Forbidden City for five days; we talked about everything under the sun, whispered countless sweet words into each other's ear – but she never talked about her husband, and I never talked about my wife. I don't know what she said to him on the phone; she told her company that she would make up the missed days at the end of the year. The explanation I gave my wife was perfectly simple: I said I was rushing to finish a story for a magazine in Beijing, and that I wasn't staying at my sister's place because a friend had an empty apartment. It was too soon to say when I'd be back in Shenyang.

Then came the fifth day.

When we woke up around noon on the fifth day, we were both weak-kneed and bleary-eyed, without even the strength to kiss or talk to each other. Exhaustion wasn't the main reason, of course. The main reason was that we had to say goodbye. Mary had to go home. We had to leave our hotel near the Forbidden City. Maybe I could come up with reasons to prolong my stay in Beijing, but she couldn't avoid going back to her home in Chongwenmen nearby. It fell to me to say the parting words, the gist of which was that all good things must come to an end.

Mary said she knew. But then she said, 'Stay another two days. Make it a week, our golden week. We're good together. If the two of us can't have a honeymoon at least we can have a golden week.'

I said, 'Yes, my love, we *are* good together – better than I ever expected. But we're not children; we don't need to mark our time off like that. You can't put it off any longer.'

Mary smiled, but tears dripped from her eyes. 'I know you're tired of me,' she said. 'You're bored, you've had enough, you can't wait to get rid of me – you've got other women in Beijing…'

The truth was that I couldn't bear to leave Mary. I had grown more and more fond of her, from her stubborn streak to the way her ideas danced to and fro – but I couldn't abandon common sense, and I wouldn't mix up real life and fiction. We weren't citizens of Utopia or the City of the Sun, after all. I grinned and bore it as she railed at me, then I helped her brush her hair, wash, and dress neatly, as if I was soothing a child. I promised her that I wouldn't just bundle her into a taxi. After we left the hotel, I'd walk with her all the way to the Beijing Obstetrics and Gynaecology Hospital, and there we would go our separate ways.

We hadn't gone outside in days, and we weren't quite ready for it. There was an autumnal chill in the air, crisp and cool; the streets were empty. We held each other tightly as we walked, leaning on each other like an old couple, propping each other up against our frailty and loneliness. 'This love of ours is something we'll savour for the rest of our lives.' That was what I said while we were still a few paces away from the cab. We had simultaneously shut our mouths after stepping out of the hotel, knowing that it would be superfluous to say anything more, that anything we said would feel threadbare and insincere. But at the thought that we would grow old, that our old selves would never get to lean on each other like this, I couldn't stop myself.

Mary pulled me to a stop at this, as if she had been waiting all along for me to open my mouth. She faced me squarely and kissed me. 'Love? You think what we had is called "love"?' I pushed her away gently and tried to explain myself, but she drew near and kissed me again, stopping my mouth. 'Ssssh. It's all right even if it wasn't love. It might not be such a bad thing, I think,' she said, a little playfully. She seemed a different person entirely than the woman I had met at Gonggar Airport, but I couldn't tell whether she was merely putting on a brave front or had radically adjusted her emotions. 'You said it yourself, didn't you? You said the longer you live, the more you think that even the word "love" is unreal, that love itself is too much like make-believe. So…'

'What I meant was –'

'What I mean is, it doesn't matter if it was love or not. What matters is, we both went to Zhangji for a while.'

And without saying goodbye or looking at me again or giving me another kiss, Mary ducked into the taxi. In the blink of an eye, May Fourth Avenue was empty except for me. I raised my hand to wave at the taxi as it receded into the distance, but Mary didn't look back. I could only see her hair, not her face. Through the rear window she looked unreal, indistinct. When I waved at her, I might as well have been waving at a dream.

Points of Origin

s.v. 'Zhangji'

THE DICTIONARY OF WORLD *Fiction* was a new release from World Literature Press. Handsomely printed and bound, with its 1,791 sextodecimo pages sandwiched between sombre mahogany covers, it sat solidly in the hand, heavy enough that if you cracked it over someone's head it would have about the same effect as a curbstone. You'd knock them half dead. I'd bought my copy the week before on a trip to the bookstore with my daughter, but hadn't yet had time to look through it properly. Though, of course, it wasn't as if you would read a dictionary cover to cover like a novel. A dictionary should be like a well-trained police officer: out walking its beat when it's not needed, appearing, as if from nowhere, only when there's a disturbance.

I had woken suddenly from dreams that morning with the novel *At Swim-Two-Birds* on my mind for some reason. This was not a novel I had read – there's no Chinese translation that I know of, and I don't speak any foreign languages – and in all likelihood I had only ever heard of it from a passing mention in some other book. But the title *At Swim-Two-Birds* had bored into my head and stuck there, and now it was nagging at me to get up and go right *now* to find out who had written it. Clearly this was a disturbance, and I was in need of a police officer. I pushed aside the covers, got out of bed, rushed to my study, and took my shiny new copy of *The Dictionary of World Fiction* down from the shelf. It was a very handsome volume indeed, save for a small spot at the lower right corner of the cover, about the size of a coin, where the lamination had flaked off to reveal an irregular patch of brown cardboard, as jarring as a blotch of mold on human skin. Naturally the book's value as a reference work was undiminished, but it was a discomfortingly obvious blemish all the same. Oh well. With any luck the book's contents would make up for it.

> O'BRIEN, FLANN (1912-1966). Irish journalist, scholar of Gaelic, inveterate toper, and author of several novels...

I brightened at the words 'inveterate toper'. Writing like that really did make up for a lot: if the entries continued in this vein, then the book was money well spent. I finished reading the entry on *At Swim-Two Birds*, but instead of replacing the book on its shelf I hugged it to my chest, left my study, and went back to the bedroom. The book would make good company for a lazy morning lie-in. The bathroom lay between me and the bedroom, and I turned in, relieved myself, and stepped absentmindedly onto the scales on which my wife checked her weight once or twice a day. I myself had never been much concerned about my figure, or particularly inclined to diet, but the number the needle pointed to startled me all the same: 77 kilos, stark naked! I bent over to take another look before realising that I was still holding the dictionary. I set it aside and reweighed myself, then set myself aside and placed the dictionary on the scale. I weighed 74 kilograms; the dictionary weighed three. Three rounds of double-checking confirmed the numbers.

That evening, my wife came home from work carrying a lot of things: the bag that she carried with her every day, three disposable containers of food, a sack of tangerines. My rear end stayed firmly planted in front of the television as she removed her shoes and switched into her slippers; she complained that I didn't care about her, that I never even paid attention. Of course I cared about her – she was my wife, after all; if I didn't care about her, who would? Flann O'Brien? If I looked like I wasn't paying attention, it was only because I had something on my mind, and had been using the TV as an excuse to let my thoughts wander. I hadn't even noticed what was on. I hurried to take the heaviest bag – the tangerines. 'Ten pounds of them,' my wife said. She straightened up and stretched her lower back, then walked briskly over to the kitchen. 'Ten pounds?' I raised the bag a little higher, hefted it in one hand and then the other. 'It doesn't feel like ten pounds.' My wife snorted from the kitchen. 'And you can tell that with your bare hands, I suppose. I double-checked on the market's general scales to make sure the seller's scales were fair.'

Holding the bag of tangerines in one hand, I went into the bedroom and took the dictionary out from under the pillow, then walked back to the kitchen, weighing them against one another, first with the tangerines in my right hand and the dictionary in my left and then with the dictionary in my right hand and the tangerines in my left. Six pounds at most, I said confidently. Three kilos. My wife was sceptical of me and my dictionary, but after we finished dinner, as she was getting ready to eat the tangerines and juice them for a facemask, she did go to weigh them. 'It *is* six pounds!' she said angrily. 'Even the market scales were rigged!' I grinned and waved my *Dictionary of World Fiction* at her, then suggested that in future she might want to think twice before saying stories weren't good for anything. My wife, working herself into a lather, shouted that she was going to go back to the market and hunt down the fruit vendor. 'That dirty cheat,' she said. 'She even had a sign on her stall saying "Quality you can trust".' I blocked her way. 'Leave it,' I said. 'At least they're good tangerines. It's not like she sold you a bag of rocks or donkey turds instead.'

(My intent with this little interlude wasn't to demonstrate the dictionary's versatility by highlighting its usefulness as a weighing tool. Verifying quantities of tangerines is only one of many possible functions. It would serve equally well as a pillow or a weapon, though you will note that I didn't emphasise its utility in bed or as an instrument of murder. This was just an amusing anecdote that I mentioned in passing.)

But back to that morning. I read the dictionary in bed for about an hour, then went back to my study to write. Before doing so, I reread the entry for *At Swim-Two-Birds* under 'O'Brien, Flann,' which took three minutes. Then I read another entry, and then other entries related to that other entry, which took a total of about 30 minutes. The rest of the hour went to reading other things: the entry for 'Gao, Xingjian' under 'Authors'; '*If on a winter's night a traveller*' under 'Works'; 'The Criticism of Solzhenitsyn' under 'Events'; '*Contemporary Writers Review of the Liaoning Writers Association*' under 'Periodicals'. I was getting ready to go back to sleep when another entry caught my eye: 'Zhangji'. The name jumped out and flashed before my eyes; all thoughts of going back to sleep vanished. Anyone familiar with my work will know that 'Zhangji' is a fictional place, one that exists only in my stories. 'A city built of words,' as the dictionary has it. 'Zhangji' was listed under 'Geography,' as were Su Tong's Fragrant Cedar Street, Mo Yan's Northeast Gaomi Township, Gabriel Garcia Márquez's Macondo, William Faulkner's Yoknapatawpha County. I don't mean to brag, but I controlled a pretty big territory, according to 'Geography'! 'Geography' also listed Wu Cheng'en's Western Paradise and Jonathan Swift's Lilliput and Brobdingnag – world-level and state-level administrative divisions, even bigger than Zhangji. But it's better to think of what you have compared with the less fortunate than of what you lack compared with the more fortunate, and I was perfectly content to list my city of Zhangji alongside other people's streets and townships, towns and counties. I'm not saying that I thought the size of Zhangji reflected on its creator, as if other people were townships and counties to my municipality. There was no chance of that, I knew; if there were, I imagine half the people in China would be rushing to join my profession, competing to see who could come up with the next Lilliput and Brobdingnag or even Western Paradise in their stories. Chinese people want so badly to become the sort of Emperor-level cadres who get their food, drinks, whores, and gambling debts covered at public expense. No – I was happy about Zhangji being bigger than the street-, township-, town-, and county-level divisions simply because the bigger the territory and the larger the population, the more leeway I would have to create twists and turns for my stories. In theory, at least.

I lay there in bed, holding the dictionary in both hands, looking over Fragrant Cedar Street, checking out Northeast Gaomi Township, visiting Macondo and dashing off to Yoknapatawpha County. Fine places all, and I enjoyed my visits to other people's territory – but you can't stay too long in foreign lands. Nice as they were, they were other people's, not mine. I felt a sudden pang of longing for my Zhangji. Setting down the dictionary, I went back to my study, turned on the computer, and re-entered my fictional world with a clear head. I was usually drowsy and bleary during the daytime, useless for anything other than sleeping. Interruptions were more common during the day, but even if my sleep was interrupted nine times I could still manage a tenth trip to dreamland. That day was an exception, though: I was stranded outside dreamland.

There's nothing wrong with sleeping during the day, as far as I'm concerned; people in this line of work tend toward the nocturnal. Ah Zuo, however, is dead-set against the habit. 'The hours between midnight and daybreak are when malign spirits are most active,' she says, never cracking a smile. The malign spirits can't do anything to people when they're asleep: people's desires are closed off when they sleep, which makes their carnal bodies impervious to temptation and renders the malign spirits powerless to harm them. When they find someone who's still awake in the middle of the night, though, they seize the chance to tempt them, resulting in physical and spiritual harm – the most obvious signs of which are dulled wits and diminished masculine energy.

Ah Zuo is a professional witch. As a witch, naturally she has a solid grounding in witch theory, and I'm willing to respect her theories, though I reserve judgment. When Ah Zuo scolds me for staying up late, I just smile and nod. I make my counter-argument in bed, where I show her that I've held onto my wits and my masculine energy – or at least the latter, being more easily demonstrable. Ah Zuo's witchiness disappears completely during these demonstrations, and suddenly she's all sweetness and light, black eyes and long legs that she sticks straight up in the air, a Snake like me but twelve years younger. 'You've still got it,' she moans, 'you've still got it, just like seven years ago.' That's right – counting on my fingers – we've known each other for seven years now.

Theories regarding wits and masculine energy notwithstanding, criticisms of my bad habits aside, Ah Zuo has maintained a fairly high opinion of me over the years. Not only on account of my sexual ability – hardly on account of that at all, even. She's more interested in my intelligence. 'What did you ever do to get so smart?' When we first began our relationship, she told me that she appreciated clever people more than successful people. Intelligence comes down to genetics, she says – she's a believer in nature over nurture. 'If you and I had a baby, he or she would grow up to be the most amazing witch.' She says this practically every time we make love. But even though we've never used birth control in all the seven years we've been together, she hasn't become pregnant. She already has a son, and I have a daughter.

It has occurred to me that Ah Zuo's recommendation that I follow the crowd and rest during the night isn't entirely unbiased. Since I rest during the day, she's reluctant to call me out of the house and disturb my sleep, but nights are even worse. Even if my wife didn't prevent me from going out, Ah Zuo can't go anywhere – and going to her place at night is out of the question, since her son would be there. Ah Zuo has no husband; she is a divorcee.

Ah Zuo's call came just as I was missing her. Whenever I find myself missing her, physically as well as mentally, she's always sure to call. I usually don't call her, since I don't know when she'll be working: she keeps irregular hours. When she's working, when she's patiently guiding a client onto the path that will route them around calamity and lead them away from misfortune, she gets upset if she's disturbed. 'What are you angry at *me* for?' I actually am a little afraid of her at those moments, when the witchiness gathers densely around her, but it doesn't stop me from trying to disabuse her of the idea that her job takes precedence over everything else. When I need her, I don't want her to be thinking about her job at all. 'Talking to me for a minute isn't going to hurt your business!' 'It isn't about business,' she explained to me once; 'If I answer the phone it makes it harder for me to enter the field. It's not fair to the supplicant.' 'Entering the field' is what she calls her process of magic-for-hire and fortune-telling; the people who believe in supernatural forces and have problems that need solving she calls 'supplicants.' The spirit world of the soul is the same as the physical world of the body, she explained. Each of them is contained within a massive magnetic field; witches are people who can pass freely between the two fields and use what they learn on both sides to decode the mysteries of Fate. If Ah Zuo was calling me now, it meant that she didn't have have any supplicants. Incidentally, Ah Zuo never explained anything about the two of us, like why we had never been able to have a child, or why she can always sense when I need her. 'A knife can't cut itself,' she said. And since I was involved with her, I was part of her 'self' too.

'Were you sleeping? I don't have anything going on here.'

'Got up a while ago. I'll be right over.'

We met just after her son's first birthday. She told me that after witches give birth, they have to rest for 770 days, which meant she wouldn't be able to 'enter the field' until her son was two. If she did 'enter', she would see nothing but a blur, and wouldn't be able to offer her supplicants services of her customary high quality. I hadn't been serious when I looked her up; I'd just heard people talking about how powerful she was, and pretty too, and I thought I'd go see her for a laugh. I wasn't bothered about her not being able to enter the field; I just struck up a conversation about parapsychology and thaumaturgy and things of that sort. We talked and talked, and though we never did manage to agree on anything, our bodies came to an agreement of their own. It wasn't just a fling, either: we got along uncommonly well, as evidence of which you may refer to our hopes of having a child together. She told me she loved me more than she had loved her fellow apprentice. This was the father of her son, another witch to whom she had briefly been married.

We enjoyed ourselves as usual when I went to Ah Zuo's home that day, but something seemed off. I said as much. I'm always teasing her about her 'superstitions' and 'feudal rubbish', but secretly I have a great respect for her. Whether she really can commune with the spirit world or not, she's an extraordinarily sharp-eyed observer; not to be dismissed, and not someone to lie to.

'I'm going to leave you for a while.'

So something *had* been wrong. 'Why?'

'I'm going to leave town so I can give birth.' Her expression was utterly sweet. She kicked the quilt aside and arched her back up, displaying her smooth, soft belly. I couldn't see anything out of the ordinary there, or anywhere else on her body.

'You're pregnant?' I reached out to stroke her belly. I couldn't feel anything there, either. 'But there's no change.'

'Of course not. It's only been three months.'

'Why do you have to go away to have the baby? You'll need me more than ever then, to look after you – and what about your son?'

'I've made arrangements. You needn't worry about it.'

'Does this mean we won't see each other again for seven or eight hundred days? And where are you going – or is that a secret too?'

'It's no secret. I'll need your help to get there, in fact. The baby should be born in Zhangji.'

'Zhangji? The Zhangji in my stories? You– it doesn't exist!'

'Yes it does. Or it will, if you'll help me.'

'It does? Where? And how can I help you?'

'In the dictionary, of course. Once you make it come out of the dictionary, I'll be able to enter it.'

'I don't understand any of this, Ah Zuo…'

'Hah! That's perfectly normal – I'd be worried if you said you did understand everything. Nobody can understand everything in this world, not even a witch like me. The only thing I need you to do is to build a new Zhangji outside the dictionary, on the foundation of the old Zhangji, before I come to term.'

'So I should write a new story about Zhangji?'

'It'll be more complicated than that. I called you today so I could explain–'

'Then will I be able to visit you in Zhangji, when the time comes?'

'No. You have no faith in miracles, no respect for the mystical, no gratitude for your good fortune. You won't be able to go.'

'That's my city you're talking about! Let your spirits punish me, then; I can keep you from leaving me, and keep you from going to Zhangji. If all this depends on me, why shouldn't I just refuse to make Zhangji come out of the dictionary?'

'Impossible.' An edge came into her voice and the cool, level look on her face reminded me that she was more than a woman with black eyes and long legs that she liked to stick straight up in the air; she was a professional witch. 'You think that just because Zhangji came from your hand, just because your dictionary says it's your creation, that it belongs to you? Making it come out of the dictionary, yes, that depends on you – but what you do or don't have to do isn't up to you, and it never was.'

Installation Piece

Ah Zuo arrived in Zhangji the week before she went into labour. Not much time, but time enough to make the necessary arrangements: a place to stay, a hospital, a nursemaid, and money to cover expenses, all of which she arranged down to the tiniest detail. A week later she gave birth, as hoped, to a baby girl, whom she called 'Serpentina.' There was a symbolism to the name, one that couldn't be shared with outsiders, which she had discussed with the father of the child before coming to Zhangji. Both of them had wanted a girl; both of them liked the name 'Serpentina.'

Serpentina was a healthy child. She had strong, resounding cries and a firm grip when she nursed, and Ah Zuo loved her so much that she couldn't bring herself to let the nursemaid hold her a moment longer than necessary. As a professional woman, however, she loved her job as a witch just as much, and she did not allow Serpentina a monopoly on her energy. She loved her job and she loved her daughter; there was no contradiction there, only evidence that she was a rational person, a person with a strong sense of responsibility – one that extended to all of her affairs, rather than the partial sense of responsibility by which people's responsibility regarding Thing A leads them to neglect their responsibilities regarding Things B, C, D, and E and serves as an excuse for slacking off, hanging back, and laying down their burdens. And so when Ah Zuo wasn't busy playing with Serpentina, the awareness that she was now only a housewife, unable to hang out a shingle and start her business – and would remain so for the next seven or eight hundred days, during which she would also be unable to see the man she loved – could still upset her so much that she would slap Serpentina on the bottom and say, 'You were the one who got me into this.' At this, Serpentina would gaze up at her with wide-open eyes that looked exactly like her own, then wave her little arms and legs around, burbling away.

One day, while Serpentina was asleep, Ah Zuo sat at one end of the sofa, reading a monograph, while the nursemaid sat at the other end of the sofa reading a fashion magazine. Ah Zuo's book was rather dry, and she felt her eyelids drooping as she read; the fashion magazine had pretty pictures and bubbly prose, and the nursemaid was clearly engrossed in it. To stave off sleep, Ah Zuo turned her attention to the cover of the magazine in the nursemaid's hands, where her gaze was drawn as if by magnets to the name Ma Tahua, printed in a handwritten font, and a picture of a man with a big beard. Immediately, she was no longer tired. She pretended to continue reading her book, but stole glances at the cover of the magazine when she could, reading it bit by bit and piece by piece until the nursemaid, having successfully sat out the remainder of her working hours, threw down the magazine and went home. She had hardly set one foot out the door before Ah Zuo snatched up Ma Tahua and held him before her eyes.

It was his figure that had piqued Ah Zuo's interest: upon closer examination of his mouth, nose, and eyes, she found him less enthralling – not that there was anything *wrong* with his features, but when you saw them clearly, when he became clearer, became more precise, she felt somewhat ashamed and afraid. She had fallen for him, she knew, but she didn't want to be unfaithful to Serpentina's father – at least, she couldn't betray Serpentina's father emotionally. So while Ah Zuo wanted to confirm to herself that Ma Tahua was just an ordinary man, she also desired that this man should help her pass the lonely time.

Ma Tahua was an installation artist. The cover of the magazine showed him assembling a heap of materials into the form of a woman selling odds and ends from a blanket spread on the ground, and the abstruse, gassy profile inside described him with gushing praise. There were more images of his works on the inside cover of the magazine. After a careful examination of all the images and text pertaining to Ma Tahua, Ah Zuo could not deny that she had fallen in love with him. There was an ambiguous quality to him and his art, a richness within their simplicity, a specificity within their abstraction, a style that fit perfectly with her own understanding of the world.

The magazine belonged to the nursemaid, who had brought it to pass the time on the job at Ah Zuo's home. She looked everywhere for the magazine when she finished her work the next day, but couldn't find it and felt too awkward to ask about it. Ah Zuo guessed the reason for the nursemaid's discomfort; fearing that the nursemaid would ask her, Ah Zuo could only deal with the situation by sending her away, saying, 'Why don't you head home early today?' The next several days went the same way: whenever she saw the nursemaid looking around for the magazine, Ah Zuo would send her home guiltily – until one day, when she could no longer stand looking into the nursemaid's confused eyes, she said, 'Well, I'm feeling just about recovered, so I should be able to look after Serpentina myself from now on – no need for you to come help anymore.' When she paid the nursemaid for her work, Ah Zuo added a little extra to the fee – several times the cost of the magazine. But the nursemaid burst into tears, snuffling, 'Did I do something wrong, Miss? Just tell me and I can fix it – you can't do it all on your own.' The nursemaid hadn't found many jobs like this one – light workload, good pay, pleasant client. At this it became Ah Zuo's turn to apologize, and the only excuse that occurred to her was, 'It's my boyfriend – he's going to come visit, and you know how it is – having a baby, not being married, he doesn't want any strangers to see him.'

Ah Zuo's burden was considerably heavier without the nursemaid's help, and she got at least two hours less sleep every night. Even so, she still had plenty of time to admire Ma Tahua's photograph in the magazine. She propped him up in the pool of sunlight by the window, in the dim shadows cast by the lamp, on the kitchen cupboard, under the blankets; he was her constant companion. Complicating matters was the fact that even being paid in full didn't stop the nursemaid from coming back. She came by on an almost daily basis, sometimes several times in one day, to ask if Ah Zuo needed anything, or whether Serpentina's father had arrived; she said she'd disappear once Serpentina's father came, but she was happy to come and help out until then, no pay necessary. Ah Zuo grew jumpy, paranoid: at the sound of the doorbell she would immediately hide the magazine; even sleep couldn't calm her nerves. Every time she hid the magazine, she worried that the nursemaid would go rummaging around for it, would turn the place upside down – Ah Zuo had stolen from her, after all.

Ah Zuo was startled awake late one night by a fusillade of thunder and lightning. As she lay there listening to the roaring rain, she realised that something would have to be done about the magazine if she wanted to make sure nobody would know she was a thief. She spent some time working out a plan, then took a pair of scissors and carefully cut Ma Tahua out of the magazine cover. With just the single cut-out, without the name of the magazine or the handwritten-font headline 'Ma Tahua' or the tools and installation piece materials in the background, even if the nursemaid spotted him she wouldn't dare say for certain that he had come from her magazine. But after appraising the cut-out several times, Ah Zuo felt that even this was not secure: Ma Tahua's facial features were still enough to identify him, after all, and if the nursemaid liked him too, if she had a strong impression of him, then just the sight of the cut-out would remind her of her magazine. To ensure perfect secrecy, Ah Zuo was left with no choice but to scrape Ma Tahua away with a fruit knife. Not all of him, of course; she only scraped away his face. His body was left intact: scraping that away as well would've meant scraping him away altogether. All she needed was to preserve the general shape of his body: given the outline of a male body, her imagination could fill in the details.

It wasn't long before Ma Tahua's face no longer belonged to Ma Tahua, or to anyone else, as there was nothing left of it but the general shape of a face: eyes, nose, mouth had all become a blank white, as if the front of his head had been replaced by a hole. She hadn't scraped it completely blank, though: to maintain the shape of a face, she had left hair on top and a beard below, with ears to the left and right. The face consisted solely of hair, beard, and ears.

'Ma Tahua' – Ah Zuo still addressed the man with a hole for a face as Ma Tahua – 'I'm sorry.'

Now that she could place Ma Tahua wherever she liked without having to worry that the nursemaid would be reminded of her magazine, Ah Zuo's nervousness eased a little. But looking down again she saw the magazine and what was left of its cover, and she couldn't think of what she should do next. Should she tear it to shreds? Burn it to ashes? Throw it in the trash? All of these seemed unbearable to her: after all, the magazine still had pictures of his work and text about him. It was afterwards, when Ah Zuo noticed that the wind and rain had stopped, that she was inspired by one of Ma Tahua's installation/performance pieces to give the magazine a proper burial. The piece that inspired her was called 'Outsiders on the Inside', and the picture of it showed a tree made of strips of calico cloth above a transparent glass coffin in which lay several photographs of a man and a woman together, peering curiously out of the coffin as if they had been disturbed at an intimate moment. Real people surrounded the coffin, dressed in mourning white and holding bouquets of flowers, their faces mournful or even anguished, paying their respects to the casket. The composition of the piece made Ah Zuo laugh, and as she laughed she placed the magazine into a bag, placed the bag into a flat cardboard clothing box, and slipped quietly outside with the box and a spade.

The air was especially fresh after the rainfall, and the trees outside her window glistened wetly. Ah Zuo looked them over, decided that the thin, frail-looking tree with the sparse leaves was the closest match for the calico tree, and began digging a hole beneath it.

The mud beneath the tree was soft and wet, and as long as she could avoid the tough, twisting roots it would take no great effort and hardly any time to dig a hole a foot deep. Ah Zuo was no shrinking violet, and years of living on her own had acquainted her with physical labour. In the blink of an eye her plan began to take shape. Of course, her nerves were badly frayed, and her emotions were stirred up, and her mind was tense, and she gazed wildly around from time to time as if she was on high alert. Not that she was afraid; it took more than pitch-black night and rustling leaves to frighten her. As a professional witch, she had a preternatural affinity for spooky atmospheres. She was just worried that someone might see what she was doing. In principle, there shouldn't have been any big deal even if someone had seen her: she wasn't doing anything *bad*, even if there was something a little fishy about digging a hole in the middle of the night to bury a magazine – but what was anyone going to do to her over something like that? But then again, this was not the sort of thing that was easy to explain, and it could lead to unnecessary speculation and suspicion if she wasn't careful. Fortunately, there were no unusual sounds or motions in her vicinity from the time she started digging until the moment when, satisfied with the pit she had dug, she laid the box with the magazine flat on the earth inside.

'Ma Tahua…'

Ah Zuo wanted to convey her apologies to Ma Tahua before filling in the earth, but –

'Thanks for letting me catch my breath. Would you mind helping me out of here?'

– but before she could say anything, she was startled into silence by a man's voice, murmuring quietly. It definitely wasn't coming from her mouth; she'd only said his name! She looked around frantically, but saw nothing out of the ordinary. And she sensed, too, that the voice was coming not from behind her but from in front of her.

'Who –' she asked, still looking behind her since there was no reason to be looking in front. There was nothing before her but the thin, frail-looking tree and the hole beneath it, while behind her there was a lawn, other trees, an asphalt road, and an apartment building.

'I didn't mean to startle you. We don't know each other – I was just hoping that since you helped me out already you could see this thing through to the end.'

This time, following the voice, Ah Zuo saw, in the glow of the distant streetlamps, that the flat box in the hole was shaking slightly. Obviously something underneath was making it move, and the man's voice was coming from beneath the box. Ah Zuo tensed, and her hands started shaking. She shook the mud from her spade and attempted to use it to lift the box she had just placed in the hole. Propping the box on edge against the side of the hole, she saw a human mouth, with red lips and white teeth, at the bottom of the hole, like a flower bud freshly sprouted from the earth. Its tongue licked back and forth, as if it was savouring the taste of something – though actually it was spitting out the flecks of mud that had fallen into it.

'What happened to you?' Ah Zuo asked, hunkering down beside the hole for a closer look. 'Did someone plant you there?'

'Don't ask me – I don't know either.' The mouth squirmed labouriously, looking somewhat impatient. 'I couldn't even breathe until just now. I don't have the strength to talk – please, I'm begging you, just hurry up and help me out of here.'

It didn't look like she had a choice – would Ah Zuo have had the heart to bury it again and let it suffocate? Don't even think about biting me, she warned it as she reached toward it. The mouth snorted: 'As if I had the strength!' And so Ah Zuo held the mouth – still flecked with mud – in her left hand while she shovelled mud back into the hole with the spade in her right. In her rush she didn't even pause long enough to lay the cardboard box flat again.

Back inside, Ah Zuo looked in on Serpentina to make sure that she was still sound asleep. Satisfied, she began a proper examination of the mouth in her hand. The mouth must have been tired as well: the lips closed lightly and it fell asleep. Ah Zuo didn't try to wake it up. She wiped away the mud and placed the mouth on her vast writing desk. The only other thing on the desk was the cut-out of Ma Tahua with the eyes nose and mouth scraped off.

Ah Zuo turned out the light and slept, though not well: she kept waking up. She felt as if there was a fly or a mosquito flying in silent circles around her, fixing her with stares that made her skin crawl. But she was too tired: when the staring woke her, she couldn't muster the energy to open her eyes and turn on the light. She only rolled over, waving her hand to beg the fly or mosquito to leave her alone. This, however, was only a temporary solution: after a while, the mosquito or fly would return, jolting her awake just as she began to drift off. So the next time she woke up, she was in no hurry to drive it off; rather she focused her attention on its flight pattern. As soon as she got a clear sense of where it was, she shot out her hand and caught it. She was able to sleep properly after that, but only for a while: soon she was startled awake again. Obviously there was more than one mosquito or fly. She snatched out with her other hand, quickly and precisely grabbing a handful of air, and her sleep was untroubled after that.

Before Ah Zuo drifted into unconsciousness, she curled her hands into loose fists, knowing that if the things she had trapped in her hands really were mosquitoes or flies, the result of tightening her grip and smashing them would be disgusting. Still, she didn't immediately get out of bed to throw them away, since she had just been woken up in the middle of the night and had neither the energy nor the inclination for any further activity. She merely reminded herself not to loosen her grip and let the mosquitoes or flies escape. She slept in this manner until the sky was bright, until Serpentina was cooing and kicking in the crib next to her.

Ah Zuo hadn't slept enough, really, but it was time to nurse Serpentina and she couldn't keep lazing in bed. She leapt up, landing on the floor, and smiled at Serpentina over the high wall of the crib, reaching out for her daughter with both hands to see if the girl would respond in kind by reaching out her own hands. Ah Zuo had long since forgotten that she had trapped two creatures in her hands. Serpentina was a bright little girl, and the way her gaze moved was proof that she recognised her mother. She stopped cooing and kicking when she saw Ah Zuo approaching, and looked at her calmly with what might have been a smile in her eyes. An instant later, though, her gaze moved from Ah Zuo's face to her hands, darting back and forth from one hand to the other, her budding smile giving way to shock, alarm, surprise, delight. She thrust her hands out toward Ah Zuo's, but hesitated, her arms reaching out and falling back like two rubber bands stretching and contracting. Just when Ah Zuo's hands were about to come into contact with her body, she moved back and pushed them away, gurgling with laughter. Only then did Ah Zuo remember the flies or mosquitoes she had caught in the middle of the night: perhaps the palms of her hands would be filthy and sticky. She straightened up quickly, withdrew her hands, and turned them over to look. To her surprise, she found neither mosquitoes nor flies in the palms of her hands, but rather two eyes. They blinked several times, shyly and awkwardly, as they caught her gaze, then crinkled as if smiling politely. An instant later, they glanced over toward the crib, as if reminding Ah Zuo to nurse her daughter.

Ah Zuo nodded and smiled back politely at the eyes in her hands, then looked over at Serpentina. Serpentina's attention had already shifted away by this point, and was now focused entirely upon a toy elephant. The elephant was made of rubber, and when a suitable amount of pressure was applied to its body its long trunk would sweep from side to side and it would make rapid or unhurried panting noises to indicate that it had shot something out of its nose: a cloth butterfly or a small plastic frog. Ah Zuo's arms were level, her hands open and extended, as she blankly watched Serpentina and the elephant. She hardly dared move for fear that she would injure the eyes in her hands. At first glance, the eyes appeared to have fused with the skin of her hands, but a more careful inspection showed that they were merely flattened against it, as if secured by loops of tape on their backs. Ah Zuo calmed down a little to see this. She went over to the writing desk in her study, carefully peeled the eyes off her palms, and placed them beside the mouth she had found in the hole the night before. The eyes stayed calmly closed throughout all of this, as if they had fallen asleep or were trusting her to take care of things.

After nursing Serpentina, Ah Zuo grabbed a quick bite to eat before pushing her daughter's wheeled crib from the bedroom to the living room to her study and back, pausing briefly every time they passed the study and she saw the mouth and the eyes – still apparently asleep – on the desk. During one of these pauses, Serpentina (who had been absorbed in playing with the elephant) flopped her arms up to prop herself against the wood slats at the side of the crib and stared wide-eyed at the writing desk. Ah Zuo moved her hands off the crib, bent slightly toward the desk, and lightly touched the mouth and the eyes. There was no response, giving Ah Zuo the courage to move them. She lifted the mouth first, placing it on Ma Tahua's hole of a face where a mouth would go, then picked up the left and right eyes and set them in their proper places. The image of Ma Tahua on the magazine cover had been several times smaller than life size, his whole body hardly half as long as an ordinary human face. But miraculously, the lips and eyes, which had been of ordinary human size to begin with, were just right once she placed them on Ma Tahua's empty face, fitting in as naturally with his hair and beard and two ears as if they had been there all along. Ah Zuo stared dumbly, not knowing what to do next. It was the sound of Serpentina shouting from next to her leg that jolted her back to consciousness: she had never heard her daughter so excited. She looked down quickly and saw that Serpentina had squeezed her rubber elephant, and that its trunk was waving back and forth and disgorging not a butterfly or a frog, but a human nose. The nose must have spent a long time blocked up and unable to breathe normally, for like the elephant's long nose it wheezed and snuffled. Its nostrils flared and narrowed; its tip glistened with sweat; pale hairs were clearly visible inside the nostrils. Serpentina pointed at it, beaming sunnily, and Ah Zuo, as if coming to a sudden realisation, reached out for the nose that the elephant had produced and placed it in the only blank spot that remained on Ma Tahua's face, where his nose had been. No sooner had she done so than Ma Tahua swelled slightly up from the glossy stock of the magazine cover, popped nimbly out of the paper, straightened and stretched, hopped to the floor, and looked up at Ah Zuo with an expression that was simultaneously friendly and somewhat irritated.

'What is it, Ah Zuo? What did you bring me here for? I still haven't finished what I'm working on.'

Ah Zuo had already backed a few paces away and pulled Serpentina's crib with her. She felt terribly embarrassed at the sight of Ma Tahua's pretty beard and his burning gaze. Though she could see now that this wasn't Ma Tahua: the eyes, nose, and mouth she had scraped off Ma Tahua's face hadn't looked like these. What the real Ma Tahua would look like, were he to turn into a real person and emerge from the magazine cover, she couldn't say – but she could be sure that it wasn't this. But if the person before her wasn't Ma Tahua, then who was it? She could only keep calling him Ma Tahua.

'I'm sorry, Ma Tahua,' Ah Zuo said. 'I was just curious – about your work – so I was playing around here and I made my own installation piece, and I pieced together a you...'

Without warning Serpentina clapped her hands together and squealed. Ma Tahua quickly turned to look at her, and she smiled and stopped squealing.

'Oh, *you*–' Ma Tahua walked past Ah Zuo toward the crib and picked up Serpentina. 'Your mother's a curious one, isn't she? All witches are, aren't they? And how about *you?* Are *you* a curious little witch…?'

He set her back in the crib and turned to face Ah Zuo, then began fishing through the pockets of his denim vest, pulling out tools – a pair of pliers and a screwdriver – as he strode out the door. Ah Zuo crooned to Serpentina and tidied up the apartment, as she did every day, then turned on the television to find something to watch. But she was terribly tired, having slept poorly the previous night, and she dozed off in front of the television until she was awoken by the sound of Ma Tahua calling her from outside.

'I'm all finished, Ah Zuo! Come take a look.'

Ah Zuo looked over at Serpentina before replying. Serpentina was sound asleep, toy elephant clutched to her chest. Ah Zuo crept quietly outside so as not to wake her, following Ma Tahua's voice toward the trees across from her apartment building, where he had set up his temporary workshop. The first thing she saw was a middle-aged woman pieced together from steel tubing, chicken wire, wood, cotton cloth, cardboard, styrofoam, and an oil painting; next, she saw the tools and materials Ma Tahua had used; finally, she saw beneath the trees a freshly dug hole in which had been thrown a flat cardboard box and a plastic bag, as well as scraps of a ruined magazine. Ah Zuo said, 'Make sure you fill that hole in when you're done so I won't have to hear about it from property management.' Ma Tahua nodded and kicked his leftover materials into the hole, shovelling spadeful after spadeful of earth on top of them. Only then did Ah Zuo return her gaze to Ma Tahua's work.

A middle-aged woman, propping her head on her hands and squatting down by the roadside, dressed in a faded army uniform without any insignia, an octagonal Mao cap with a Red Star badge askew on her head: somewhere between a woman from a military household during peacetime and a

Red Army soldier from the old days at Mount Jinggang, before the Party liberated China. Her looks suggested an old-fashioned sort of beauty, but her blank eyes and stiff posture, as well as her apparent apathy, defied any attempt at a heroic depiction. At her feet was a large canvas military tarpaulin strewn with random odds and ends: national grain ration coupons from decades before; a Red Guard armband; an old wooden spear point; an enamel pin bearing the likeness of Chairman Mao; a pamphlet from the Cultural Revolution, as well as a video CD with a cover featuring buxom women; pictures of Andy Lau, Maggie Cheung, David Beckham, Ronaldo, and other stars; mobile phone cases; digital watches; masks of ghosts and demons...

'What do you think?' Ma Tahua had finished filling in the hole.

'It's so lifelike! But... I don't know why, but it makes me feel sad for some reason.' Ah Zuo's expression looked a little like the constructed woman's. 'She just feels familiar for some reason. She reminds me of a supplicant I had named Wang Yingzi.'

'Is that so? Well, that's just the effect I wanted.' Ma Tahua appraised his work from a different angle, a look of utter satisfaction on his face. Sometime later he started, seeming to react to what Ah Zuo had said. 'Wang Yingzi? Then I'll call it "Laid-off Worker: Wang Yingzi." Or maybe just "Wang Yingzi". What do you think?'

'"Wang Yingzi"? You must be joking – what a lame title. What were you thinking of calling it before?'

'It wasn't plain enough, the name I had. I was going to call it "The Age of Chasing Stars".'

The Age of Chasing Stars

Old Wang first started writing poetry in middle school. He laid his pen down in 1957, for fear that his poetry would get him branded a Rightist, and didn't pick it up again for more than a dozen years. Even though he stopped writing poetry, and often publicly scorned his years as a poet, he was always pleased, and sometimes even moved to tears, whenever someone referred to him as one. Given this background, it's not difficult to see why for many years, whenever he spoke of China's political leader Mao Zedong, the epithet with which Old Wang described him was invariably 'the great poet.' 'Oh children,' he often instructed his son and daughter, 'the great poet Chairman Mao is our great mentor, our great leader, our great commander in chief, our great helmsman: you must start following him in rebellion at a young age and swear not to stop until all under heaven is a vast expanse of red.' The same background led him to have his son and daughter memorise the entire published poetic oeuvre of Mao Zedong at a very young age. He had in fact chosen his son's and daughter's names, respectively, from two of Mao's heptasyllabic quatrains: 'On Comrade Li Jin's Photograph of the Transcendents' Cave on Mt. Lushan' and 'On a Photograph of the Women's Militia.' From a line in the former poem, 'a boundless view atop the perilous peaks,' came his son's name, Xianfeng ('perilous peaks'); from the latter's 'undaunted and heroic with their five-foot spears' came his daughter's name, Yingzi ('heroic').

These had not been their original names. Old Wang's son had been born Wang Erxiao ('Little Two') and his daughter had been Wang Fangniu ('Cowherd'). These were not cultured-sounding names, and looking at them, one might be forgiven for thinking that Old Wang was nothing more than an amateur poet who hadn't read his canon. In fact both names had cultural and poetic overtones, and there was even a story behind them. During Old Wang's days as a poet, he encountered the most famous person he would ever meet in all his average

175

and unexceptional life, a poet by the name of Fang Bing. Old Wang had published a few lyric poems in the newspapers, which had instantly rendered the primary school teacher a star of the educational system. Once, when a senior official from the local Department of Education took him out to a hotel to write a report, Old Wang saw at the door of the hotel Fang Bing, who was visiting a friend staying at the hotel. Fang Bing had a senior position at the local Department of Culture, as a result of which he often attended the same meetings as the leader from the Department of Education, whom he recognised. He paused to chat with him briefly. It wasn't until they had finished their conversation and were about to take their leave of one another that the leader from the Department of Education remembered Old Wang. By way of introduction, he said, 'This is young Mr. Wang, our own writer – a poet like yourself.' Fang Bing shook Old Wang's hand and said, 'Good good good – write on.' Old Wang was so moved he could hardly say, 'Thank thank thank – you quickly enough.' He learned later that Fang Bing had only paused between the three 'goods' and the 'write' because he had a stutter. By responding with three 'thanks' and a pause before the 'you,' Old Wang had appeared to be making fun of the man's speech impediment, a thing for which he did not forgive himself for a long, long time. That was only a minor mistake, however; his major mistake was that he had seen Fang Bing, shaken his hand, and spoken with him. Old Wang had just had a son, and had a daughter not long afterwards, and in commemoration of his meeting with Fang Bing he chose the names 'Erxiao' and 'Cowherd' from Fang Bing's best-known work, 'The Song of Erxiao the Cowherd,' which had been widely sung after being set to music by Li Jiefu:

> *The cows all still graze on the hillside;*
> *The cowherd's nowhere to be found.*
> *But it's not that he's skiving off for fun;*
> *...... The young cowherd, Wang Erxiao...*

During the Cultural Revolution, when Fang Bing was roundly denounced and struggled against, Old Wang – thinking to repudiate his admiration for Fang Bing, and to reserve all his adulation for Mao Zedong – chose new names for his son and daughter. Two years later, when his son Wang Xianfeng avoided being rusticated in the 'Up to the Mountains and Down to the Countryside' campaign and enlisted in the military instead, it was generally accepted that his name had played a part. The people in charge of military recruitment certainly didn't want the child of an intellectual – a Stinking Old Ninth! – in their army. The urban militias wanted only the children of soldiers and workers. But one recruitment chief, happening to see Wang Xianfeng's application, sighed in admiration. 'What a name,' he said. 'That's the sort of name a soldier should have.' And so it was that Wang Xianfeng made his way into an army uniform.

Wang Xianfeng's luck was almost as good as his name: despite his near-total lack of connections, he had the unbelievable good fortune to be stationed practically next door to his home, a mere 40 kilometres north-east of Shenyang at the Magang Commune. Naturally, there were too many people in his brigade for them all to live in Magang Town, so they lived up on Magang Shan – Mount Magang – within the bounds of Magang Commune. Many years later, when Magang Shan was made a national forest park, the newspapers revealed that from the early 1950s to the early 1970s, soldiers at the military base there had dug an artificial cave of major strategic significance into the mountainside to serve as an air command centre. It subsequently became known as the 'Mile-High Mountain Fortress.' The cave was deep and long, fully fitted with airtight shelters, electrical transformers, a generator room, a boiler room, conference rooms, lavatories, one-person offices complete with armchairs, two-person office suites with double beds, and even a dance hall. It had, without question, the most advanced preparations for war anywhere. Lei Feng, that most famous of warriors for

Communism, had personally applied pick and spade to rock and earth there, and major government leaders from Peng Dehuai to He Long to Chen Yi to Luo Ruiqing to Chen Xilian to Madame Mao herself had all, on various occasions, inspected and praised the project. At the time, however, the locals knew only that there were always troops on Magang Shan: they guessed, speaking amongst themselves, that the troops were digging fortifications, but nobody dared bring it up in public. A carter who talked about the fortifications on a visit to market was arrested on the spot for leaking state secrets. It followed from this that whatever the detachment on the mountain was doing was a secret assignment. As far as the military was concerned, not even locals from Shenyang like Wang Xianfeng were permitted to reveal the specifics of their location to family members, not even if the place was within walking distance of home. The carter wasn't the only one who had to eat a charge of leaking state secrets. A soldier who had been stationed there before had told his family he was digging out a cave on Magang Shan, and ended up in front of a military tribunal. It was the early 1970s when Wang Xianfeng arrived, however, and excavations on the cave had been going on long enough to be common knowledge. The secret of Magang Shan had become an open secret, and open secrets were of no great concern to anyone in or out of the army. Not only was Wang Xianfeng able to tell his family where he had been stationed and what he was doing; he was even able to take time out to visit them and invite his father and sister to spend a night with the detachment.

Old Wang and Wang Yingzi were both very excited to spend the night at the heavily fortified base, but they had different reasons for their excitement. Old Wang was excited to see the thoroughness of his country's preparedness for battle, as well as the implications for his son's future career. Knowing that China need no longer fear American imperialism or Soviet revisionism, and that his son was a 'five-good' fighter, he was as excited as he had been when he published his first poems many years before. His daughter Wang Yingzi, a romantic at heart, didn't care about the significance of the fortifications or about her older brother's advancement. What impressed her was the list of names connected with the massive cavern: Lei Feng, Peng Dehuai, He Long, Chen Yi, Luo Ruiqing, Chen Xilian, Madame Mao. These were names she had only encountered in books or on the radio, but now, through Magang Shan and her brother, they were connected to her. This made her feel special, though the owners of the names – except for Lei Feng, Chen Xilian, and Madame Mao – had long since become infamous. Even so, she thought, 'infamous' was still a kind of 'famous,' and it was such 'famous people' that the 15-year-old girl most adored.

From then on, in her occasional phone calls and letters to her brother, or on visits he paid them while on official business, Wang Yingzi was always extremely interested in those 'famous people,' and pleaded with her brother in hope of finding out what 'famous people' would next visit Magang Shan for an inspection. She dreamed, sweetly, that some day when she was visiting her brother at Magang Shan her visit would just happen to coincide with that of a 'famous person.' How blissful their chance encounter would be. Wang Xianfeng laughed at her. He said she was dreaming and that he wouldn't be bringing his father and sister to the base anymore. 'Well then,' Wang Yingzi said, 'just tell me the next time someone important is going to visit and I'll go there myself.' 'Not a chance,' Wang Xianfeng said. This wasn't a reaction against his sister's obsession with 'famous people' – he worshipped 'famous people' too. He and his sister took after their father: the entire Wang household worshipped 'famous people.' He was firm in dashing his sister's hopes only because they were unrealistic. 'Who's coming and when are both military secrets,' he said. 'Civilians don't understand secrecy.' 'It's not like I'm a Kuomintang agent,' Wang Yingzi said. 'Why would you be afraid to tell me? Besides, I don't care about the military stuff; I just want to see a leader with my own eyes.' In fact, though

Wang Xianfeng was too embarrassed to say so, there was no chance of his being informed of these military secrets in advance. Sometimes a senior cadre – someone his sister wouldn't be interested in – would arrive and he wouldn't even find out about it until after they'd left. As for the 'famous people' his sister was so fascinated by, he might not find out they'd visited until days after the fact. But there was a downside to dashing his sister's enthusiasm: she started to doubt whether Peng Dehuai and Madame Mao and the others had ever really visited Magang Shan. She even decided that Wang Xianfeng and the rest of the detachment were lying or exaggerating. To preserve the honour of the Magang Shan detachment, Wang Xianfeng, too, wished that some 'famous person' would visit, even if he only found out about it afterwards, so that the next time he saw his little sister he would be able to defend Magang Shan from the position of an eyewitness. Even if he embellished a little, it would still be true.

Fortunately, he didn't have to wait long for his opportunity. Word of the visit spread privately from soldier to soldier, perhaps because the news was too shocking for anyone to keep it to themselves. After Army Day on August 1, there might be a visit from a senior figure in the government. Wang Xianfeng knew how dangerous it would be to divulge any word of this to a civilian, but he had always known his little sister to be capable of locking her lips, and besides, this wasn't just bragging: if he didn't pass the news on he was going to explode.

'Senior? Maybe a regional army cadre at most. I'm not interested in *that* level.'

'No.' Wang Xianfeng was almost bursting. 'The *most* senior leader.'

'The Commander?'

'No, the Party Centre. It's – whatever you do, you have to keep this – '

'Huh! Don't tell me then, if you don't trust me. If you want to trick me, at least make the lie more believable. The Party Centre!'

'It really *is* the Party Centre! It's Chairman Mao himself!'

'What?' The colour drained instantly from Wang Yingzi's face; her eyes became unfocused, her hands trembled, and sweat beaded on her forehead. 'B-b-b-brother, y-y-you m-must be j-j-joking–'

'R-r-r-really! I wouldn't have the g-guts to m-make th-that kind of j-joke, not even if I borrowed y-your guts…' Wang Yingzi's stutter was infectious, but Wang Xianfeng quickly composed himself. 'Niuniu,' he said, calling his sister by her nickname, 'listen to me very carefully. Ever since the clashes over Zhenbao Island, the forces of Soviet revision have been plotting their next move against us. Chairman Mao has taken a particular interest in Manchuria's readiness for battle, and he plans to visit for an inspection on August 1. Of course, Chairman Mao has so many things on his plate, so if something comes up he may send Vice-Chairman Lin…'

'Lin Biao? Just imagine if Chairman Mao and Vice-Chairman Lin both visited at once! What a joy that would be for the people of Manchuria!'

'Yes, I hope they can both come and look at our 'mountain fortress' too. But it's also possible, from some people's analysis, that if they're both too busy with other things, then…'

'I don't want to hear about any stupid analysis! Don't jinx it!' Wang Yingzi covered her brother's mouth with her hand and burst into tears.

'All right, all right, I won't jinx it. I was just reminding you so you won't say I was making things up. One guy thinks that Chairman Mao and Vice-Chairman Lin might both send Vice-Minister Lin…'

'You're so lucky! When they come, make sure you get a good, long look at them for me – shake their hands, if you can! And then make sure you don't wash your hand, and then come back and shake my hand – oh, wait, I have to run to the bathroom…'

Excitement stimulates the bladder; Wang Xianfeng understood that. He felt like he could go himself. He was excited on two fronts. First, to see Chairman Mao or Vice-Chairman Lin himself was an honour thousands of times greater than his father's encounter with Fang Bing, if not tens of thousands of times. And he was happy to see that his little sister was so mature and sensible. Even though she wanted more than anything else in the world to see one of the senior leaders for herself, she knew that they belonged to the soldiers at Magang Shan, not to her. She didn't try wheedling for him to take her along with him; she just told him to shake her hand when he came back. In his excitement, Wang Xianfeng resolved not to let her down. If the opportunity presented itself, he would definitely try to get word of the visit before it happened, and would tell his sister so that she could share simultaneously in his happiness, at a remove of 40 kilometres.

August 1 came and went without any whisper of a visit from a senior head of state, or even of a district commandant. But just as Wang Xianfeng, like all the officers and enlisted men, was beginning to lose hope, he caught word on the morning of August 8 as he was helping in the kitchen that two vehicles would be leaving the Magang Shan base that afternoon and going into Shenyang. One of them would be going to Dongta Airport to bring back a shipment of foods that had been sent in by air freight, as well as a cook who specialized in Hunan cuisine. The other vehicle would be going to the song and dance troupe in Shenyang to pick up revolutionary opera performers, as well as their costumes and props. The reason behind the preparations – especially when you added Hunan food into the mix – went without saying. Wang Xianfeng grew instantly excited, thinking that this must mean Chairman Mao would join all the officers and enlisted men in celebration. It must be that Himself hadn't come on August 1 because he had first visited Heilongjiang and Jilin, and was now completing his trip to Manchuria with a visit to Liaoning. Wang Xianfeng couldn't go on working: he threw down the radishes and cabbage in his hands and walked to the phone room, feigning nonchalance and humming 'The Road to Jinggangshan' as he went.

'Hello? Could I trouble you to fetch Wang Yingzi? She lives in the Japanese building, Block 1, number 24.'

Wang Xianfeng had called a public telephone located outside the gate of the compound where his family lived. School was out for the summer, and if his sister wasn't out playing with her classmates, she would probably get his call. If she *was* out, then at least he'd be able to tell her he'd tried. As it happened, she was at home.

'Xianfeng! As soon as Auntie Luo said there was a call for me, I knew it must be you. What's up?'

'Oh, nothing much. Have you been well?'

'Your voice – is there someone–'

'Mm. Pretty smart!'

'Really? Really? Is it really Number One?'

'Of course.'

'Heaven! Did you shake his hand?'

'Well – I'll do my best…'

'He's not there yet? Is he coming today? This afternoon? Or the evening? It's the evening, isn't it?'

'Pretty much.'

'That's, that's – I want to go, Xianfeng! I want to go see him!'

'That's impossible. Completely out of the question. Don't even think about it.'

'Please? Pleeeeease?'

'That's enough. I've got work to do here – I'll shake your hand soon, all right?'

'No! Xianf–'

Wang Xianfeng hung up the telephone, satisfied that he had done his duty, but at the other end of the line, Wang Yingzi's heart was shredded into a tangled clump. She tried to sit quietly for a while to settle down, but was unable to calm herself. All she could do was pace back and forth vigorously, as if she were on a cross-country march, loudly reciting the opening of Chairman Mao's poem 'The Long March': 'The Red Army fears not the hardships of its march / Ten thousand rivers, a thousand mountains, it holds lightly.' She calmed down as she repeated the poem, her increasing calmness reflected by the decision that she would go to Magang Shan. First she changed into a new army uniform her brother had given her. Then she put on her army boots and army cap and fastened her Red Guard armband neatly around her left arm. Then she emptied out her savings jar, counted the money inside, and wrapped it all up in a handkerchief. This she placed into her backpack, along with two steamed buns and a chunk of pickled cabbage. The addition of these to the original contents of her backpack – a copy of *Quotations from Chairman Mao*, a copy of *Quotations from Vice-Chairman Lin*, a copy of *Quotations from Marx, Engels, and Lenin*, a notebook, and a ballpoint pen – made the bag somewhat heavy. She slung it over one shoulder as she fastened an army belt around her waist. She looked the way her brother had several years before, when he set out from Shenyang for Beijing as part of the exchanges between Red Guard factions across the country. The difference was that her brother hadn't seen Chairman Mao when he visited Beijing: Chairman Mao hadn't held a ninth review of the Red Guards. This time, she was certain that she would receive a personal inspection from Chairman Mao.

The heroic Wang Yingzi left a note for her father on the table and set out. To protect her brother's secret and keep her father from worrying about her, she wrote that she was going to a classmate's house, and would probably spend the night there.

The first two-thirds of the journey went smoothly: she took a Shenyang public bus to Xiaodongmen, where after a brief wait she caught the hourly bus that ran from the city to the outlying counties. She got off at Xinchengzi, under whose administrative jurisdiction the Magang commune fell. But there were only two buses a day from Xinchengzi Town to

Magang Town: one at eight in the morning, the other at one in the afternoon, and it was already half past one by the time Wang Yingzi arrived. She cursed herself silently for having hesitated after she got off the phone, but quickly rallied. She had prepared herself for the possibility that she would encounter difficulties in her journey. If worse came to worst, she'd just walk. Her brother and the other Red Guards had walked to Beijing, so why should she have to wait for a bus to go to Magang Shan? She ate one of her steamed buns and half the salted cabbage, then drank two dipperfuls of water that she got from a lady carrying water by the roadside. Wang Yingzi was a clever girl: instead of just asking one person for directions, she asked people every now and then as she went, to make sure she hadn't been pointed in the wrong direction by someone too embarrassed to admit that they didn't know the way. Also, she asked for directions to Hushitai and Qingshuitai, which she knew lay between Xinchengzi and Magang. If the person giving her directions was a bad person, and wanted to do something bad, the proximity of Hushitai and Qingshuitai should be enough to make them think twice. Bad people usually preferred to go after people on longer journeys. It was only after she had passed Hushitai and Qingshuitai, as Magang Town was just coming into view, that she encountered a bad person. Though strictly speaking you couldn't necessarily call the person bad.

It was a woman who was talking to a few other women at the edge of a field. Wang Yingzi felt a sense of warm familiarity upon seeing them, since they were obviously 'Educated Youth' – city kids sent down to the countryside to get a taste of the hard life. The Educated Youth who got sent down to Xinchengzi were all from Shenyang, so they were from the same city as her. And they were the ones who greeted her first: one of the women called out, 'Where are you going, Little Miss Eighth Route?' Wang Yingzi said she was going to Magang, and as soon as she opened her mouth they could hear that she was from Shenyang. 'A hometown girl!' another girl called. 'Looking pretty swell there – where are you going, visiting your husband's family? How'd you end up with in-laws out in the country?' Wang Yingzi's sweaty face went a deep red. Another one of the young women said, 'Don't talk like that, she's still a little girl.' Another one of them said, 'I'm a little girl too, aren't I? How come I've got to work like those old hags in the village?' Another one replied, 'Don't let the villagers hear you saying that,' then turned back to Wang Yingzi. 'Rest a while and have a drink of water.' Wang Yingzi really was thirsty, so she thanked the young woman and had a drink, then asked the girls how to get to the mountain. She hadn't dared ask for directions to the mountain before, since she knew that people would instantly remember that the mountain was a military base, and that the troops stationed there had dug out a huge command centre. Questions like that could lead to trouble if she wasn't careful. She felt more at ease asking the Educated Youth for directions: they weren't likely to make a huge deal about small things, and they were hardly likely to be Kuomintang agents snooping around for military secrets, or spies in the employ of the revisionist Soviets or the imperialist Americans. And indeed, they told her about a road that would take her through the mountain without having to go through Magang Town, and guessed instantly what her background was. 'Huh – going to visit a brother in the Red Army?' one of them asked. She said she was. The Educated Youth instantly fell over themselves laughing. Wang Yingzi remembered that in movies and books set during the war, whenever a young woman talked about a brother in the Red Army, she always meant her lover. She tried to explain: 'No, not in the Red Army – he's my brother, my *real* –' but the more she tried to explain, the harder the girls laughed, and she began to tear up with frustration. Fortunately one of the women stopped laughing before the others and helped her out of the situation: 'I know, I know – a girl your age wouldn't have a lover; "brother" means "brother"…' After that, Wang Yingzi thanked the girls again and set back out on the road. Before she had gotten far, however, one of the Educated Youth ran up behind her and shouted for her to stop. Wang Yingzi turned around, smiling, to see what the young woman wanted, but the young woman reached out and snatched off her army cap. 'Water's not free, sister. I'll keep the cap – you go on looking for your brother.' Wang Yingzi froze for an instant in shock. She tried to snatch the cap back, but the young woman pulled out a sickle from the back of her trousers and said, 'I'll cut you.' Then she said, 'If you don't get the fuck out of here right fucking now I'll take the rest of the uniform too, you see if I don't.' Wang Yingzi believed that if the young woman got angry she might well strip away her army uniform. She turned and walked away, but as she went she said, 'Just you wait until I find my brother.' 'Go on then,' the Educated Youth said, obviously relieved that things had gone no further. 'You go get your brother.'

All things military were so fashionable that it wasn't uncommon for civilians to steal army caps or uniforms – that much Wang Yingzi knew. But it was something men did: she'd never heard of women robbing people. She had hesitated before setting out, unsure whether she should wear the outfit or not. Under ordinary circumstances, she would never have dressed up like that – it was too eye-catching, and it was bound to attract the notice of thieves too. But once she was in the uniform, all she could think was: *if anyone tries to take this, I'll say I'm wearing these clothes to visit Chairman Mao!* She reckoned that thieves would be afraid of Chairman Mao, and that this would be enough to avert all danger. It wasn't until she got on the first bus that she realised she couldn't tell a thief that Chairman Mao was coming. If the thief wasn't just a thief, if he was a landlord fat-cat reactionary bad element Rightist or a secret agent, then she'd have just divulged information about Chairman Mao's movements. But there was no way for her to go back and change out of the uniform, and she had been fortunate enough to have a smooth journey up until this point. She'd never imagined that here, on the very edge of her brother's turf, she would run into a thief – much less that the thief would be a woman.

Wang Yingzi walked on, crying as she went, but it wasn't long before she had bigger things to think about than the army cap. She was making her way up a mountain path by this point. The path, lonely as her, wended between sheer cliff faces, over ground shaded so deeply that it might as well have been under a canopy. But the path was luckier than she was, she thought: it had no feelings, no consciousness, while she knew fear and was conscious of both her own solitude and the frightening sounds that came from all around her. Was that the wind shrieking? Was that an animal howling? Was that a boulder tumbling? She didn't even know what the things frightening her were; she saw only that the sky above the mountain seemed to be getting darker earlier than usual.

Wang Yingzi's body produced wave after wave of sweat, and shook with wave after wave of shivers. She remembered that when her brother had brought her here in the army jeep, it had taken no time at all to get to the base at the saddle of the mountain, but when she looked ahead now, all she could see was an unbroken stretch of mountain, with no sign of any depression. Could she have taken the wrong road? But mountain roads aren't like roads through the flatlands, which can tangle and snarl like vines and branches; she was sure that this was the only road on the mountain, and that as long as she followed it there was no chance of getting lost. Wang Yingzi gritted her teeth, driving all thoughts from her mind and putting all her energy into walking forward. As she walked, she took *Quotations from Chairman Mao*, *Quotations from Vice-Chairman Lin*, and *Quotations from Marx, Engels, and Lenin* out of her bag, and, imitating the way her teacher led the class in reciting from the books every day, served as a teacher for the rocks and trees of Magang Shan:

'Everybody take out your copy of *Quotations from Chairman Mao* and turn to – follow my lead – and everybody recite one passage three times each, starting from "Be resolute." Ready? and: "Be resolute, fear no sacrifice, and surmount every difficulty to achieve victory…"' That was very good, but I don't think I could hear *everybody's* voice. Now everybody, let us turn, our hearts filled with proletarian revolutionary emotions, to page 301 in *Quotations from Vice-Chairman Lin*. Starting from the first line. 'Ready? and: "We will respond to the mighty call of Chairman Mao, not only by utterly destroying the bourgeois headquarters at an institutional level, but also by engaging in broader and deeper revolutionary criticism in order to completely detect and root out the faction of 'capitalist roaders' within the Party, led by Liu Shaoqi, the Khrushchev of China, and engaging in political, mental, and theoretical struggle against them to ensure that they will never rise again." That was *very* good, everybody. Now if everybody would turn to page 249 of *Quotations from Marx, Engels, and Lenin*, starting with "We Communists," and, all together: "We Communists are people of a special mould. We are made of a special stuff. We are those who form the army of the great proletarian strategist, the army of Comrade Lenin. There is nothing higher than the honour of belonging to this army. There is nothing higher than the title of member of the Party whose founder and leader was Comrade Lenin. It is not given to everyone to be a member of such a party. It is the sons of the working class, the sons of want and struggle, the sons of incredible privation and heroic effort…"'

There was a series of low rumbles right beside her as she declaimed this, and by the time she realised that this was not the sound of a packed classroom full of students responding to her but rather the kind of thunder that immediately precedes a massive downpour, the mountain – which already offered a narrow field of view – was completely shrouded in mist. Heavy raindrops, driven by the wind, battered down an eye-blink later. Fortunately, Wang Yingzi had the cliff face and trees to shield her, and she darted into a recess in the cliff face as soon as she felt the first drops. It was a very shallow recess, only deep enough to keep her back dry – but it was enough to protect the copies of *Quotations from Chairman Mao*, *Quotations from Vice-Chairman Lin*, and *Quotations from Marx, Engels, and Lenin* in her backpack. There was another string of ear-splitting thunderclaps. Wang Yingzi saw a flash of red light before her eyes, and then everything went dark…

Someone shook Wang Yingzi awake, and she opened her eyes to see Li Tiemei, from the opera *The Legend of the Red Lantern*, with her single long braid; Auntie Ah Qing, with her hair up in a bun; and young Chang Bao with his fur hat. Not far away, she saw a jeep half-full of soldiers wearing make-up, and through the branches behind it the rays of the setting sun. A surge of excitement rushed through her. 'Chairman Mao…' she said, 'Wang Xianfeng…–' and then she fainted again.

The jeep was full of performers from the Shenyang song and dance troupe, on their way to a banquet with the officials and soldiers at Magang Shan. Li Tiemei, Auntie Ah Qing, and young Chang Bao knew who Chairman Mao was, but they hadn't heard of Wang Xianfeng. The driver of their jeep, however, knew both names. So they brought Wang Yingzi with them to the base at the saddle of the mountain and turned her over to Wang Xianfeng. The next time Wang Yingzi woke up, the first thing she saw was her brother, who looked both distressed and delighted. But she had no time to pay attention to him. She turned her head quickly, looking all around. She was, she saw, lying down in the infirmary.

Wang Xianfeng squeezed her hand. 'Oh, Niuniu, Niuniu, you're awake!' he said, his voice quavering. 'Thank goodness you weren't too close to that tree – the lightning blew it to pieces…'

'What time is it?' Wang Yingzi said. 'Are they all asleep?'

'Who? Oh – it's two o'clock in the morning,' Wang Xianfeng said. 'They finished their act and left. – Oh, oh, you mean – Oh, I'm sorry, I'm sorry – I gave you bad information. It was only the director of the Logistics Department paying a visit…'

Wang Yingzi sat up, bawling, and pounded her brother with her fists. 'No! You're lying, you're rotten, you just didn't wake me up in time…' But her body, weak as it was, wouldn't let her sit up for long, and Wang Xianfeng had to help her lie back down. 'You kept all the happiness for yourself! You didn't wake me… if it wasn't Chairman Mao I bet it was Vice-Chairman Lin…'

Wang Xianfeng quickly clamped a hand over her mouth. 'For heaven's sake, don't go naming names like that here – are you trying to get me court-martialed?'

But Wang Yingzi didn't care how tense or scared her brother was, or how reasonable his explanation was; eyes wild and emotions surging, as soon as her brother removed his hand from her mouth she began yelling: 'Chairman Mao! Vice-Chairman Lin! Chairman Mao! Vice-Chairman Lin!' Even as her brother was reaching out to cover her mouth, she leapt up and made for the doorway.

Wang Xianfeng hesitated, caught between wanting to grab his sister and wanting to stop her from shouting. He could see that she was hysterical; it was no use trying to talk sense into her. He would've liked to knock her out with a quick punch to the head, but couldn't bring himself to do it. Then inspiration struck. It had been Deputy Director Lin who visited, he told her. 'He's only deputy director of the Office of the Air Force Command,' he said. Lin Liguo wasn't a major leader, he meant, so Wang Yingzi hadn't missed anything special. She disagreed: 'Deputy Director Lin might not have a very high rank,' she said, 'but he's still the son of Vice-Chairman Lin Biao, the flesh and blood of the great leader Chairman Mao's war comrade. I love and respect him just as much as his father.' 'Well, all right,' Wang Xianfeng said unhappily. 'You sit here quietly for a few minutes while I go and check with my superiors to see if he'll be willing to grant you an audience.' Wang Yingzi lay down obediently. 'Thank you, brother,' she said weakly. Wang Xianfeng returned about five minutes later. 'Deputy Director Lin can only see you for a moment,' he said.

'He's got to leave and go back to Beijing tonight.' Another ten minutes or so later, two young soldiers walked into the infirmary. The one in front, a young man of middling height but with fair, noble features, walked straight to the side of Wang Yingzi's bed, followed by a muscle-bound man who couldn't stop yawning – a serviceman or a bodyguard, obviously. He had a herringbone army overcoat draped over the crook of one arm; his other hand never strayed far from the holster at his waist.

Before Wang Xianfeng could make introductions, Wang Yingzi leapt up from the bed: 'Deputy Director Lin!' Tears streamed down her face, and she gripped both of 'Lin Liguo's' hands tightly.

'Lin Liguo' withdrew one hand, smiling, and patted her lightly on the head, twice: 'Young Red Guard Wang Yingzi, I see that your feelings for Chairman Mao and Vice-Chairman Lin are very deep indeed. That's good, very good. For now, your mission is to rest well so you'll be even better able to protect the Chairman and the Vice-Chairman.'

Wang Yingzi snapped to attention. 'Yes sir!'

'Very well then. It's time for me to go back to Beijing to make my report to Chairman Mao and Vice-Chairman Lin.' 'Lin Liguo' stood up, turned smartly, and walked out of the infirmary. By the time Wang Yingzi staggered to the doorway to shout, 'Give my regards to Chairman Mao and Vice-Chairman Lin!' there was nothing outside but gusts of wind and the flickering shadows of the trees.

At the start of the new school year, the Composition teacher assigned her class the essay prompt 'I Thought/Noticed/Saw/ Heard/Gathered/Smelled/Got/Caught/Felt…' After some thought – and the careful alteration of 'Magang Shan' to 'Mt. X' – Wang Yingzi wrote an essay entitled 'I Saw the Son of the Great Leader Chairman Mao's Close Wartime Comrade Vice-Chairman Lin, Deputy Director Lin Liguo.' Her teacher, thrilled, gave the essay an 'A+' and passed it along to the local newspaper for publication. The newspaper set Wang Yingzi's essay in type a few days later, and was preparing to publish it in the next day's paper when Old Wang, who secretly listened to enemy radio broadcasts every evening, heard from the Voice of America that Lin Biao and his son had died in a plane crash over Öndörkhaan, Mongolia, while fleeing to the USSR after a failed attempt at a coup. Shocking as the enemy broadcast was, Old Wang still believed it, and he went to the newspaper late that night to get his daughter's essay back.

Mouth and Piece

Lin Liguo was doing an on-the-job doctorate. He had passed his thesis defence and was getting ready to receive the degree: by all rights, he should have been happy. But the past few days he had been unusually depressed. It's popular to talk about 'depression' these days, but although Lin Liguo had never been particularly up on fashion, this was the word that came to mind lately whenever he thought of his degree. It was, he felt, the only word that could express his state of mind. And so that day when he went online to chat, he changed his screen name to 'dPressed.'

Accompanied by a profile pic of a girl, a screen name like that would be guaranteed to attract a raft of chatty male netizens – but the avatar next to Lin Liguo's 'dPressed' was a man, and he spent ages in the chatroom without a single person paying him any attention. He'd tried making the first move a few times, but the responses were all along the lines of: 'I'm depressed too'; or 'I could use some comfort myself'; or 'Grow a pair'; until he was both depressed and deeply annoyed. He was just about to leave the chatroom and go offline when he noticed a screen name: 'mouth_n_piece,' and was instantly inspired to write a cod-classical couplet:

Pieces at the ready, mouths open everywhere;
A bellyful of thoughts, and nowhere I can share.

Whoever was on the other end was quick on the draw; the response came back unusually quickly:

Gag the mouths; toss the pieces; what have I to fear?
This girl's got her own turf on the Internet – right here.

And that was how Lin Liguo met Guan Miao.

Guan Miao asked Lin Liguo later if the sexual connotations of 'mouth_n_piece' hadn't occurred to him. 'What kind of person do you think I am,' Lin Liguo said. 'All I thought of was *Mouthpiece* magazine. The way I am at the moment, I could have people perform sex right in front of me and I'd probably just wonder if they had a sex licence or not.'

Indeed, Lin Liguo's depression was intrinsically tied up with the word 'Mouthpiece.'

Lin Liguo was a college instructor who taught journalism – 'Mass Communications,' more properly. He held a master's degree and hadn't planned on getting a doctorate, but the trend over the past few years had been for institutions of higher education to require their instructors to have doctorates. Plenty of people who had PhDs but could barely string a sentence together had done well out of the new policy, to the consternation of Lin Liguo, who was a practiced, composed lecturer. What bothered him wasn't that there were idiots wearing doctors' robes; it was that the robes had been practically bought and paid for, and with public funds at that. There was a policy at his school: if instructors completed an on-the-job doctoral programme, the school would cover 80% of tuition costs. So it was that Lin Liguo joined the ranks of PhD students. It wasn't too difficult to do a doctorate these days, all things considered; it was no great stress for Lin Liguo. As long as you passed the exams for your two foreign languages, filled your publication quota, and turned in a dissertation of no fewer than X-many words, you were good to go. And that was for one of the more legitimate programmes. There were others that would waive the foreign languages and the publications and award the degree based solely on the dissertation. Naturally, the latter programmes were only open to cadres in leadership positions of a certain rank, or members of families of a certain standing. Lin Liguo, being neither a leader nor a moneybags, had to take the legitimate route. This was of no great concern to him – he spoke his first and second foreign languages passably, and had published more than the requisite number of articles; more importantly, his dissertation topic and defence of it had met with the approval of his committee, and a publisher had even suggested that he expand his dissertation into a book later that year. So why was he depressed?

The problem was with his publications.

When doctoral candidates submitted their list of publications to the school before graduation, they were supposed to attach official documentation from the newspapers or publishers affirming that the student was the author of the published piece. Even if you were, say, Jin Yong, and your martial-arts novel, *Demi-Gods and Semi-Devils,* had been serialised in the *Ming Pao*, and everyone on the planet knew that you were Jin Yong and that you'd written *Demi-Gods and Semi-Devils* – even if you'd taken everyone out for beers with your payment for the novel, even if your supervisor was green with envy, having worked all his life without producing anything like *Demi-Gods and Semi-Devils*, you'd still have to go to the Ming Pao offices and get a letter, complete with official red seal, before the school would accept that you, Jin Yong, had indeed written a novel called *Demi-Gods and Semi-Devils.* Explained in this way, the reasoning should be clear – and we can follow this train of thought to find the root of Lin Liguo's depression. He had published quite a substantial piece, 'On the Responsibilities of Journalism to the Party and the People,' in a magazine called *Mouthpiece*, and although he had put this on the list of publications he'd submitted to the school, he had been unable to get written confirmation from *Mouthpiece*, the reason being that *Mouthpiece* had ceased publication half a year prior.

As mentioned, Lin Liguo had published more than the required number of articles, enough that even if *Mouthpiece* could no longer give him a letter of certification, he could still submit his list; one article fewer wouldn't make much difference either. Everyone knew that no one looked at these lists once they were submitted; no one cared which articles were serious and which were trivial. The problem was that another requirement for PhD candidates was to publish a piece in a 'key periodical.' Lin Liguo had published mostly in *Practical Journalism*, *Modern Communication*, and *Frontlines*, none of which was sufficiently 'key.' The shuttered *Mouthpiece* was the only key periodical in which he had published, which meant that he had no choice but to include 'On the Responsibilities of Journalism to the Party and the People' among his publications.

Mouthpiece, once a major organ in the field of journalism theory, had been headquartered in Beijing. Lin Liguo didn't know the editors well, but they had called him when they selected his article for publication, so he had the managing editor's number. Lin Liguo contacted him and explained the situation. The man was perfectly polite, but said that the seal that they used for all official documents had been thrown away when the magazine shut down. The best he could offer was an unofficial letter of certification. Lin Liguo went to talk to the relevant administrator at his school to see if an exception could be made for 'On the Responsibilities of Journalism to the Party and the People.' But the relevant administrator said that to make such an exception would be an affront to scholarship and an insult to the degree. An unofficial letter would not do at all.

'How can you prove that you didn't write the letter yourself?'

Lin Liguo didn't have an answer for that. All he could say was, 'It wouldn't just be the letter – my name's in the magazine too.'

'And it'd be even worse if your name weren't there,' the relevant administrator said. 'The point of the letter is to certify that the name attached to the article belongs to you and not someone else with that name.'

'It's me, it's me,' Lin Liguo said. 'Of *course* it's me – it's on my national ID card and my household registration booklet. I've never heard of anyone else being called Lin Liguo, never mind anyone else working in journalism studies.'

'Well, I have,' the relevant administrator said, his poker face suddenly crinkling into a smile. 'Maybe you're too young to know – Lin Biao? Lin Biao had a son with the same name as you.'

Lin Biao and his son were dead by the time Lin Liguo was born, but of course he had heard of the two of them – how could he not have? The relevant administrator was playing with him, he decided, but he had no choice but to put up with it. 'You can trust me – I'm an honest person, a Party member.'

The relevant administrator grew stern again: 'And are there any corrupt elements who *aren't* Party members? And is there anyone who'll *say* they're dishonest?'

Lin Liguo's throat went dry and he could say nothing more. He could only go see his supervisor, in the hope that his supervisor would verify that he was indeed capable of writing an article like 'On the Responsibilities of Journalism to the Party and the People.' His supervisor expressed his understanding and stated his confidence in Lin Liguo's abilities – but said, 'Even if they're being sticklers, you've got to play by their rules,' because 'otherwise who'll certify that the certification I gave them isn't fake?'

This line of reasoning struck Lin Liguo as bullshit, bullshit even more objectionable than the reasoning employed by the hack bureaucrat who had just been giving him a hard time. He said, 'Do they actually believe you can be a PhD supervisor, but not believe you're an honest person?' His unimpeachably honest supervisor laughed. 'If they don't, they don't. Can't say I blame them.'

Lin Liguo left his supervisor's office in an angry fog and with a sense of failure. He bought two cartons of cigarettes and two bottles of liquor, and that evening he went to the home of the relevant administrator. He opened by saying that the relevant administrator's strict adherence to principle had been a great lesson to him; then he once again requested that the relevant administrator make an exception and allow him to use the unofficial document. The relevant administrator looked at the cigarettes and liquor without acknowledging them, but after further emphasising the importance of notarisation and certification, he expressed his sympathies regarding the closing down of *Mouthpiece* and the inconvenience it had caused, and – in the end – assured Lin Liguo that he could use the unofficial document – if, and only if, the editor-in-chief of *Mouthpiece* signed it himself.

After thanking the relevant administrator profusely, Lin Liguo phoned the managing editor once again to ask for the phone number of the editor-in-chief of *Mouthpiece* so that he could get a letter of certification from him. Tracking down the editor-in-chief proved to be an easy task: after *Mouthpiece* shut down, the original staff had stayed where they were, the office hadn't moved anywhere, and the magazine had continued to use the original magazine publication number to start up a new magazine, *Celebrity Pictorial*. The editor-in-chief picked up the phone, and at the sound of Lin Liguo's Manchurian accent, he was reminded of the exquisite prose of 'On the Responsibilities of Journalism to the Party and the People,' 'a mixture of the literary and the rational.' Without pausing to find out why Lin Liguo was calling, he launched into a pitch: 'How about doing a feature for us on Zhao Benshan? Our rate will be enough to make it worth your while.' Only after he finished his pitch did he grasp what Lin Liguo was saying. 'Oh,' he said. 'I'm afraid this isn't going to work…' Lin Liguo hadn't been expecting the editor-in-chief to turn him down. 'Even if I didn't have to sign my name to it, it wouldn't work. You've got to understand, Lin, as the editor-in-chief I have to abide by all the rules and regulations pertaining to journalism. Do you know the back story for why *Mouthpiece* shut down? We were promoting adversarial journalism, in direct contravention of all accepted principles; we were running pieces about media involvement being more effective than the law in conflict resolution, which is to say that we were covertly advocating personal advocacy rather than rule by law, which is to say that we were committing a "Major Error". Fortunately for us, the higher-ups responded to the Error, not to the individuals responsible for the Error, so as the chief editor I got off with nothing more than some criticism and a lesson learned the hard way – but I've got to learn from experience, right? If I write up a letter of certification for you, who's to say someone won't claim I was protesting against the way the higher-ups handled the case, or trying to resurrect the ghost of the wrongfully killed *Mouthpiece*, and then who's to say the higher-ups won't come down harder on me? Forget all about *Mouthpiece,* Lin; forget you ever published a piece in our ill-fated little magazine.'

Lin Liguo hung up the phone in tears and sat down at his computer, where he logged into a chatroom under the screen name 'dPressed' to lighten his depression. And this was how he encountered, under the name 'mouth_n_piece,' the similarly depressed Guan Miao.

Guan Miao hosted the entertainment channel's 'LOLOL' show at the local radio station. When Lin Liguo teasingly called her a big celebrity, she replied that she was a celebrity with a short shelf life. 'I could get laid off any day.' Her tone was a mixture of nonchalance and hurt.

Guan Miao had graduated with a major in early childhood education. Scoring a job as an announcer at a state mouthpiece like the radio station after a few years as a teacher was sheer good luck. The station was holding a competition to find new announcers. Contestants were judged on the basis of their skills, rather than their educational backgrounds. In addition to the prizes on offer, the top three contestants would receive official jobs at the station. In actuality, the station had decided that it would hire three well-connected people, but of the three they had in mind only one had an undergraduate degree – hence the part about not considering contestants' educational backgrounds. Hiring them through an open competition was a chance for the station to make a little extra money from application fees, training costs, and spectator tickets, while at the same time ensuring that the chosen contestants' 'connections' wouldn't come to light. It was a sensitive period for the local government and the 'higher-ups' were best pleased when the 'lower-downs' appeared to be conducting their backroom deals in broad daylight, making everything appear to be on the level. The radio station was one of the 'lower-downs' most skilled at pleasing the 'higher-ups.' But two hours before the contest, one of the three selectees backed out – presumably having found a better job elsewhere – and the station, caught flatfooted, had no time to discuss whom to give the open position to before the contest began. With a broad range of general knowledge, fast reaction times, a good voice, and a pretty face, Guan Miao lucked into third place behind the two selectees, who had been given the questions beforehand. Guan Miao was no dummy, and she hadn't been on the job long before she figured out what had happened. She had always had a strong personality, but at the station she kept her head down, worked hard, and kept to herself, hoping that she would make it through the half-year trial period. But sometimes the more you worry about trouble, the more trouble comes looking for you. Her line manager, for instance – the deputy director of the station's lifestyle and entertainment channel – had failed on multiple occasions to keep his hands to himself, on one occasion coming up behind her and embracing her from behind, pressing the side of his scratchy face up against hers. She broke away, but she was nauseous for the rest of the day. That morning, the same deputy director had backed her into a deserted corner of the studio and looked her over, his eyes unreadable. Other than being unsubtle in his harassment and unable to take a hint, Guan Miao could tell that the deputy director wasn't a bad guy. He was kindly and straightforward, and there was no chance of him getting violent if she didn't respond to his advances. Even so, she certainly couldn't let this slide – who'd be able to tolerate that sort of thing day in, day out? Besides, if the studio door was closed, the little room would be completely cut off from the outside world: you could set off a bomb inside and nobody would hear it. She couldn't help worrying about what would happen if the deputy director really did go crazy all of a sudden. And so, rather than doing as she had done up till now and feigning panic like a delicate little girl, Guan Miao set her face, stopped pretending, and revealed her hard, contrary, worldly side.

'I understand where you're coming from,' she said. 'But you can't force this sort of thing. It's wrong and it's lame.' She placed a chair between herself and the deputy director and stared him down.

The deputy director got an awkward look on his face. 'What are – I was just, I wanted to talk… if I gave you the wrong impression, I apologise. I wasn't, I didn't mean…'

Seeing how quickly he crumbled, Guan Miao felt a little bad for the deputy director. He was her superior, after all, and considerably older than her – she should give him an out. 'So,' she said. 'You're a nice person, I know that. But I'm not – it's not just you. Any man. I'm not…'

'Don't!' the deputy director blurted, as if he'd been stung. 'Don't tell m– I don't need to know anything about your personal life. Just listen to me, all right? Just – don't tell anybody about our conversation today. I brought you into the studio because I didn't want anyone to overhear… I don't like to go stirring up trouble, all right? I'm a coward, OK? Any time I don't look like a coward, it's a front, it's me imitating them. So, I mean, it's not as if I like the way I am…' He seemed sincere, but Guan Miao wondered what he was getting at. 'So, old Mrs Jin –' Guan Miao knew who old Mrs

Jin was: the organisational Party secretary, or the disciplinary Party secretary, or anyway some sort of secretary, alternately severe and earnest, hot and cold by turns. Mrs Jin had chatted with her a few days before, and asked Guan Miao what she thought separated a Party newspaper or a Party station from a cheap tabloid. 'She's got relatives in high places, you know. She has a lot of clout at the station. And she takes an interest. Has a habit of micromanaging. Miss Qi, who came in along with you, is a distant relative of hers, but… She has always aimed for purity: pure news with a pure news team. The way she sees it, the station shouldn't have anyone on staff who uses drugs, or sleeps around, or dresses inappropriately – no men with long hair, or women with revealing clothing…'

Guan Miao couldn't take any more. 'What are you trying to say?'

'…or homosexuals,' the deputy director concluded, not allowing Guan Miao to cut him off. He paused, but Guan Miao no longer had anything to say. The deputy director cast a significant look at her, then continued. 'And she won't stand by and watch as any of these things happen. She wants everyone working at the station to have a full and happy family life… and you – your trial period isn't over, but she would like to see you with a perfect family and a loving husband. But here you are, 29 and you haven't got a partner…'

'I do, Director –' Guan Miao saw what was going on, and inspiration struck. Clearly when old Mrs. Jin had chatted with her a few days earlier and asked casually whether she had a partner, it was because she had heard the rumours about her. 'Actually, I do, Director – I told Mrs Jin that I didn't because I was afraid she'd think that my love life was taking away from my work…'

'Oh yes! At the meeting, Liu Ying said your boyfriend was a policeman, named Wang Xuebing, and that she could prove it…'

A chill went down Guan Miao's back. Liu Ying was the director of the Entertainment station, and she was younger than the deputy director. A couple of days earlier, she had, out of the blue, said to Guan Miao: 'So your boyfriend's a policeman?' Guan Miao had only laughed, not knowing what she was talking about. Liu Ying continued: 'When I was leaving the station yesterday I saw you getting into his police car.' 'What–' said Guan Miao, but Liu Ying cut her off: 'There's nothing wrong with a policeman. What's his name?' 'Wang Xuebing,' Guan Miao answered with a grin. That morning, they had done a programme called 'The Inescapable Cop Complex' with an actor named Wang Xuebing, who was always getting cast as police officers.

Liu Ying's face clouded. She had been speaking casually before, but her expression was growing less and less casual. 'Like the actor?' she asked. '"*Bing*" as in "soldier"?' 'Oh,' said Guan Miao, remembering that she had to keep a straight face at all times and not joke around with everybody she met. 'No, not that "bing." "*Bing*" as in "ice".' She couldn't very well say anything else. Liu Ying relaxed visibly: 'Wang Xuebing, policeman. Good. See if you can borrow his car sometime.' Liu Ying left, but Guan Miao's thoughts were a blur: Liu Ying had a brand-new Mazda of her own; what would she want a police car for? Now she understood what it had all been about.

'That's right, Director – my boyfriend's name is Wang Xuebing, and he's a policeman. I suppose you all have opinions about the police, but it's not an easy job – he can't even afford to buy an apartment, or we'd have been married long ago…'

'Ah, yes – well, keep up the good work, Ms Guan. I'm sure you'll continue to dazzle us.' With these friendly parting words, the deputy director stood up and walked toward the studio door.

'Thank you, Director Liu,' Guan Miao called after him. 'Don't let Mrs Jin fire me…' But this last sentence she spoke very quietly, and the deputy director may not have heard it. After this she sat there on her own, and cried a little.

After Guan Miao finished telling Lin Liguo about the causes of her own depression, she asked if they couldn't help one another out. 'I mean, it's not like I give a fuck if they fire me, but if I can find a way to avoid it, I like being a host. Heh – I've even got a bunch of dipshit fans. It's pretty funny.' She straightened her neck and squinted her eyes like a tough girl in a movie. Lin Liguo had a hard time picturing this brassy, unshakable woman crying.

'How can I help?' Guan Miao's story had only made Lin Liguo more depressed. 'I mean, why does life have to be so damn *hard*?' But Guan Miao's brashness was contagious, and he adopted a cocky, joking tone a moment later: 'So are you really gay?'

Guan Miao wanted to take care of Lin Liguo's problem first. The next time they met, she handed him two sheets of A4 paper with a flourish. The words on the two pages, tidily handwritten with a fountain pen, were nearly identical and were to the effect that (1) *Mouthpiece* was a key Chinese-language periodical, and (2) the article 'On the Responsibilities of Journalism to the Party and the People' that appeared in 2003 Issue 1 was indeed the work of Lin Liguo, Ph.D. candidate at —— University. The only difference between the two pages was the signature: one page bore the words '*Mouthpiece* Magazine,' stamped with the round official seal of the magazine; the other signed off with the words 'Yang Guangwei, former editor, *Mouthpiece*,' and was stamped with Yang Guangwei's oblong personal seal.

'My god, you *know* him?' Lin Liguo cried. Yang Guangwei was none other than the editor-in-chief who had declined to write him a letter of certification. But an instant later his excitement faded and his face paled. 'Guan Miao, you– you– these are fake?'

Guan Miao snorted. 'Oh, grow a pair.' She handed him the round official seal of *Mouthpiece* and the oblong personal seal of Yang Guangwei, and although Lin Liguo withdrew his hand, he reached out again a moment later and accepted them with trembling hands.

He was trembling even harder when it was his turn to take care of Guan Miao's problem. Compared with Guan Miao's problem, he realised, his own hadn't been worth trembling over. At least he had Guan Miao's determination to inspire him. At least his philosophy of life included the three-word maxim, 'Be a man.' Otherwise he would've pissed his pants several times over.

Guan Miao placed absolute faith in Lin Liguo. She kept no secrets from him. He was extremely moved by that. When he wasn't busy trembling, he assured Guan Miao and her girlfriend that no matter how long this took, no matter how much effort it required, no matter what kind of unforeseeable problems or dangers it led to, he would do everything in his power to help them.

Put simply, Lin Liguo's job was to pose as Guan Miao's imaginary fiancé – but it wasn't that simple. If it had just been an ordinary impersonation, posing as her future husband would have been no big deal. The problem lay mainly in the fact that he had to pose as a police officer.

Guan Miao's girlfriend was a section chief of some authority in the Public Security Bureau, and it was within her power to get Lin Liguo the full costume, including badge and identification, of a Police Superintendent Second Class. If anyone took a close look at Guan Miao's fiancé's documentation, they would find all of Wang Xuebing's papers in order. Lin Liguo didn't have to be Wang Xuebing, the police officer, all the time; mostly he was still Lin Liguo, lecturer and doctoral candidate. It was only once or twice a week, at Guan Miao's instruction, that he needed to become Wang Xuebing, Police Superintendent Second Class. Guan Miao usually sent her instructions in the morning or evening. Sometimes she needed him to come to the station looking for her; sometimes she needed him to pick her up from work or an after-work dinner with her co-workers. In the latter case, Lin Liguo's picking-up of Guan Miao would take one of two forms: either he would arrive on foot and wait for her in front of the station or the restaurant, or he would drive up in a squad car with Guan Miao's girlfriend. When he had a car, the driver – Guan Miao's girlfriend – would duck down and hide, while Lin Liguo, who didn't know how to drive, would stand in front of the driver's-side door and look around idly, or pretend to be engrossed in checking the trunk or kicking the front tires. He would keep up this act until Guan Miao's sweet voice, like a baby bird returning to its nest, flew out of the gaggle of co-workers and drifted toward his ears: 'Wang Xuebing…'

Household Registrations

They were short-handed at the station, so they took turns: every nine days, each of the male officers had to work the night shift. Everyone thought the night shift was boring; Wang Xuebing was the only one who didn't mind it.

In point of fact, day shifts at the station were boring too. The difference was that during the day you had people coming and going with their petty quarrels and complaints, which could at least dilute, distract from, or cover over the boredom, and make the dullness seem less dull, even if this was only a facade and what lay beneath was still deadly dull. But there was nothing wrong with that if you could use it to fool yourself. At least it was better than facing true boredom. The boredom of the night shift was the genuine article, too thick and treacly to stir into motion or melt away. At one point, a bumptious young recruit reckoned he'd fight the boredom by getting in a hooker to help pass the night whenever he was on duty. His plan did not take into account the possibility that an old busybody retired cadre would hear them at it and write angry letters about corruption in the police force to anyone who might pay attention. The higher-ups were irate, and they would have kicked the guy off the force if his co-workers and wife hadn't made statements en masse saying that the hooker wasn't a hooker but his wife. He got off with a disciplinary warning in the end. Imagine getting a disciplinary warning for sleeping with your own wife. Nobody on night duty tried to fight the boredom after that.

Of course, everyone knew that working at the police station – day shift or night shift – already had a fairly low boredom index. After all, there were murders and arsons and rapes to stimulate the nerves, family feuds and neighbourhood disputes to lift the mood. At any other work unit – stifled in an office, day in and day out, writing reports for your bosses, or stuck outside exposed to the elements year after year grafting grapes to cantaloupes for scientific research, or working as a short order cook or a schoolteacher – basically any other job would have a higher boredom index. There aren't very many things in this world that aren't boring. Being a mayor isn't boring, but it's busy. Being a prostitute isn't boring, but it's dangerous. Being a real estate developer might not seem boring, but you'll never get a loan if you haven't got backing. Being a pop star or a pro athlete might not leave you time to be bored, but you'll never make it into the spotlight if you haven't put in the practice on the fundamentals... If working at a police station was boring, this was only in comparison to working at Headquarters, where they had *real* power, or working as a traffic cop, where they could earn *real* money on the side, or working in Criminal Investigations or on the riot squad, where they saw *real* excitement.'

The station had originally stocked a few items to help people on the night shift keep the boredom at bay – a telephone, a computer, a television, all possible sources of diversion. These subsequently became unusable – not because of any defects, but because the station chief had identified them as instruments of pornography, off-limits to anyone on the night shift without express permission from the chief himself. It started when someone called Hong Kong had phoned a sex line, costing the station a considerable sum of money; then someone had had text-sex with an online friend and downloaded pornographic images onto the station computer. The person responsible neglected to delete the text or the images afterwards, and in the end two female staffers elevated the mistake to the status of sexual harassment and registered their concerns. Finally, there had been a case of someone bringing in DVDs and old video CDs and using a publicly owned television, as well as previously confiscated porn videos, to satisfy their own base urges. Sometime after that, they hauled in a carpenter from Anhui who didn't have the appropriate residence permit, and instead of fining him, the station chief had him make several precisely shaped little wooden boxes. At the end of every day, the station chief would meticulously lock up the boxes, which contained the telephone, computer, and television, to await unlocking by the chief the next morning. The box for the telephone was a testament to the carpenter's skill: a painstakingly crafted little opening ensured that incoming calls could be received as normal, while preventing the placing of outgoing calls. And so the people on night duty were as good as locked into a boring little box of their own.

A few of the officers were airing grievances against each other one day – 'You say it's my fault for calling sex lines? I blame *you* for downloading smutty pictures' – and it almost came to blows. 'I don't blame any of you,' Wang Xuebing said. 'It's your wives' fault for not keeping you on short enough leashes.' Everyone burst out laughing. 'Who's keeping *you* on a leash?' they asked him. True enough: Wang Xuebing was the only widower at the station. His wife and son had died in a car crash several years before, and he had not only not remarried, but hadn't even looked for anyone else. And yet, strangely, of all the various things that had provoked the ire of the station chief, he had not been responsible for a single one. Wang Xuebing smiled but said nothing, an unreadable look in his eyes. He had spoken without thinking, and he hadn't given any thought to what was keeping his heart on a leash or how he would defeat boredom. But having been asked this follow-up question, he suddenly understood himself. But now that he did, he couldn't keep smiling – or rather, he couldn't maintain anything but a dismissive, perfunctory smile.

Whenever Wang Xuebing was up for night duty, he would bring a few books with him: the new edition of a police academy textbook, *Criminal Psychology* for instance, or the American novel *Interview with the Vampire*, or the trendy, illustrated *BuchBilderBuch, Geschichten zu Bildern*, or the popular scholarship of *Ever Since Darwin: Reflections in Natural History*. Seeing how he alleviated the boredom with books, his co-workers would sigh to themselves over their own lack of patience for reading anything even as short as a newspaper. Wang Xuebing, however, thought it was both right and wrong to say that he alleviated the boredom with reading. On the one hand, he had enjoyed light, casual reading ever since he was a child, and books could indeed bring him a certain romantic pleasure. He was middle-aged, on the other hand, and people of his age had long since learnt to appreciate the pleasures of realism – and would admit that the pleasures of realism were the only thing that could combat boredom. In this he thought he was no different from his co-workers who called sex lines or downloaded smutty pictures or watched pornographic videos.

Wang Xuebing was on duty again that night. As with every other time he had night duty, once the hand of the quartz clock pointed to nine, he decided that nobody else was likely to come knocking or calling. He rose, stretched lazily, put down the book he had been holding, left the duty room, walked down the short corridor, took out his keys, opened the iron security door at the inner end of the corridor, and strolled casually into the still, stifling air of the storeroom.

The station's storeroom wasn't for general storage; it was a file room, like a miniature library. Within stood row after row of imposing filing cabinets, each filled with household registration files for the station's jurisdiction, each file an inch or more thick, neatly wrapped in buff brown paper, dozens, hundreds of families condensed within. Wang Xuebing walked purposefully to Cabinet 3, turned his key in the lock, moved his finger to the third shelf from the top, and counted from left to right until he got to the ninth file. He reached in and withdrew it. Household registrations had long since been switched over to computerised systems, so the written files, worthless now, were almost never consulted. A layer of dust covered them, though a closer look would reveal a thin coating of dust on volumes one through eight, and a heavier coating on volumes nine and onward. Wang Xuebing walked toward the door with File 339 in his hands, dusting it off with a shoe brush as he went, and sat down at the desk beside the storeroom door. With the door opened a little wider, he could stay in the storeroom while keeping an eye on the station entrance and the duty room phone.

Sitting ramrod-straight in his chair, Wang Xuebing paged through the papers in his hand. He seemed to flush – not with a guilty conscience, obviously, but with excitement. Someone who didn't know what was going on would have assumed he was reading an adventure novel or a smutty magazine. In point of fact, what he was reading was duller than pharmaceutical instructions or appliance manuals: surnames and given names, sexes, birthplaces, ethnicities, dates of birth, religious affiliations, marital statuses, degrees of education… these should only have had a soporific effect. Yet Wang Xuebing read them with relish, like a gourmand at a banquet. Some pages he skipped past without a second glance; others he read again and again, reflectively; still others he read, turned past, then turned back to and pored over again, apparently having thought of something, or perhaps having been inspired by something on another page. He looked over the forms and their dry contents as if he was scanning for a secret signal, hatching a plan. Slowly, as he honed in on the signal, as inspiration came, he closed his eyes, dropped his shoulders, relaxed his body, and buried his head between the pages, not rising for some time. There were two possible interpretations of this position. One was that he was thoroughly worn out and was slumping forward to rest a while; the other was that he was trying to vanish, to become invisible, the better to squeeze into the rooms and apartments contained in the forms, to approach the people inside the words...

Being a reader, Wang Xuebing was familiar with Leo Tolstoy

and the old Russian's famous remark that 'Happy families are all alike; every unhappy family is unhappy in its own way.' The death of Wang Xuebing's wife and son in a car crash had brought unhappiness upon his family, but when he reminisced about the family's happiness before the accident he found that it really was little different from that of other families. The family of three he had just entered, for instance: Wang Xuebing looked at the patriarch and matriarch, thinking that they could just as easily be him and his wife, though of course they had a daughter and he had a bouncing baby boy. It was a Friday night, and their household was especially lively on Friday nights, since this was the daughter's first night home from school for the weekend. She would be there Saturday and Sunday too, but for the girl, who had been away for a week, everything at home was fresh on Friday nights. She had a ton of things that she was itching to share with her mother and father; there was TV to watch and games to play and books to read; more importantly, she could be as princessy or bratty or naughty as she pleased. Whereas on Saturday and Sunday nights, as on her nights at the school, she had to spend all her time on housework or sessions with her private tutor to prepare for the college entrance exam that she would be taking in a few years time. The fourteen year-old daughter, a middle school student, went to a boarding school.

Actually, Wang Xuebing knew that without any singing or dancing, without football or hide-and-seek, without raucous drinking or clamorous games of cards, even a 'lively' household of three was lively only in relative terms – compared, say, to when it was only the husband and wife at home. Right now, there was a stronger sense of family; for instance, the daughter, having just read a short book on the subject of evolution, was bouncing around excitedly and barraging her parents with questions.

'"Specialisation?" Oh, here.' The mother looked at the book, then closed it and did her best to present its contents from memory, the way a teacher would. 'Some forms of life, once they're in a stable environment, evolve over time to suit it so perfectly that they're no longer suited to any other environments, and they evolve specialised features. Like the branch of the hominids that evolved into human beings: that branch shares a common ancestor with the chimpanzee, but for some unknowable reason, it chose to develop and propagate in completely different regions and environments, and so in the end it "specialised" into human beings, while chimpanzees – oh!' The wife turned to look at her husband. 'Isn't that amazing – people are more closely related to chimpanzees than chimpanzees are to gorillas. Humans share 98% of their genes with chimpanzees, but chimpanzees share only 97% of their genes with gorillas…'

The daughter took umbrage at this, assuming that her mother was ignoring her. She snatched the book out of her mother's hands and went over to her father.

'…All these things you're studying, they're ancient history and cutting-edge science at the same time. Your poor old dad doesn't even have a layman's understanding of it,' the father said as he paged quickly through the book. 'So in the cell nucleus, see, there are these long or ring-shaped things, and those are chains of deoxyribonucleic acid. I'll get to those later once I've looked them up – and if you stain those with an alkaline dye and look at them under a microscope, you'll see that some parts are more heavily stained and easier to pick out, and those are called chromosomes. There are 23 pairs of chromosomes, and they're made of nucleic acid and protein – well, protein is, it's what's responsible for the formation and operation of the body's cells and organs. Just about everything in us, from our hair to our hormones, is either made of proteins or it's made *by* proteins. What the word refers to is a kind of chemical reaction – look, see, chemical reaction. And that's why it's important to study chemistry. Once you've learned about chemistry, you'll understand everything –'

'What are you talking about? That doesn't even make any sense – you're a scientific illiterate.'

Wang Xuebing stifled a laugh. His son had done this too.

His son used to call him a football illiterate.

'What am I going to do with you—' the father looked a little embarrassed. 'Your mother and I were liberal arts students. We were sort of cut off from these sorts of things, you see. I'll get you a medical dictionary at the bookstore tomorrow, and that should answer all your questions.'

'You mean it? You'll get me a medical dictionary? Tomorrow?' The daughter went over and took the father's hand.

The father may have just been saying it, but seeing how earnest his daughter was, how eager and excited, he couldn't very well go back on his word now. 'Of course I mean it. I haven't been to the bookstore in almost a whole month.'

'Then — take me? Just think how jealous everyone'll be of the old man with a pretty young thing on his arm…' As she entreated her father, the daughter seemed suddenly to remember her mother, at which she naturally regained her normal composure. 'But I can only keep you company for an hour — I have to be back here by ten for the tutor. And I'm going to have to watch you to make sure you don't spend all your money on literature and history and philosophy…'

This girl was a quick little operator, Wang Xuebing thought, the way she could turn everything to her own advantage. His own son hadn't been nearly as sharp; he only knew how to get what he wanted by fighting for it.

'When did you get so bossy? Fine, then, if I can't buy anything then I can't buy anything. Believe it or not, I bet if you ask your mother or me anything about literature or history or philosophy, we'll—'

'Really? All right, I have a philosophy question,' the daughter said challengingly.

'Why don't you ever ask about the things you're supposed to be learning?' the mother said from the side.

'The question, if you're ready,' the daughter said, pretending not to hear her mother, 'is: which came first — the chicken or the egg?'

The father stopped short: 'You're — a question like that…

213

you're just trying to trip me up. That's not a question, that's a cheap trick.'

The mother butted in: 'A philosophy question? You're not exactly posing the question very philosophically, are you?'

'See? See?' The daughter shook her head scornfully and shrugged. 'You want to cover up your own ignorance, so you reject the question itself. Pah!' The two adults wanted to respond, but seeing that the daughter already had an answer ready, they made no further protest. This was for the best: any further opposition would have resulted in charges of bullying as well as ignorance. 'The latest studies have shown that the egg existed long before the chicken. The reptiles were the ancestors of the avians, and reptiles all lay eggs.' The girl walked smugly toward her room before her stupefied parents could respond, pausing and turning back at the door to call: 'Remember, dad, you promised! Tomorrow you're taking me to get that medical dictionary.' Like a grandmother admonishing a grandchild.

This was a typical example of what a lively Friday night looked like for families. The child of the family would butter up, annoy, inquire of, or speak down to their parents, and then, while they were still feeling pleased with themselves, decide unilaterally to place a full stop at the end of the evening's liveliness without pausing to think how their parents might feel. It might not have been wrong of them to ignore their parents' feelings; parents everywhere basically have only one feeling: happiness at their child's happiness, contentment at their child's contentment. Why did their relationship with their children have to be that way? It was as if once children did their part by carrying on their parents' genes and incorporating their parents' chromosomes into their own bodies, they became the heroes of the story and gained the qualifications and capital to dictate their parents' emotions and direct their wills. Nobody could say for sure why children suddenly became the heroes of the story, or where their qualifications and capital came from. Blame it on the genes and chromosomes, maybe. They survive and propagate by using the invisible hand of bloodlines to pass all the power on to the next generation without so much as a by-your-leave, and they stick parents with all the duties and responsibilities. Wang Xuebing had read about genetic inheritance, but it was all too complicated for him. He hadn't been able to figure out what it was all about, and hadn't particularly wanted to. Now, though, with his wife and son gone and himself buried in other people's day-to-day lives, it was as if he suddenly reached some essential understanding. Wang Xuebing's mind was suddenly flooded with feelings. At that moment, the woman in the role of the mother, taking her cue from her daughter's departure, was getting ready for bed. He watched as she turned into the bathroom, stripped off her clothes, and stood on the scales – Wang Xuebing averted his gaze politely, shifting it to the man in the role of the father.

The man in the role of father would usually be in his study now, but the following day's arrangement and the knowledge that his customary morning sleep would be ruined seemed to have left him unsure of what to do. If he turned on the computer, he worried that he wouldn't be able to keep himself from working too late, so that when he went out with his daughter the next day his fatigue and torpor would make him look like 'an old man' for real, and he would embarrass her. But his biological clock was still running according to his usual schedule. If he went to bed now, his habit-induced jet-lag would keep him from feeling drowsy and he would be stuck lying there miserably, unable to sleep. Instead of filling out the night with work, he would fall into a night-long tedium. With this obviously in mind, he dimmed the lights of his study and started paging through a dull magazine, nurturing the sleepiness within himself for his daughter's sake.

Fortunately, father and daughter both awoke at the same time the next morning. They rose, showered, ate, and departed, both of them in fine fettle, for the bookstore.

Since they had a prior agreement that the father wasn't allowed to purchase any books of a literary, historical, or philosophical bent, after entering the bookstore, the two of them briefly browsed the first floor, where they purchased a colourful contact-paper book cover, then perused the second floor, where they purchased a new English-study book; subsequently they proceeded via the escalator to the fourth floor. The third floor they skipped. The first floor sold video discs, coffee table books, and other trendy knick-knacks; the second floor sold textbooks and study materials; the third floor sold books about literature, history, philosophy, economics, politics, religion and war; the fourth floor sold dictionaries, as well as books on engineering, sciences, agriculture, medicine, stocks and computers.

With the daughter in front and the father behind, they made a beeline for the dictionary counter. The employee at the counter enthusiastically directed their attention to Chinese-language dictionaries, dictionaries of idioms and set phrases, English-language dictionaries, Japanese dictionaries, dictionaries of music, dictionaries of fine arts. But father and daughter had their own views when it came to choosing and buying books, and they shook their heads in knowledgeable unison and said, 'Thank you, but we'll look ourselves.' As they spoke, their eyes fell on the *Medical Dictionary (Life Sciences Volume)*, and before her father could say a word, the girl piped up.

'Excuse me? Would you mind handing me the *Life Sciences* volume from that set?'

The daughter accepted the book politely and paged through it. The father stepped behind her, gazing at the bookshelves longingly.

'This looks right.' The father took the book from her and looked at the cover. 'Can we buy just this volume?' he asked hesitantly.

The store employee answered immediately, but even if she hadn't, father and daughter could see at the bottom of the cover that the book was not for individual sale: it was the whole set or nothing. There were seven volumes in all, grey-jacketed books of varying lengths lined up on the shelves. The daughter looked at the book, then at the father. The father looked at the daughter, then at the book.

'Dad, I want to study medicine when I grow up. I don't just mean being a doctor, I mean research, how to keep people from getting sick.'

'I understand. Dad's happy that you've got a direction....' The father asked the employee to bring over the whole set, and he looked at each volume in turn. 'Even if you don't study medicine, it's important to understand the body, understand life. Let's get the whole set. Dad's brought enough money.'

The daughter stood on tiptoe to kiss her father. 'Thanks, Dad!' She turned to look at another spot on the bookshelves. 'Dad, do you have enough, I mean after you buy this set, to buy something else? Something expensive?'

Wang Xuebing could imagine the rush of happiness the father must have felt when his daughter kissed him, but he hadn't imagined that her affection came with conditions. That was... Wang Xuebing wished he could step in and protect the father's wallet for him.

The father's enthusiasm was flagging, of course, but after the daughter's sweet kiss he barely hesitated at all. 'Sure, sure, I've got enough. I've got my card, anyway, so we can always find a bank machine if I don't have enough cash. There's never a downside to reading. Anything you want to read, I'll support – What were you looking at?'

'Excuse me? Could you bring us that brown book? *The Dictionary of World Fiction?*' The daughter looked at her surprised father and smiled slyly. 'I saw you eyeing it. Take a look – if you like it and it's useful, why not get it too?' Like a grandmother speaking to a grandchild again, but in a different tone this time.

The father managed to maintain his composure, doing no more than poking his daughter lightly, but Wang Xuebing's throat caught and he felt his eyes growing damp. He had a strong urge to rush up and join the father in caressing the heavy *Dictionary of World Fiction*. He could do no such thing, of course. The man's hand was his only point of contact with the dictionary, which was a new release from World Literature Press. Handsomely printed and bound, with its 1,791 sextodecimo pages sandwiched between sombre mahogany covers, it sat solidly in the hand, heavy enough that if cracked over someone's head it would have roughly the same effect as a curbstone. You'd knock them halfway dead. It was a very handsome volume indeed, save for a small spot at the lower right corner of the cover, about the size of a coin, where the lamination had flaked off to reveal an irregular patch of brown cardboard, as jarring as a blotch of mold on human skin. Naturally the book's value as a reference work was undiminished, but it was a discomfortingly obvious blemish all the same.

'Do you have another copy of this?' The father showed the store employee the blotch on the cover.

'I'm afraid not – we don't get many copies of such expensive books.' The employee was appropriately apologetic.

'In that case, what about a discount?' He spoke a little shyly.

'Not possible.' The employee answered decisively: she had been asked that question before, apparently, or had gotten instructions from her bosses.

'Whatever,' the daughter whispered. 'When I win the Nobel Prize for Medicine, I'll give you and mom all the prize money.'

Father and daughter looked at each other and burst out laughing, to the consternation of the store employee, who must have thought they had been whispering about her. Wang Xuebing laughed too, watching the two of them from behind and feeling also a sudden urge to go up and remind the daughter that the full name of the prize she intended to get was the 'Nobel Prize in Physiology or Medicine'.